Lakeshire Park

Other Proper Romance Regency Titles

Nancy Campbell Allen

My Fair Gentleman

The Secret of the India Orchid

Julianne Donaldson

Edenbrooke

Blackmoore

Leah Garriott

Promised

Josi S. Kilpack

A Heart Revealed

Lord Fenton's Folly

The Vicar's Daughter

Miss Wilton's Waltz

Promises and Primroses

Daises and Devotion

Lakeshire Park

MEGAN WALKER

Visit us at shadowmountain.com

Proper Romance is a registered trademark.

Library of Congress Cataloging-in-Publication Data

Names: Walker, Megan, 1990– author.
Title: Lakeshire Park / Megan Walker.
Other titles: Proper romance.
Description: Salt Lake City : Shadow Mountain, [2020] | Series: Proper romance | Summary: "Amelia Moore needs to secure her sister's engagement to Sir Ronald or else the two sisters will be left destitute. The only problem is that Peter Wood has the same goal for his own sister. Amelia and Peter begin a rivalry—one that Amelia has no choice but to win—but competing against Peter makes Amelia vulnerable to losing the only thing she has left to claim—her heart"— Provided by publisher.
Identifiers: LCCN 2019045245 | ISBN 9781629727349 (trade paperback)
Subjects: LCSH: Courtship—Fiction. | LCGFT: Romance fiction. | Historical fiction.
Classification: LCC PS3623.A3595516 L35 2020 | DDC 813/.6—dc23
LC record available at https://lccn.loc.gov/2019045245

Printed in the United States of America
LSC Communications, Crawfordsville, IN

2 3 4 5 6 LBC 27 26 25 24 23

To my Simon,
King of the NICU,
for teaching me everything I know about
hope, courage, and genuine love.

Chapter One

Brighton, England, 1820

My fingers held the last chord on the pianoforte a beat longer than necessary. Another morning filled with Father's song. When he was alive, I'd play the music over and over while he read his correspondence in the morning, and he'd hum along to the rise and fall of the melody. If I played just right, I could almost hear him still, almost feel that same exhilaration that comes from childhood, where worries are few and the future full of hope.

But the end of the song and the strike of the clock meant it was time to prepare for my stepfather, Lord Gray, who would be returning soon from his daily bath in the sea, and I was loath to give up my freedom.

Tucking in the bench, I picked up my stitching basket from the window seat where I'd been working earlier. I carefully collected each wayward thread, making sure to leave the cushion as clean and as plush as I'd found it.

Golden light streamed through the glass, beckoning me to tarry. Lifting my face to feel the sun's warmth, my eyes instinctively sought out the Royal Pavilion framed inside the uppermost right corner of the window. The building sat upon the hill a quarter mile from Gray House, its exotic domes and minarets piercing the clear England sky. What I wouldn't give to walk inside those walls, to feel the security and ease that must come from a life of such grandeur.

"Brighton is a bit different from London, is it not?" Clara's reflection met mine in the window.

"A bit more eccentric, to be sure." I turned to face my younger sister. "But far less crowded, I'll give it that."

Clara sighed. "Would you believe I miss the Season already? The society, the dinners, dancing until morning . . ." A smile touched her eyes, a first since we'd arrived back in Brighton three weeks before.

I let out a happy sigh of my own. "And falling asleep in the coach to the clip-clopping of the horses' hooves on cobblestone." When had I ever fallen asleep so easily? Years ago, perhaps. Before life struck us with spades and dug up our roots.

Clara bit her lip. "I thought for sure we'd hear from . . . *someone.*"

"We shall." I squeezed her arm, offering her my most genuine smile. But the words rang false to my ears. Three weeks with no calls. We'd met plenty of eligible gentlemen who lived within easy distance to Gray House, but still, our door was silent.

"Amelia," Clara's voice was small. "What will we do if . . . What will happen if neither of us marries before—"

"Do not worry over such things." I tucked a loose curl behind her ear. Worrying was my responsibility.

"Lord Gray has worsened since our return. His coughing never ceases." Clara's eyes were pained, her voice dejected.

"He promised Mama he would see to our security. For all his faults, and for all his resentment toward us, he loved her. We must trust he will see his promise through."

Clara looked down, unconvinced.

"Did he not give us a Season? And your dress—we haven't had new dresses like these in years."

Heaven knew I'd endured headaches for a week from all his shouting when I'd pled our case. But if I could convince the man to fund both our Season and new gowns certainly I could convince him to use his connections to our benefit. Couldn't I?

Clara tugged on a loose curl by her ear. "Aunt Evelyn nearly ripped my silk gown to pieces when she saw it."

"Do not call her that. She is hardly our aunt." I frowned. Lord Gray's family did not claim us so why should we claim them?

Evelyn had been our chaperone, meeting us in London only because Lord Gray paid her royally for the task. Yet she'd kept us behind her heavy elbow at every introduction, her prized daughter directly in front of us. I had to crane my neck around Catherine's curls every night to carry any semblance of a conversation, forcing smiles while Evelyn told nearly every gentleman who'd inquired after my dance card that I was either too sickly or too overtired to exert myself. Catherine, however, willingly obliged every one of my suitors.

My cheeks colored at the memory. Why had I been so quiet? So timid and so easily tossed aside? Never again.

Straightening from the window, I refocused my thoughts.

"Where have you been this morning? I did not hear you come in."

"Mary accompanied me on a walk along the shore. I thought perhaps the ocean could lift my spirits. The sunrise over the Channel was breathtaking." Clara's smile faded, and I caught her gaze lingering on the Pavilion for a moment. Her eyes looked sad and hopeless.

My heart fell at the thought of her longing for something out of her reach. Knowing my sister—the peacekeeper, the kindest, gentlest woman I'd ever met—felt trapped in a life forced upon her was nearly more than I could bear. Mama had married Lord Gray after Father's death to relieve us of such burdens. Only it hadn't worked that way; our worries only escalated after she too was taken from us. And now it was my job alone to ensure Clara's happiness. Clara's success in society. Clara's future.

"Lord Gray is not far behind me, I'm afraid," Clara said flatly, breaking the trance that held us at the window.

I drew a heavy breath, and the familiar scent of stale smoke in the air brought me back to the present. "Then we must be quick." I squeezed her arm and tugged her alongside me.

Preparing for our stepfather was like preparing to walk onto a battlefield. His newspaper needed adjusting, his pillows fluffed, and his cigar box at the ready. The slightest misstep—from dropping a book to walking too heavily across the floor— could anger him.

Sewing basket in hand, I scanned my surroundings for anything out of place. No one could find fault in this room. But Lord Gray would. That much was certain.

As though on cue, the drawing room doors flew open

with a bang that echoed through the house. Lord Gray stomped in with shoulders hunched, eyes set on his dark chair in the back corner.

"Where is my cigar?" He bellowed hoarsely.

"Just here." I set my basket on the window seat and fetched Lord Gray's cigar box from under the newspaper beside his chair. His habits were the same every afternoon, but he'd only started smoking in the drawing room since our return from London. Though I hated the smell of the smoke, and even more how it lingered on my clothes and in my hair, neither Clara nor I dared mention a word to him.

"How was sea bathing today, Stepfather?" I asked, my shoulders tensed.

"Cold," he muttered. Barely bothering to clip the head, he lit a match and took a long pull from his cigar. He finally seemed to relax as he fell into his gray velvet chair.

"Shall I fetch some tea?" Clara's voice sounded small, pinched.

"No," Lord Gray growled. Without warning, he curled into himself, an alarming wheeze lifting his back up and down, up and down, followed by a deep, retching cough that rattled his breath. All was silent for a beat, and then, like the rush of an ocean wave, his voice crashed upon us. "What on earth are you doing standing around? Is there not work to be done? Look at this room, the absolute shame of it! If anyone of matter came into Gray House, they would think we live like rats."

I kept my voice calm, despite his rage. "Of course, Stepfather. The floor needs attending, to be sure." I took a few careful steps backward, angling myself in front of Clara, and bent down to pick imaginary threads from the rug beneath the settee. All for guests who would never come.

A knock sounded on the door, and our butler, Mr. Jones, walked in, bowing. "A letter for you, my lord."

Clara glanced at me with questioning eyes, and I could feel her wondering, hoping.

"I shall have it." Lord Gray steadied his voice and raised his empty hand in expectation.

I forced my heart to settle as he broke the seal.

It wouldn't do to hope. Evelyn had made sure of that. I hadn't wanted to worry Clara, but I was sure Evelyn had spoken ill of us, spreading rumors amongst the *ton*. Why else would we have no correspondence after spending two months in London?

Lord Gray folded the paper into crisp lines while taking another long draw from his cigar. He endured another wheeze and another shaking cough that I could practically feel in my own lungs.

"Tea." His voice was hoarse and rough.

Clara sucked in an audible breath and turned on her heels, nearly running from the room in pursuit of it.

Lord Gray's dreadful cough had brought us to Brighton, or rather to the healing waters of the English Channel, following in the footsteps of the Prince Regent himself. The doctor had initially diagnosed pneumonia, but after every remedy was administered and every option exhausted, Lord Gray ignored his doctor and uprooted us to Brighton. Clearly, the ocean held no magic elixir for the lungs, either.

"Sit," Lord Gray snapped at me. His fingers twirled the cigar, his eyes watching its embers blaze at the tip, lips pursed.

I sat in the chair beside him and nervously straightened the pink linen skirt of my dress.

"This letter is from Sir Ronald Demsworth of Hampshire. A well-spoken man clearly besotted by one of you."

My jaw threatened to fall open. Sir Ronald? The smiling, curly-headed young man Clara had chattered about incessantly? The one who'd inherited both a title and a Royal Pavilion–sized estate? Yes, he'd paid particular attention to Clara in London, but not once had he called on us through Evelyn. Why was he writing to us now?

Lord Gray cleared his throat. "I have your interest, then? I will not waste my breath on you, Amelia, as I have already wasted enough money trying to secure a future for you—to no avail, I might add, despite affording you every luxury of a London Season. Catherine has been home for three weeks, same as you, yet she is nearly engaged. I admit I was surprised when our doors remained silent, no letters inquiring after either of you. But here we are." He gestured briefly to the paper he held. "A baronet, no less, and an invitation to his home for a fortnight."

My heart jumped into my throat, and I felt a surge of relief at the idea of escape. London had seemed too good to be true, and I'd all but armored myself against the hope of leaving Gray House again so soon.

His sunken eyes bored into mine, willing me to ask, to beg. He knew as well as I did that this invitation bore a deeper meaning, a blooming interest, and was a greater opportunity for us—for Clara—than we could possibly hope for. I also knew that neither I nor Clara had any money or means to reply affirmatively without help from our stepfather. We'd need a coach for travel, a maid to share between us, and an allowance. Asking, and certainly begging, did not come naturally to me. Clara's reflection flashed in my memory—her sad eyes, softened from weariness and disappointed dreams.

"Lord Gray, you have been so generous to us." The words tasted like lemon on my tongue. "After Mama died, you've still protected and provided for us these past two years."

He rolled his eyes. "Do you honestly think I do any of this for you?" He spat. "Neither of you deserve this life, not with the blood of the Moores running through your veins. There is not enough of her in you to make me care beyond the promise I made regarding your protection. A promise that dies with me."

He'd said such things a thousand times, but the sting of such open disdain burned fresh upon my cheeks. His invocation of death lingered between us, the word billowing along with the smoke from Lord Gray's cigar until both filled the room.

My own life was before me, more fragile and more uncertain than I had ever imagined before, a future cracking like glass. My gaze found the bluish-gray carpet beneath his feet. "I see."

"Look at me," Lord Gray demanded coldly, and I forced myself to meet his sunken eyes. I noted the darkened hollowing to his cheekbones, the dryness of his cracked lips, and thinness of his graying hair. I wanted to look away from him, to pretend I didn't see the truth in the labored rise and fall of his chest. But after six months with no improvements, it was glaring so obviously at me, I could not turn away.

"Have you called for the doctor, Stepfather?"

His countenance changed from anger to liberation. "I've already spoken with Dr. Wyles. He says I have no hope of recovery." He spoke as if he were more inconvenienced than troubled by the news. "Unlike your father, you are smart. Certainly you can deduce that very shortly, everything I have will be given to Catherine's brother, Trenton, and you will be left with nothing."

His words buzzed in my head like flies, blurring my vision. A tightness squeezed my chest, and my lungs fought for air.

"*Look at me, Amelia!*" Urgency thundered in his voice. He waved the letter in my face, his cold eyes full of disdain. "My family will take my money and turn their backs on you when I am gone, and I would not have it any other way. Fool that I am, I bound myself for your mother's sake before she died, or I would have rid my house of you long ago. This invitation compels me to offer one last alternative. You will go to Hampshire and secure this match. Then I shall meet Arabella again with a clear conscience."

"Y-yes," I whispered, my mind swimming in thought. I'd known he resented us, known that our father had ruined his life, but I'd never imagined that his hatred ran so deep. I could no longer sit. Rising from my chair in stunned silence, my legs instinctively carried me to the door.

"And you haven't much time to prepare."

Turning, my hand loosely gripping the door handle, I watched him take another slow pull of his cigar. "How long?"

"It appears the letter was delayed in transit. You must leave tomorrow."

Chapter Two

The morning sun burst through my curtains, which were open enough to allow in an unwelcome stream of light. My forehead ached from the stress of last night's rushed gathering of a fortnight's worth of necessities. Had I slept at all?

I rubbed my temples as Mary tiptoed in and set a tea tray on my side table before opening the curtains the rest of the way.

"What time is it, Mary?" I yawned.

"Just after seven, Miss Amelia," she replied, adding a spoonful of sugar to my cup of tea.

So I'd slept for three hours. Not enough. Perhaps I'd be able to nap in the coach. I sipped my warm tea, easing out of my covers with cup in hand. A floor below us, Lord Gray's coughing shook the air. The start of a new day, and perhaps for him, one of his last. My stomach knotted at the thought, and I lost my appetite.

"Amelia?" Clara rushed in, fully dressed, her hair perfectly curled and pinned. Her eyes were as bright as the morning sun, nearly bursting with excitement. "I've told Mr. Jones to ready the coach. We must be off if we are to make it in time for dinner at *Sir Ronald's* house. Can you believe it?"

"I cannot." I smiled, despite knowing the truth of Lord Gray's confession. Any knowledge of our true circumstances would ruin the party for Clara, and she deserved a chance to create a genuine connection with Sir Ronald. Not something forced out of fear for her future. "His home must be magnificent."

"Oh, I am sure it is. Five floors and two wings, and a library he admires. He even has a room entirely dedicated to yellow, which is his favorite color. And his holding encompasses hundreds of acres of land." Clara's eyes brightened as she recalled the details.

My mouth fell open, and it took me a minute to find my voice. "How do you know all of this, Clara?"

"Well, dances and dinners, of course. We escaped to the terrace a few times. And once we hid away under a grand staircase when a certain woman would not leave him alone. He is not overly fond of large parties."

Half-laughing at my sister whose secrets were more than I possibly could have assumed, I shook my head in amazement. "This is why you've been so glum. Did he tell you he would write to us?"

"I am not glum. We are friends, that is all. Miss Wood, I hear, has held his affection for some time. So, no, he did not inform me of his party. But I am happy for the invitation regardless."

"I see. Well, we shall see if Miss Wood was also extended an invitation when we arrive. It sounds to me like Sir Ronald's interests may lie in another direction." I shot her a pointed glance, and she scrunched her nose.

"Please don't say such things, Amelia. I only want his happiness. Promise me you will not try to persuade him otherwise? Or meddle between us? If Miss Wood is as amiable as I have heard, then I doubt it will do any good. I am thrilled to have been invited at all."

"Miss Wood," I huffed. "She sounds plain."

"Amelia." Clara shook my shoulders with her hands. "Promise me."

If only she knew what she asked of me. I could not lie, but I could not make such a promise either. A middle ground would have to do. "I promise to do nothing that would make you unhappy, Clara."

Downstairs, Mr. Jones informed us that Lord Gray was feeling especially unwell this morning and was unable to see us off. I was unsurprised by his absence, but I also felt a tinge of relief. What would I say to him if these words were my last? I had little to thank him for beyond the sustenance he provided and the roof over my head. Even then, I was not entirely sure I felt grateful for that.

Mr. Jones helped us into the carriage, and just before closing our door, said, "Lord Gray asked me to wish you luck in your journey. Safe travels, Miss Moore, Miss Clara."

"Luck?" Clara questioned as we rode out of Brighton. "I wonder why he thinks we need luck. Such a strange, peculiar man. I am glad to be away again so soon."

"As am I." I sighed, listening to the sounds of the squeaky coach. "I am sure he meant for our travels." Nothing to do with our uncertain future.

"Yes, but that would imply he meant to be kind, and Lord Gray is the most unfeeling man I have ever met." Clara tsked. "I will never understand why Mama chose *him*. After a man like Father. Elevating our status is not a worthy enough excuse to be tied to such a person."

I could not disagree with her, but I had a sinking feeling that if Clara did not win Sir Ronald's heart, I could more easily understand marrying for protection, without much say as to whom.

"Be grateful you know so little of the subject to be able to wonder on it." I gave in to another yawn and closed my eyes. There was something about a ride in a coach, heading far away from Lord Gray with Clara as my companion and the soft sound of Mary's knitting needles, that was so comforting and so familiar, I fell asleep every time.

We stopped at a small inn for a meal before continuing on our way, but then a few miles outside of Hampshire, Clara sat bolt upright. "My gloves! Amelia, my gloves! I took them off for lunch. I've left them."

I sat up straight. "Are you sure?"

"Yes." She moaned, covering her face with bare hands. "They were my last short pair."

I took a deep breath. Our allowance was small, but gloves were a necessity. Clara couldn't wear evening gloves during the day. "We will have to stop at a shop in town."

"I am sorry, Amelia. How could I be so careless? Wasting money on new gloves."

"It is an inexpensive mistake. And easily remedied," I assured her, though inwardly I groaned too. What would happen when our reticules emptied?

A few hours later, we pulled up to a row of shops lined side by side down a broad street in the middle of a small farm town. Clara had fallen asleep in the coach, and I did not want to worry her. Our hands were nearly the same size, though it would be a miracle if the glove maker could accommodate us on such short notice. I could only hope to persuade him to sell me another person's order at an inflated cost. Or with a hefty tip in the least.

The store was much larger on the inside than it appeared and looked as though the owner was in the middle of a remodeling. At the front, a clerk sat at a long, rectangular wooden desk, writing in a thick book. He looked up through his spectacles as I approached.

"Welcome, ma'am, I am just finishing this order. I shall be with you in a moment."

"If you could point me in the direction of the gloves you offer, then I shall wait for you there."

"Oh." The man removed his spectacles, uncovering a furrowed brow. "I am sorry to disappoint you, but our glove maker has recently moved his business elsewhere. Unfortunately, I can take no further orders until our new man arrives next month."

Would luck ever find us? I could handle disappointment, but I could not bear to see it in my sister. "I'm afraid our need is great. I must ask you to sell me anything you have on hand, sir. Anything at all. I can pay you well."

"Well, we've sold quite a lot of his old things already—patterns, samples, and the like—but I think there's one pair of sample gloves left on the table. Smaller in size, which appears to suit you, and I believe they are a fashionable beige.

Just there, on the back corner table. I will assist you in a moment." He motioned me forward, and I nodded my thanks, hurrying to the back corner of the shop.

Squeezing around a large sign, I spotted the table, my eyes searching desperately for beige fabric. Just as I approached the edge of the table, a rustling sounded directly underneath it. I drew an anxious breath, taking a step back.

A man appeared near my shoes, climbing out from below the table. My eyes widened in shock as he recovered himself. Where on earth had he come from? He bore no resemblance to a shopkeeper.

In fact, he looked quite the gentleman. A fashionable coat clung tightly to broad shoulders and a wide chest. He had a breezy air about him, with full, smiling lips and a clean-shaven jaw, his dark, wavy hair loosely drifting over his forehead. But it was his eyes that captivated me. They were the clearest green, boring into mine without reservation. The man chuckled through my scrutiny, and I burned to my ears with embarrassment. My gaze had lingered too long.

"Pardon me," he said, a smile wrinkling the corners of his eyes as he dusted off his knees. "My search led me to a pile of stray fabrics under the table. This shop is rather disorganized, is it not?"

What a strange man. The corners of my lips twitched as he ruffled his hair. "Terribly," I responded. "Excuse me."

Reminding myself of my goal and my limited time, I twisted around him and began sorting through the dreadfully unorganized accessories on the table.

But the man did not leave. He moved closer to me, lifting a cherry-colored ribbon from the table. An odd bubbling sensation filled my chest, and I did not like how flustered it made me.

"Perhaps I can help you find what you are looking for," he offered, clearing his throat.

I turned, eyebrows raised in interest. "Have you seen a pair of beige gloves? I've been sent back for the very last pair, and I'm in a bit of hurry."

The smile on his lips fell instantly, and I dropped my gaze to his rising hand—and the gloves he held.

"Oh, you've found them. You won't mind, will you? My sister left her last short pair at an inn, and I—"

"I am sorry." He shook his head. "But I cannot give these up. *My* younger sister, who is, I am sure, far more commanding and much whinier than yours, will have my head if I return without these. She's found a spot on hers that will not do, and these happen to be just the right size."

"A spot? That can be remedied. My sister is without gloves entirely, sir. I am afraid this little shop is our only hope of acquiring a pair before arriving at a rather important house party. Surely your sister will understand." I held out my palm, hoping I'd pled my case sufficiently. The man had done his duty to his sister by arguing her case, but clearly Clara's need was greater.

"I assure you she would not, unfortunately." He flashed me a look of meaningful regret with a deep sigh, and I retracted my hand. "Allow me to offer you their value in currency as recompense for her disappointment. You seem like a reasonable woman."

"I do not want your money, sir. And I assure you, I am not at all a reasonable woman." I folded my arms across my chest, the ridiculousness of my last statement bringing heat to my cheeks.

The stranger tilted his head, eyes studying me, before allowing himself a light laugh. "Well, then, in that case, allow me to seek out another pair and deliver them to you. Where will you be staying?"

"If it is so easy for you to secure another pair of gloves, can you not give me the one in your hand and seek out another for yourself?" I bit my lip. I had little experience swaying men, charming them even, and if London was any judge, I failed more than I succeeded.

"I'm afraid I am pressed for time. If these gloves were not so desperately desired, I believe you would be well worth the scolding." A teasing glint sparkled in his eyes.

The nerve of this man! Did he wish to humiliate me? I'd all but begged for his mercy and was refused, and now, mortified. What a terrible advocate I was turning out to be.

"Name your price." I lifted my reticule, praying silently this was not a man of too great a fortune or I would make myself into an even greater fool to deny him. But how could Clara face Sir Ronald without gloves? We would be finished before we even began. "I must have those gloves."

"You reject my money and offer me yours?" He narrowed his gaze almost pityingly. "Money is not something I have in short supply. I am sorry, but I must insist on maintaining my hold."

I frowned dejectedly, heat flaming up my neck. I could not argue with him without risk of further embarrassment. "Good day to you," I said, managing a brief curtsy.

Snatching a peach-colored ribbon from the table, I

hurried to the front of the store. I would not return to Clara empty-handed.

"Wait," he called after me. But I did not spare a second glance.

Just as I rounded the corner to the counter, the arrogant man quickened his pace and stole ahead of me. I imagined pushing him aside and demanding service, but he was already in conversation with the clerk. For all his charm, he was decidedly not a gentleman in the honorable sense of the word. I gritted my teeth.

After paying his fees, he took the brown paper package from the clerk and turned to me again, a gentleness touching his voice. "You must tell me where you are staying. I want to make this right for you, and for your sister."

"You are being impertinent. I do not know you at all, sir. And honestly, after this interaction, I do not wish to." Humiliation welled in my chest like a fire that refused to be extinguished, and I choked on the fumes.

"Allow me to change your mind. At least tell me your name." He stepped sideways, blocking me from moving forward to the clerk with my ribbon.

"I rarely change my mind. Do not waste your time. Excuse me." I lifted the ribbon in my hand to the clerk, but the presumptuous man grabbed my arm.

"Your name?"

"Amelia," I said curtly. Impertinence matched with impertinence. Knowing only my Christian name would not help him find me. "My name is Amelia."

I elbowed him aside and opened my reticule as the clerk packaged up Clara's new ribbon.

"I hope I see you again, Amelia," the man said.

Staring straight at the clerk, I waited for the clang of the closing door. Satisfied that the man had departed, I finally let out the breath I'd been holding.

The clerk handed me a brown package. "Good day to you, miss."

"I have not yet paid, sir." I rolled the package over in my hands. It was much too big to contain one small ribbon.

"The gentleman added your ribbon with his others and paid for you. Good day."

I stood, mouth agape, as the clerk returned to his paperwork as though nothing amiss had happened, and an anger rose in my chest that rivaled even Lord Gray's foulest of moods. Who was this man? Had I not plainly told him I was uninterested in his money or his help? I bolted toward the door, furiously bent on finding him, on telling that irritable man exactly what I thought of him and his unwanted recompense.

But he was gone.

Chapter Three

"Perhaps they are poor, Amelia. His sister could well have needed the gloves more than I," Clara said after I told her of my encounter with the stranger.

"They are not poor." I handed her the bag of ribbons, full to the brim. Apparently, the man had been quite generous.

Clara pulled them out one by one, exclaiming over the colors and fabric and praising the generosity of the man who'd denied her what she currently needed most. It was just like a man of wealth to think he could buy a good opinion with money, as though I would easily forget his selfishness. I shook my head to rid my thoughts of him. He'd made his choice, and he was gone. And there was only one thing I could do now.

"Here." I pinched off my buff-colored gloves, handing them to Clara.

"What are you doing? I will not accept your gloves; it is my own fault mine are gone." Clara shook her head, scooting away from me.

"Take them, Clara. I care little for what Sir Ronald's company thinks of me. I can hide my hands in my skirts."

"Surely someone belowstairs will have a pair I can sew up for you, Miss Amelia," Mary said from her corner of the coach.

"There. You see? Mary and I will sort out another pair." I tossed the gloves to Clara, who tugged them on reluctantly.

Moments later, the coachman rapped on the roof, and we looked out the east window just as the coach drove out of the lined woods and into an expansive clearing. There in the middle of the freshly cut lawn sat a grand estate, sandy-colored with four stories of parallel windows lining the front, reflecting the light from the setting sun. The double doors to the house were open. Our coach pulled into the drive, and a footman hurried out.

He opened my door and helped me down, followed by Clara. Just as my nerves started to get the best of me, a beautifully dressed, ginger-headed woman walked out to greet us. She was elegant and fair, bearing an air of authority as she approached us.

"Welcome, ladies. You must be the Misses Moore. I am Lady Demsworth, Ronald's mother. Ronald has told me so much about you both, and it is such a joy to have you here at Lakeshire Park." Sincerity flowed through every word, and she reached out for us, inviting us near.

"Thank you so much, Lady Demsworth." I urged Clara ahead, following behind her. "We are very happy to be here."

"Yes," agreed Clara. "What a lovely estate. Amelia and I have missed the countryside dearly."

Lady Demsworth took Clara's arm affectionately. "That's right. Ronald told me you were raised in Kent. I am sure

Brighton is a vastly different environment. I hope this visit is a comfortable reminder of fond memories."

Clara smiled graciously. "Thank you, Lady Demsworth. It already is."

"I am sure you're both ready to dress, but everyone is so excited to make your acquaintance. Might I introduce you to the party first? We've kept it rather small in hopes of a casual gathering and creating an opportunity to become better acquainted with Ronald's closest friends."

"Of course we do not mind," Clara said. "Mary will have just enough time to ready our things."

I followed closely behind the two as they entered the house, comfort enfolding me like a warm, heavy blanket. I tried to place the feeling, to name the unfamiliar warmth that relaxed my heart. All I knew was that here, nestled in the middle of nowhere, I could breathe. How I hoped these next two weeks were only the beginning, that we could finally find refuge within these walls once Clara made a match with Sir Ronald.

We'd just reached the foot of the grand marble staircase when Lady Demsworth veered left. Another set of double doors, white and trimmed with gold, stood as the entrance to the bustling drawing room.

Lady Demsworth fiddled with a string of pearls around her neck as though she, too, held high hopes for these next two weeks. As we entered the room, a click of the door signaled to me that the clock had finally begun.

Two weeks to secure my sister's happiness.

My pulse quickened as Clara and I were introduced to the company. First was Mrs. Turnball, a refined woman of few words, though her gaze spoke volumes of her character. Her eyes were soft but focused, her head held high and resolute as she greeted us.

Meanwhile, her daughter, Miss Beatrice Turnball, fawned over Clara's golden hair, claiming her own brown and my auburn to be far inferior. "You must call me Beatrice," she said. "We shall be fast friends."

Next were two gentlemen sitting on the settee across from the window engaged in boisterous conversation. Both men stood at our approach, bowing deeply.

"Mr. Bratten of London," Lady Demsworth introduced. The tall, skinny man with a youthful countenance smiled proudly. "And Lieutenant Rawles, who dutifully serves our country."

"At present, my services are not required," the lieutenant corrected. "I am on half-pay until the king has better need of me." His rough, unkempt exterior, including an unshaven jaw and scarred right eyebrow, was intimidating, despite his smile.

I could've sworn the two men cast each other a knowing glance as we walked away.

"Where is Sir Ronald?" Clara shyly asked Lady Demsworth as we rounded the room.

"Getting another arrival settled. The Woods arrived just before you, and Ronald is very good friends with Mr. Wood. The two haven't seen each other in nearly a year."

"Miss Wood is here?" Clara's voice fell flat, but she recovered with a generous smile.

Blast our bad luck.

"Yes." Lady Demsworth nodded. "Ronald said you'd be

eager to meet her. In fact, your rooms are beside each other upstairs."

Just then, the doors burst open, and Sir Ronald's laughter filled the quiet room. Everyone stood to greet their host. Clara rose on her tiptoes, aiding his view of her.

"Miss Clara! You've arrived." Sir Ronald made his way to her, guiding a bustling, curly-headed blonde by his side. "I trust your journey was uneventful."

"Indeed." Clara grinned. "We were so pleased for the invitation."

"It is I who am pleased . . . to see you again so soon." Sir Ronald's smile grew serious and sweet, and my heart swooned for Clara.

The blonde girl, who Sir Ronald introduced as Miss Georgiana Wood, wedged herself perfectly between him and Clara. Her smile was fixed as she said, "Surely you are tired from such a long journey."

"Not at all," I said, raising my chin. Her presence alone put me on guard. Georgiana was a certain kink in our plans.

Sir Ronald pulled both ladies into conversation, and a comfortable murmur filled the room as the company fell into pairs and trios. I stepped back, suddenly out of place, like a stranger among a group of old friends. Now was the perfect time to dress for dinner. I could be back down before Clara noticed I'd gone.

Rubbing my face with my hands, I turned to exit through the double doors. With a whoosh of my skirts, I ran straight into something tall and hard. Stunned, I grasped wildly for balance, my discomfort magnified as I was caught in an embrace.

"Amelia?" A low voice said, sounding much too pleased—and much too familiar.

My senses realigned, and I drew my head back, meeting the green eyes of the man from the shop. I stepped out of his hold, my mind spinning.

No. It could not be. Had he followed me?

"How did you find me here?" He leaned against the doorway with a wicked grin, echoing my own question.

"Excuse me?" Did he honestly think I would look for *him*? "I am a guest here."

He stood up straighter, eyes flooded with interest. "You know Demsworth? How?"

"Never mind. What are *you* doing here? And when are you leaving?" I could not hide the sudden worry that filled my voice. This fortnight was about Clara. I could not have any distractions.

"As it happens, I know Demsworth rather well." He shook his head in disbelief, laughing. "Amelia, I cannot believe you are here."

I crossed my arms, glancing over my shoulder, fearful someone might overhear our conversation. "You should address me as Miss Moore, sir. I have not given you permission to use my Christian name so openly."

"I beg to differ." He lowered his chin, eyes glinting. "And so would the shopkeeper four miles down the road."

Embarrassment wafted through me, igniting my pride. Perhaps I had not behaved as ladylike as I should have, but he'd not acted his part either. I huffed at the thought. "What kind of honorable gentleman steals a pair of gloves from a lady? And then throws his money at her to solve the problem?"

He glanced to my bare hands, and I quickly tucked them behind me.

"In the first place, I never professed myself honorable," he said, rubbing the back of his neck. "But I have regretted leaving that shop from the moment I stepped out its door."

His eyes met mine curiously, like he wanted me to react to his regret. But the only emotion I felt was anger. His regret did not change his choices. And choices defined a person.

"Forgive me if I do not offer adequate sympathy." At this point, it would be safer for me to retreat into the room to get away from him. A conversation with Lieutenant Rawles was more enticing than being forced to address the guilty conscience of this man.

"Wait," he called as I stepped into the light of the drawing room.

"Peter!" Georgiana waved, and I turned, locking eyes with the strange man who'd followed me.

Sir Ronald also turned. "Wood, just in time. The Misses Moore have arrived."

The man kept his eyes on me as Sir Ronald, Clara, and Georgiana moved toward us.

"Ladies, this is Peter Wood, a great friend of mine, and as I am sure you know, Georgiana's brother," Sir Ronald explained.

Mr. Wood—*Peter*, though I would never dare such informality aloud—offered a low bow. "How very fortunate I am to be in your company."

If this was luck, then Lord Gray had cursed me.

"It has been too long." Sir Ronald looked pleased. "Inheritance is such a tricky trade, is it not? I mourn the loss of your father as I have mourned my own, but I am glad to have you near. Have you finished things in London at last?"

"Finally, yes. A year's worth of settling affairs. And thank you, Demsworth. Georgiana is thrilled to be closer as well."

And then it hit me, like the weight of a thousand bricks pressing into my chest. Miss Georgiana Wood. The woman Clara claimed to be in competition with for Sir Ronald's heart was this man's sister. Frustration boiled hot within me as I clenched my skirts with my bare hands. To have lost Clara's gloves to Georgiana Wood, whose nose could touch the ceiling for how high she held it, was unacceptable. Judging by her expensive blue silk dress and shiny pearl necklace that rivaled Lady Demsworth's, Georgiana did not often fail to acquire her heart's wishes.

"Dinner will be ready in a half hour," Lady Demsworth declared from the doorway.

"Perhaps we should dress," Clara said into my ear.

I caught Georgiana motioning to her brother, and Peter turned to Sir Ronald. "I fear we have missed quite a lot of each other's lives. You have much to tell me."

"Shall we sit? Your travels surely rival mine." Sir Ronald grasped Peter's shoulder.

"Georgiana, join us, won't you?" Peter edged the three of them toward a settee near the window, pointedly away from the rest of the company.

Clara looked back at them, frowning, and I realized my mistake. We should have dressed for dinner first instead of making introductions. Clearly, Peter had not hesitated to navigate his sister into the center of Sir Ronald's attention. Meekness or timorousness would not be afforded here if I was to keep up with the competition.

"Yes," I whispered back to Clara. "Let us dress quickly. The sooner we dress, the faster we will be back down."

Our room, large and square, held two beds with brown wooden headboards occupying the rightmost wall and a fire crackling in the hearth on the opposite side. The fireplace was framed in white marble with light blue velvet chairs placed in front of it. A bouquet of lilacs in front of the open window filled the room with a sweet scent.

Mary had placed our gowns and long evening gloves over our beds, and she quickly pulled Clara over to the dressing table.

Despite the urgency I felt to return to the drawing room, I couldn't help but lean my elbows on the windowsill and take in a deep breath as the chill of the early evening breeze brushed across my face. Daylight waned, casting shadows in the crevices of the rolling hills outside. It was a beautiful scene.

My bones ached from being caged in the carriage all day, but worse, my mind spun with the faces of all the people I'd just met. Each seemed kind enough, save the Woods. Georgiana would be trouble. And her brother was intimidating to say the least.

"Amelia," Clara chided. "If you start dressing now, Mary can attend to you when I am finished."

"Of course," I said, tearing myself away from the window. There was no time to waste.

Dinner was a boisterous event and more casual in seating

arrangements and conversation than Lady Demsworth could possibly have anticipated. Between the men, no one else could get a word in, and their stories from past hunting adventures turned poor Lady Demsworth green as she picked at the lamb on her plate.

I took a small bite of roasted potatoes and risked a glance at Peter. He was grinning at something Lieutenant Rawles was saying, his arms crossed as he leaned back in his chair. Before reason called me to my senses, I caught his eyes with my own for a brief second. Nerves seizing, I stared down at my plate. What was it about his gaze that intimidated me so? I moved the remaining vegetables around with my fork while Georgiana encouraged the men with perfectly framed questions, batting her eyelashes as she sipped from her cup.

After dinner, Mr. Bratten entered the drawing room ahead of the other men, choosing a card table with Mrs. Turnball and Beatrice and motioning for Lieutenant Rawles, who was piling a stack of books next to a chair, to join them. Sir Ronald began a game of whist with Clara, Georgiana, and Peter, which left me alone with Lady Demsworth.

"I am feeling rather tired. I think I will do some stitching by the fire," Lady Demsworth said. "Would you care to join me? You should know that I appreciate honesty over obligation."

"In that case, I would love to join you and enjoy the fire *without* the stitching." I stifled a yawn, and she nodded.

"You look exhausted, Miss Moore. Should I call for a cup of chocolate with our tea?"

"That would be lovely."

Lady Demsworth led me to the coziest chair I'd ever sat

in, the velvety fabric as soft as the plump pillow at my back. A cup of chocolate arrived shortly after with the tea tray, and I leaned into my chair, listening to the muffled voices in the room.

Clara was laughing, a gloved hand covering her lips, clearly taken with something Sir Ronald had said. The striking transformation of my sister over the course of a single day was astounding. Yesterday her sadness had been overwhelming, but today her countenance was filled to the brim with elation. To keep her like this, happy and free, I would do anything.

Lady Demsworth was drifting off, stitching only once every few minutes. Her casual nature permeated the Demworths' home. I felt so at ease already, and we'd only just arrived. Half of me still expected Lord Gray to march in and demand his cigar, his relentless cough shaking the walls. I was glad Clara did not fully understand the gravity of this visit, of how quickly we needed security. But a small part of me wished there was someone who felt the weight of my burden too.

Peter's loud laugh echoed off the ceiling, and I straightened. That man. How could I keep him—and more importantly his sister—from getting between Clara and Sir Ronald? Certainly not by sitting in a corner sipping hot chocolate.

Careful not to disturb Lady Demsworth, I rose and made my way across the room. Sir Ronald and Peter stood at my approach.

"Miss Moore. If only whist could be played with five instead of four." Sir Ronald smiled regrettably. "But, please, join us if you'd like to watch Georgiana and I rob your sister and Wood of their dignity."

Clara scowled playfully at him, eliciting a grin from Sir Ronald that creased his cheeks. Peter cleared his throat, and I met his gaze. His eyes held curiosity, and I shot back as much indifference as I could muster. I would no longer be timid. If a battle raged between his sister and mine, Clara would win.

"Now I am invested wholeheartedly," I said. "I cannot see Clara losing at whist, unless Mr. Wood is a terribly unskilled player."

"That I am not." He winked at me, and my nerves tightened. "But if we have an audience we should raise the stakes. What do you say, Demsworth? What should the winning pair get?"

"Tea on the veranda," Georgiana said, leaning closer to Sir Ronald. "Under the stars."

Clara exhaled, eyes dropping to her cards. I could not blame her. Who would want to spend an evening with Peter Wood on the veranda?

"Agreed." Peter smiled as if he'd already won. Clara's slumping shoulders conceded. "Miss Moore, allow me to offer you my chair."

I wanted to say no. I would have stood all night before taking anything from him. But Sir Ronald looked expectantly at me, and I nodded my acceptance. For Clara's sake.

I thanked my stars for Peter's formality in front of the company. Perhaps he meant to keep our secret after all. He slid his chair nearer to Clara so I could sit by her, and then retrieved another from a nearby table.

The game continued another half hour until, as predicted,

Clara and Peter lost three points to one. I clenched my jaw, knowing Clara had played her best. Peter had obviously thrown the game so his sister would win.

"I thought you said you were skilled, Mr. Wood?" I cast him a disparaging frown.

"Every man has his day. Apparently, this was not mine." His easy grin added fuel to my fire.

"No, it was not," I grumbled. And neither would tomorrow be, nor the rest of the days we might spend in each other's company. My patience for Peter Wood and his scheming had just run dry.

Chapter Four

A gentle breeze rustled my skirts as I walked upon the soft grass, farther and farther from Sir Ronald's house. He'd taken our company on a tour of the grounds, and I was determined to find them. If only I hadn't slept away the morning like an old spinster. With aching feet and not a man in sight I could almost claim the part. Plopping down on a lonely stump at the edge of the tree line, I wiped a trace of sweat from my brow.

I was lost. I must've already walked an hour or so but was no closer to Clara than I'd been at the house. What if she was struggling? What if she needed me to laugh at her jokes or boast of her successes? Neither of us had experience with winning a gentleman's heart. The only example we had was my mother's, and Father had not been her *choice* at all.

On the bright side, at least I had gloves. I pulled Lady Demsworth's old pair tighter upon my hands as though they had imbued me with power and courage. Mary's stitching was masterful. An eighth of an inch proved precisely the difference in our measurement. And according to Lady

Demsworth's maid, there were a dozen more pairs waiting to be mended, so these gloves would not be missed.

Hooves pounded in the distance, startling flocks of birds in the trees.

When a small carriage rounded the bend, I waved my arms like a stranded islander lost at sea, and the coachman pulled up beside me.

"Ma'am, what are you doing all the way out here?" a servant asked.

"I fear I've walked too far. I am trying to find Sir Ronald and his party."

"I see. We're meeting them up north with the picnic he requested. There is room in the carriage for anyone too tired to return by foot. Would you like a seat? The ride is bumpier in the pasture, but you'll get there all the same." The coachman dismounted, guiding me to the carriage door and helping me inside.

The drive was indeed bumpy, but my sore muscles welcomed the respite anyway. When the carriage stopped, I peered outside and there, just up the hill, stood Clara. Her hair was loosely curled and pinned under her bonnet, crowning her face like an angel. She wore a wispy pink dress that flowed with the breeze, the color matching the hue in her cheeks. She stood out just enough in the party without being overly conspicuous in appearance.

I stepped out of the carriage and approached the group.

"Miss Moore, you've arrived just in time." Sir Ronald waved me over. Clara, Georgiana, and Peter stood in a half circle at the base of a hill. Peter looked annoyingly handsome in his navy overcoat, his hair windswept as though he'd just rescued a dozen damsels in distress. I felt his stare as I approached the group, though I pretended not to. He'd had his fun last night, but today was a new day.

"I've brought your picnic with me," I teased, latching arms with Clara and looking to Sir Ronald. "I'm terribly sorry to have slept so late. How was your morning?"

"Much fun," Clara said with a softer than usual smile. Something was wrong.

"Yes, the grounds here are breathtaking." Georgiana placed a hand on Sir Ronald's arm. A perfectly beige gloved hand.

As servants set up the picnic, I took the opportunity to pull Clara away a few feet, just out of earshot.

"How was the morning? Really?" I asked.

"Fine." Clara looked away into the distance. "Sir Ronald's lands are truly lovely."

"Only, what? Tell me at once, Clara. Did something happen?"

"Not something. *Someone*." She glanced over her shoulder to where Georgiana was laughing at something her brother said. I could almost guarantee it was not as funny as that.

"What can I do? I could force her down the hill. Roll her ankle?" I tried to lace humor in the idea, though I was frighteningly willing to follow through with it.

"Georgiana? She is tolerable. As I've told you, Amelia, I only want Ronald to be happy. I just want an *equal* chance at being his happiness." She spoke with determination, as though she had to convince herself she was capable. "He is a good man, and he'd make a good match for me. For us.

We could stop worrying about Lord Gray and live our lives." Clara sighed, brooding again. "But I can hardly get a word in edgewise with Georgiana's *brother* here."

"Mr. Wood?" My voice squeaked on his name.

"Yes," she exclaimed, annoyed. "With every bit of conversation, even the weather, he finds a way to turn it in Georgiana's favor. It is maddening. For half a minute, I'd like to talk to Sir Ronald about his life here, what it's like to be master of all this. But when I try, guess what the conversation turns into?"

"Georgiana." I groaned, feeling her frustration. "Perhaps I can pull her into conversation, distract her."

"No." Clara shook her head. "It is not so much Georgiana as it is Mr. Wood. Amelia, I need you to distract *him*."

"What?" Surely I'd misheard her. My confidence in swaying that man to my will was infinitesimal, if it existed at all. Not to mention that I loathed him and nearly every word that came from his mouth.

"Just for the afternoon. Please, Amelia. I will go mad if I have to hear him spout on about his sister for one more minute."

One afternoon. I rubbed my temples. Suddenly, the miles I'd walked earlier were not so exhausting. The ache in my feet, welcomed. But having to spend time alone with Peter Wood? That was misery indeed. I peered over my shoulder and saw him standing between Sir Ronald and Georgiana like mortar between bricks. Clara was right. Something had to be done.

Lifting my shoulders and straightening my back, I anchored my resolve.

"Well, Clara, you are fortunate now more than ever to have a clever sister. I may not be the most beautiful woman here, but I can find a way to keep Mr. Wood at bay." I set my chin. "Do take advantage of whatever time I can give you. It will not be earned painlessly."

Clara's eyes brightened in excitement, and she pulled me into a happy embrace as she squealed into my ear. "For all that is bad in my life, you, dear sister, keep the good at an equal balance."

I heartily agreed. We rejoined the company just as the servants finished laying out the picnic.

Cold meats, cheese, fruit, and breads were offered along with lemonade. It was quite a handsome feast.

Sir Ronald beckoned Clara over to his blanket to share the small spread he'd prepared, and as she settled in beside him, Georgiana positioned herself on his right.

Realizing my duty, I searched for wavy brown hair and listened for a deep, velvety voice, finally finding Peter dallying near a servant at the carriage. For now, at least, he was occupied on his own.

I grabbed a small plate, filling it with bites of everything that looked appealing. I was ravenous from walking miles, not to mention having missed breakfast, and just thinking about enduring Peter's attention made my stomach grow three sizes. Undoubtedly, a lady with my current burdens needed ample nourishment. I claimed a spot on an empty, smaller blanket near Clara's, training one eye on Peter. Some way or another, I'd have to convince him to join me before anyone else did.

After a few bites of ham, I savored the cheese and fresh bread, a bite-sized pastry, and a biscuit. A gentle breeze brushed across my face, and for a moment, I was entirely content with my circumstances.

A very precious, short-lived moment.

Glancing up to where Peter had been, I realized the servant stood alone. Worse, Peter was mere steps from walking past me—and heading straight toward Sir Ronald and Clara. I had to act, and fast.

"Mr. Wood!" I said too enthusiastically through a mouthful of biscuit. I swallowed behind my hand, forcing myself to meet his eyes despite the painful embarrassment I felt having his attention in its entirety. Curse my appetite and the desperation in my voice.

"Miss Moore," he said brightly, as though surprised to see me. I glanced to Clara, who laughed openly beside Sir Ronald, and then back to Peter, who stood above me with raised brows. My stomach clenched, and I regretted the amount of food I'd just consumed. For such small portions, I'd filled myself to the brim.

If only I'd been thinking more than eating. How could I capture Peter's interest long enough to give Clara adequate time with Sir Ronald? Anything dull would not do. I needed to truly surprise him. But what about me would surprise Peter Wood? Too often I kept to myself, a creature comfortable with solitude, prone to laughing about thoughts in her head. What tactics did I have to keep a man's attention? What did men even want to hear? A compliment, perhaps?

I straightened my back, brushing my hands with a napkin. "You look well today."

The compliment felt as insincere as a horse telling a fly it was missed. Judging by the mirth in Peter's eyes, my tone was not lost on him. But at least he found it funny. He cleared his throat, wiping away the smile he clearly did not want to share so freely. "I feel it. And how are you faring this beautiful sunny afternoon?"

"Wonderfully. Join me, won't you? We could chat about the weather or . . . whatever it is you enjoy talking about. You can hold a lady's interest, can you not?" I raised a brow to challenge him. Though I knew little of his personality and character, I had an inkling that Peter enjoyed a challenge.

Again, his lips twitched, and I felt entirely unsatisfied by his reaction. Did he mean to laugh at me? Or was there some other reason for his desire to force down his smile?

"As you wish, my lady. Allow me to get a plate, and I'll return right away. May I fill your cup, or offer you more pastry?"

"No, thank you. I am quite content."

Those bright eyes peered curiously into mine as he offered a deep bow and continued past me toward the spread. His walk—or saunter, really—was as carefree as though the wind itself carried him. His hair wisped with each step, and he threw a half grin to every person who greeted him. I bit my lip, letting out a heavy breath. Could I keep up with this game we were playing? Peter's confidence far outweighed my own.

He seemed keen to continue our acquaintance, but for what purpose? The worst of it all was the feeling of deceitfulness that surged within me. I had not actually lied to Peter, or to anyone else, and yet I felt as though I had. Creating an illusion of a friendship based on such pretenses did not satisfy my moral compass, and yet I had no choice. Clara depended on me. Her very livelihood, her happiness, depended on these next thirteen days.

Before I resolved my emotional dilemma, Peter was back. He rested easily beside me, stretching out his legs in a lazy fashion and situating his plate beside mine. What would I say now that I had his attention? How could I entertain him?

"Gloves today, hmm?" He graciously broke the silence, motioning to the borrowed pair in my lap as he took a bite of cheese. He must've wondered where I'd found them. Or perhaps he assumed I'd lied about my desperation. I might have to toy with him to get the time I needed for Clara, but I did not wish to lie to him.

"Lent by a friend who happens to be much kinder than a man I met in a little shop down the way." I sipped my lemonade, looking innocently along the back of Sir Ronald's estate. It seemed to never end, even as it melted into a perfectly blue sky dotted with fluffy white clouds.

"As it so happens, I know that man." Peter took a swig of his own drink, peering out into my same scene. "And I can tell you honestly that he is truly sorry for taking them from you."

I highly doubted that. "Is he? Well, I hope he learned a great lesson about his actions. You never know who you are hurting by denying kindness."

Peter hung his head, a gentle smile creasing his cheeks handsomely, and stared down at his plate like a troubled child. "I know." He jerked his head up and met my gaze teasingly. "That is to say . . . *he* knows. And he will spend a great while thinking more on his actions. I promise he is not usually so narrow-minded."

"Good." I set down my cup and stole another glance at Clara. Her companions were in happy conversation, and it was clear to me that their trio worked best alone. But what game was Sir Ronald playing? And would it work out well for Clara? The question unnerved me. For her happiness, I would do anything.

"Now." Peter turned to face me, the seriousness that had touched his features smoothed over with his original placidity. Apparently, the business between us was resolved. "Tell me something, Miss Moore. No one else has heard of you, nor of your sister. It is as if you've been in hiding and just brought to light. Why do you think that is?"

"In hiding" was a kind way to imagine our lives in Brighton. Without callers or friends, we likely seemed like recluses, though the truth was as simple as having no choice. Peter waited patiently for my response, as though my answer would unlock other important questions in his head. Unfortunately for him, I had more sense than to indulge him in our private affairs. Peter Wood, with all his charm, was nothing but an enemy to me.

"We live in Brighton with our stepfather, Lord Gray. We are no great mystery, I assure you. Clara and I have moved around quite a bit this last decade, so perhaps we've simply confused the *ton*."

Peter furrowed his brow. Even frustrated, he was irritatingly attractive. "That is a deeply unsatisfying answer, Miss Moore."

"You expect me to tell a stranger my secrets? Unlock the cavities of my heart, bare for the taking?" I mimicked his furrowed brow sarcastically.

"Yes. That would be fantastic, actually." Peter grinned, leaning in closer. "I am eager to hear them."

Too eager, in my opinion. What game was Peter playing? He was far too keen to get to know me. "Where do *you* hail from, Mr. Wood?"

Peter cast me a disappointed look before crossing his arms and staring at his plate. "Most recently London. Before that, I studied in Paris. My father thought it best for me to continue my education abroad for a time." He paused for a moment before continuing. "Or perhaps he sent me because he could not adequately oversee my studies on his own. Heaven knows my mother had enough work for him to do. But it matters not. Everything my father worked for is now mine, and I have every intention of creating what I want from his labors."

"Which would be?" I could not pull my attention from the curve of Peter's smile, the gentle way he shrugged when he finished speaking.

"Home." The word was soft and full of longing. Whatever Peter described, he ached for it and cherished what was not yet his.

My heart suddenly beat, as though it awoke from a deep sleep, and an overwhelming longing overcame me. *Home.* I could almost hear Father's low voice, see his bushy eyebrows, his nose wrinkling as he laughed, and feel his embrace swallow me whole.

"That sounds lovely," I said with feeling, meeting Peter's eyes with my own.

"Yes, well. Four-and-twenty years as their son. I think I've earned it." Peter's face fell as he looked away. An untold story lingered between us for a moment, filled with unanswered questions that itched to be asked. Who was this Peter Wood with a perfectly cut coat and tempting smile?

Before I could ask, the moment passed, and servants began clearing away empty platters, plates, and cups. Guests moved away from their blankets, and I saw Clara was still with Sir Ronald, Georgiana on his opposite side.

“Shall we?” Peter stood, offering me his hand.

Could I trust this man? He whose primary motive surely opposed mine? If my intuition was correct, he wanted Sir Ronald for Georgiana. And if his loyalty to her was half as strong as mine to Clara, he would stop at nothing to secure the match. Yet some mystery lurked just under his friendly facade. Some piece of him that was different, real.

No. This was *Peter Wood.* Though I took his hand, I could not trust him. He’d proven his character once already, and I did not need a second chance to form an opinion. Gloves would be the last thing he took from my sister.

Chapter Five

I dropped Peter's hand once I was on my feet and followed him to the gathering a few paces away from the picnic.

"How is everyone faring?" Sir Ronald asked with enthusiasm. "The end of the tour is just up this hill. The view from there encompasses the northern end of my estate, with all the lands run by my tenants. I will warn you—it is a bit of a steep climb."

"I am up for the challenge," Georgiana said airily, and the rest of the company agreed.

"Shall we?" Peter extended his arm to me, smiling mischievously.

Sitting next to each other in close proximity was one thing, but to take his arm felt as though it crossed some invisible line I'd drawn between us. Peter was not a friend, and would likely never become a friend, especially after Clara won Sir Ronald's heart and broke Georgiana's. But Clara's timid smile reminded me of my purpose. Like it or not, I was pinned to Peter for the afternoon.

"Thank you," I said, holding onto his arm as loosely as I

could. It felt odd to be so near him as he led me behind the others. A warmth radiated from him that compelled me to enjoy it to the smallest degree. I shook the thought away. This was the same man who scurried from underneath a table and refused to relinquish a pair of gloves he did not even truly need.

I stole a sideways glance at Peter, whose peaceful gaze seemed quite content with his circumstances. Not a single worry wrinkled his brow. Clearly, Peter and I led vastly different lives. He had the world in his hands for the shaping, and in a few weeks or even days, given Lord Gray's failing health, I would have not a penny to my name. How could I find common ground with Peter? I had no special accomplishments to speak of, nor beauty to flaunt. But I needed to appear interesting enough to keep his attention away from Sir Ronald. At the pace we were moving, we'd soon catch up with Clara and Sir Ronald, and my arm linked through Peter's would be entirely in vain. I had to distract him and slow him down with some sort of intrigue. And quickly.

"Heavens." Lifting a hand to my forehead, I tightened my hold on his arm, drawing a shallow breath to accentuate the facade. "What a climb."

"Indeed." Peter raised a brow, biting his lip. We stopped, and I took several deep breaths, each one longer than the one before. Up ahead, the group faded as they climbed over the hilltop. Even if I could give Clara only a few minutes with Sir Ronald, any embarrassment I afforded myself would be worth it.

Peter hesitated, and then reached around for my other arm. "Are you alright?"

"No. I am quite out of breath. I cannot take another step." I moved in front of him, blocking his way upward. A few more labored breaths and a slower than usual walk up the hill would satisfy my goal.

Peter stared at me oddly, as though piecing together a puzzle. "You do look ill, Miss Moore." His voice was smooth, cool, and a tease twitched the corners of his lips. "Allow me to carry you the rest of the way. I assure you I am more than capable."

My eyes widened. Surely he was not serious. But then he started to bend down, his free hand brushing my skirts, and I jolted forward, away from him. "No, thank you."

"Oh." He feigned innocence, straightening himself. "Well, it appears as though you are moving just fine now. Shall we continue?"

"I am not moving fine. I am decidedly out of breath." I glared angrily at him.

"Allow me to aid you. As an honorable gentleman, I cannot allow you to suffer." He moved closer, arms outstretched, the most infuriating grin upon his face.

"I thought you said you were not honorable in the least?" My voice was rushed, anxious, as I stepped backward, holding up my skirts. I had the most ridiculous notion that Peter would lift me in the air despite my weak attempts to dissuade him, and I would be mortified like I'd never been before.

"Nothing gets past you, does it, Miss Moore?" He took a larger, closer step, and I could no longer remain impassive. "In that case, since I should very much like to assist you up this hill, and if I am not honorable, then I shall not think to ask for your approval."

His hand grazed my wrist, and I bolted upward at a most unladylike pace. Peter was on my heels, and I shrieked as he reached for me. Faster and faster, higher and higher, I ran, eyes focused on the grass beneath my feet. Would he truly humiliate me? My side ached with sharp, shooting pains, and I sucked in a breath.

The incline had steepened before rounding out, and when I turned, Peter was only steps behind me, having just reached the top as well. He placed his hands on his hips as his chest heaved with exertion.

"Well done. That was much faster than I thought. And much easier than carrying you myself." He glanced heavenward. "This, by the way, is what breathlessness feels like. You should study the feeling before you take up acting again. A valiant effort, but nothing about your figure would convince me that you could not climb such a minor hill as this one after resting at a picnic."

My breathing was slowing, but my heart raged with anger. "I was not acting." I winced at the lie.

"Of course you were. But why were you so intent on keeping me from the party? That much is unclear. You are a clever woman, Amelia. But even I can see that you are still angry with me over those gloves."

I gritted my teeth. Having Peter openly reveal my motive was nearly as bad as being outwitted. He was right. Despite my scheming, I'd climbed the hill faster than I would've had we continued walking at our previous pace. Peter had won again. And heavens, it irked me.

I did not spare him a second glance as I left him to his certainty and confidence. I would not give him the satisfaction of having affected me. My anger with him went beyond those ridiculous gloves. In truth, I cared less for what he had taken, and more for what he *could* take from us if given the chance.

Fortunately, the company was in raptures over the view, so no one noticed my plight. I found Clara walking along the front of the hill with Sir Ronald and Georgiana, but she tore away from them when she saw me.

Clara led me to the back edge of the hill, far away from the others. We appreciated the low-lying farmlands, rich and lush with life, the shades of green changing where the sun hit, and the tiniest hints of color from budding flowers and weeds.

"Thank you," she said, lacing her arm through mine. "That picnic was perfect. And this view. Is it not the loveliest thing you've ever seen?"

"It is," I replied, heart calming with my sister's enthusiasm.

"I could see it every day for all of my life and never tire of it." Clara's eyes grew hopeful, full of longing, but she quickly caught herself and blinked the dream away.

"Were you able to offer such compliments to Sir Ronald?" I asked slyly.

Clara smiled. "We spoke openly about his estate, yes, and of my admiration for it. I think he was pleased."

"Good. Then my time with Mr. Wood was not spent in vain."

"The way Georgiana describes him, he is quite generous and kind." Clara's voice rose in pitch.

"Conceited and pompous are more accurate descriptions," I muttered.

"Amelia, hush. He will hear us." Clara laughed behind a gloved hand. "To think we've hardly been here a full day—"

"And already he irks me." I stretched my neck, rubbing it between my hands. If Clara knew Peter was the man from the shop, she likely would not keep quiet about her opinion.

"If he really is so terrible, I do not want you to sacrifice for me," Clara said in a firm voice.

"Come, ladies!" Sir Ronald called. "Shall we stop by the gardens before returning to the house?"

I pulled Clara close as we moved toward the group. "Nothing for you is a sacrifice. I can manage Mr. Wood." Though even I was not convinced. Peter Wood was different than any other man I'd ever met. In everything he did, he gave too much. He was too bold, too aware. And entirely too handsome.

Chapter Six

Dressed for dinner, I tugged on my evening gloves and pinched my cheeks for a final touch of color. Clara had already descended to the drawing room after I insisted she not wait for Mary to finish my hair. The delicate curls she fashioned atop my head had taken longer than I'd wanted, and I hated to be late.

No one seemed to notice me slide in, condensed together as they were, conversing merrily in the center of the room. I kept to the side wall, searching for a view between heads. Surely Clara was in the middle of the group.

Crackling from the nearby hearth drew my attention, where Peter sat with his back toward me. My nerves ignited, pulsing through my body, when I realized Clara sat opposite him.

"Amelia." Clara waved me over, a desperate look in her countenance.

Peter rose to greet me, bowing as I approached. His wavy hair was tamed, and I could smell the freshness of soap from his shaved jaw.

"Good evening, Miss Moore," he said innocently.

"Mr. Wood." I curtsied ever so slightly. "I see you have found my sister."

"Georgiana admires her. I thought it only fitting that I come to know her better as well."

Did he? That seemed an unlikely motive.

Clara looked questioningly to me, and I nodded toward Sir Ronald. With even the slightest of gestures, Clara could read my mind.

"Excuse me," she said. "I think I will join Sir Ronald and see what all the men are laughing about just now."

Once she had retreated, Peter relaxed, sinking into his chair like a thief giving up his mask.

"You seem a bit too interested in my sister. Perhaps you would be better suited to Miss Turnball." I hovered over him, arms folded across my chest.

"Bratten has set his sights on her. Not that I disagree with you, though, about your sister. She is too sweet."

"Right, you need someone as cunning and as overconfident as you." The words slipped from my tongue like water flowing in a stream. Why could he not just leave Clara be?

Peter reared back slightly. "You are as brash as you are beautiful this evening, Amelia."

I raised a hand to my neck, glancing around the room, though no one was in earshot of us. "I shall take that as a compliment."

"Shall we go in, Ronald?" Lady Demsworth called from the settee.

"Of course, Mother." The men stood, and without hesitation, Sir Ronald offered his arm to Clara.

"Well done," Peter muttered under his breath. "She left me just in time. Georgiana could learn a thing or two by watching your sister."

What was that supposed to mean? Did Peter believe that everyone schemed as he did? That he and Clara were compatible in their attempts? The thought was insulting.

I anticipated Peter would offer his arm to me, willed it almost, as it would give me a chance to reject him. But the words spoken were not his.

"Might I escort you inside, Miss Moore?" Lieutenant Rawles asked from behind.

"I would like that." I took the lieutenant's arm, narrowing my eyes at Peter. His lips were pursed, eyes set at Lieutenant Rawles as we turned toward the doors. Never had I been so pleased to attend a small, more informal dinner party where the guests could choose their own seats. If I played my cards right, I would not have to sit by Peter Wood for the duration of the fortnight here.

"How are you this evening?" Lieutenant Rawles asked, his voice kind and low.

"Very well, thank you. And you?"

"I am exhausted," he admitted with a laugh, his posture slumping as we passed into the dining room and toward the mirrored, candlelit table. "Demsworth's little tour turned into quite the trek, did it not?"

"To be sure," I agreed, taking the seat he offered me. What a gentleman. From his gruff exterior, I'd half expected him to behave more like he looked.

"Are you comfortable?" Lieutenant Rawles stopped above me, waiting.

"Yes, thank you." My face must have registered surprise at his gentleness for when I met Clara's eyes, she exaggerated a smile for me to emulate. Were all gentleman supposed to be this amiable? This thoughtful and caring? Peter's chair scratched loudly as he pulled it from under the table. He sat, scowling at his plate. No. Some gentlemen were brooding and self-involved.

Lady Demsworth directed the course of the dinner, asking general questions to each member of our company.

When it was my turn, I sipped from my glass, waiting for her question, as a servant placed a sweet-smelling pudding in front of me.

"Miss Moore, how is your stepfather faring? There are rumors his illness has worsened, heightened by a lack of his presence during the Season. But surely they are untrue?"

I stilled, unable to meet Clara's gaze. Lord Gray's secret itched in the back of my throat, choking me. Clara knew our stepfather was sick, guessed he likely would not recover, but she did not know with certainty as I did.

"His doctors have unfortunately been unable to find a diagnosis, nor any useful treatment," I said.

"What is it that ails him?" Sir Ronald asked, dipping his spoon in his own dessert.

"An illness of the lungs." I tucked my hands under the table, looking up to find Peter's eyes. They were curious and almost sad.

"How very unfortunate," Lady Demsworth continued. "First the loss of your father, then your dear mother, and now . . . He is smart to have relocated to Brighton. Medicine is advancing there."

That I doubted, though I would not say as much. The mention of my parents stung, but it always did.

"He is well taken care of," I said, which was not a lie in the least. Lord Gray hired more help than he needed.

"And Lieutenant Rawles, how are you enjoying your time away? We did not find you in the Season this year."

I let out a breath, happy to escape further questioning, and picked up my spoon. Our story was still unfolding, and the present company would learn of our destitution soon enough. When I raised my head, Peter was still staring at me, but this time he quickly looked away, busying himself with stirring his pudding.

Lady Demsworth rose from her chair before I'd finished my dessert, and I snuck one last sweet bite before politely wiping my lips and following her into the drawing room with the other ladies.

Before I could speak to Clara, Sir Ronald entered the room with all four men behind him. "Shall we play a game? A bit of blindman's bluff?"

Voices mounted in approval as the group gathered around.

"I haven't played since we were children," Clara whispered from behind me. "I will embarrass myself."

I turned to face her, finding fear and worry in her brown eyes. "It is only a game, Clara. You will not have to go first, and if you hide yourself well, not at all. I shall help you. Stay beside me."

"Mrs. Turnball and I will be in the corner conversing. Do see that you maintain propriety, Ronald." Lady Demsworth pursed her lips.

"Of course, Mother, of course. None shall lose her reputation in my house," he joked, pulling a handkerchief from his pocket. "Who should like to go first?"

"Georgiana," Peter called with a smirk.

"I couldn't," Georgiana demurred in a voice that wasn't at all convincing.

But perhaps if Georgiana made herself a fool, Clara would feel less ridiculous to play in Sir Ronald's company.

"Come, Miss Wood, let us start out with a lady and make the men look all the more foolish," I prodded.

Georgiana smiled. "Oh, all right. But I do not wish to guess names. I am terrible at guessing."

"But you must." Sir Ronald tied the yellow handkerchief over Georgiana's eyes as the rest of us scattered about the room. "That is my favorite part."

"Don't forget to spin her," Beatrice called, an edge of competition in her voice.

Georgiana smiled as she reached out her hand to Sir Ronald. He took it and lifted their joined hands above her head. She twirled under the arch of his arm, giggling as she spun. At the count of ten, he released her, then darted across the room to find his own spot. Clara sucked at her teeth, glaring at Georgiana's aimless steps.

"You should've volunteered," I whispered into her ear on a breath, but Clara only rolled her eyes.

Georgiana giggled with outstretched arms, turning on a heel in pursuit of any sound. She walked dangerously close by Mr. Bratten, who stood straight as a board.

As she neared Peter, he jumped a chair, knocking over Lieutenant Rawles's stack of military books in his wake.

"Who was that?" Georgiana asked.

"He's to your left!" Peter called breathless, and Georgiana hurled herself leftward directly into Sir Ronald's chest.

"Who do you have?" Beatrice called. "She must guess! It's the rule of the game!"

"Oh, let her be. She's uncomfortable," Lieutenant Rawles grumbled admirably.

But Georgiana simply grasped Sir Ronald by the arms to examine him. He stood perfectly still as she traced up his coat with her fingers, further up to his neck and then to his face. She giggled as she thumbed his smooth jaw, ran her hands over his nose, and tugged at his hair. "Sir Ronald?"

He took off her blindfold, gazing at her with mirth, and she shrieked in delight, hugging him around his neck. Surprise rippled through the company. Even Peter, whose frown and raised brow were in contrast to his usual smile, seemed taken aback by Georgiana's forwardness. Everyone relaxed in the next moment, though, save Clara, who looked as though she wanted to pop Georgiana on the nose with her clenched fist.

"Well done," Peter clapped. "Demsworth's turn."

"I think I am ready to retire," Clara whispered softly, pulling my arm into hers. I could not blame her. We were certainly the odd ones out in the room, knowing no one beyond our host, while they all knew each other so well. But then, why had we been invited? There must be something here for Clara.

"One more round," I whispered. "Let us watch Sir Ronald make a fool of himself."

While Georgiana twirled Sir Ronald, I distracted Clara

by pointing out Mr. Bratten, who was smoothing his hair in a mirror along the wall.

"Ten," Georgiana called, racing behind a nearby chair. Sir Ronald was neither slow nor timid, taking long strides toward walls, tables, and chairs. He barely missed Lieutenant Rawles, who leaped backward behind the pianoforte just in time.

"Where are you, Rawles? I can hear your breathing every time you move." Sir Ronald tilted his head, waiting.

"Trying to pin me?" the lieutenant said, poking Sir Ronald in the back before flying to his left. "There is nothing like a sea of bullets flying at your rear to make you learn how to dodge rather quickly in war, Demsworth."

Just then, Peter pushed Georgiana straight at Sir Ronald. He was mere moments from reaching out and grasping her again. She feigned terror, backtracking slowly. Clara pursed her lips, shaking her head slightly. Not again. Clara could not be subject to this again.

Thinking fast, I tipped over the chair beside me, but I hadn't considered my own proximity to Sir Ronald, and he whipped around, grasping a handful of my skirts.

"There you are!" he laughed. "But wait. Who *are* you?"

Georgiana's smile held disappointment, but Clara beamed. Whether at my intervention or my being caught I could not know, but her brightened countenance was worth it all.

"Hmm." Sir Ronald found my hands, tracing them with his thumbs, then up my arms with a half nervous smile upon his face. I blushed to be touched so freely, and by the man my sister hoped to marry. His hands reached my face, where he felt my cheeks, my eyebrows, and the curve of my nose.

Then to my hair, where he tugged on a curl, chewing his lip in thought. After a moment, he ventured, "Miss Clara?"

The room waited in silence as I lifted his blindfold, peeking under it at him. The hope in his eyes dissipated when he saw me, replaced by humor and embarrassment.

"Ah, Miss Moore! You bear a likeness to your sister. A fool, I am!"

"We are nearly the same size, though I am older. You should have felt for wrinkles and gray hair, Sir Ronald."

Everyone laughed, and I looked to Clara. Her smile had faded, but she reclaimed it when she caught my stare. If only she could be standing in my position. I was not interested in the least in playing the blind man.

But I had no choice. Sightless and wobbly with the blindfold in place, I followed the sounds of light footsteps which seemed to come from every direction.

"This is the worst sort of game," I said, feeling blindly in front of me. "Clara, tell me where you are at once and save me from this."

"Never," Mr. Bratten called, but his voice was too far away.

A hushed whispering turned into laughter on my left, and I moved toward it, arms flailing like kites in the wind.

Rustling sounds from all around tempted me, then I felt a sudden movement behind me and heard a man's easy laugh. I whirled around, leaping toward the sound, and bumped hard into the figure of a man. I grasped his arms, and he held me steady in an embrace. The most awkward embrace imaginable.

"I've caught you," I said. It was impossible not to smile,

though I knew I looked ridiculous with a handkerchief covering my eyes.

"Who did you catch?" Beatrice called.

My fingers searched nervously to decipher the identity of my prey. If only I'd paid better attention to the men tonight. This man's coat was thick and smooth. Expensive. Except . . .

"No medallion, so not the lieutenant." Though the figure was indeed a fine form, strong and broad and tall. He stood as still as a statue as I traced lines over his chest, which rose and fell with even breaths. My hands reached his shoulders, and the man drew a deeper breath.

"Am I taking too long?" I asked.

A rough hand took mine and placed it on his face. He shook his head mutely as though to answer "no" to my question.

"He is having too much fun," Beatrice said with humor.

"Or perhaps he is ticklish." Georgiana laughed.

I blushed, imagining what I must look like. How improper the entire situation was. Moving my hands quickly to his neck, I grazed upward to his smooth, strong jawline. "Not Mr. Bratten, who I believe neglected a shave tonight."

"She is not wrong," Mr. Bratten chortled from across the room, and I smiled. That left Sir Ronald and Peter.

As I traced his face, I felt a distinct crease in his cheek, a dimple from a smile he likely bore as I humiliated myself trying to discover him. My heart jumped. This had to be Peter. I raised onto my tiptoes to run my fingers through his hair. It was wavy and smooth, unlike Sir Ronald's coarse tufts. I ruffled it up before huffing and taking a step back.

"Mr. Wood?" *Please say it isn't you.*

As my handkerchief lifted, green eyes pierced into mine, twinkling above a wicked grin. "Miss Moore. I did not expect to be so fully scoured this evening with your lingering touches."

Laughter filled the room, and I pushed Peter away with a scoff, decidedly through with blindman's bluff. Why did Peter Wood always ruin everything?

"Would anyone like their tea?" Lady Demsworth stood, motioning to the butler. "How flushed you are, Beatrice. Do come sit for a moment. And you, Miss Moore, do join me."

Anything to escape what I'd just endured. Had Peter been laughing at me the entire time? Likely so. He'd made me a fool. And yet, my fingertips still tingled from his touch.

The tray was brought in, cups and saucers clinking. I followed Lady Demsworth's direction and took my cup from her after she poured. The company followed suit, and I was soon surrounded in activity. To my left, Mrs. Turnball and Lady Demsworth conversed about the upcoming ball, while Lieutenant Rawles sat on my right, restacking his pile of books. Neither drew my interest, and I placed my empty teacup on the tray before turning around in my seat to examine the room.

Mr. Bratten and Sir Ronald were at a card table in the front with Beatrice and Georgiana. Where on earth was Clara? More importantly, where was Peter? My answer came a moment later when I saw them a few paces away on the window seat. Clara looked absolutely discouraged with her chin lowered, gazing out the window while Peter gave some monologue that appeared uninspiring. How dare he steal her away twice in one evening?

Offering my thanks to Lady Demsworth, I squeezed from between my neighbors and strode toward Peter. Anger from being manipulated boiled within me, and I could no longer control my tongue.

"Clara." I tried to keep my voice even as I approached them. "I need a word with Mr. Wood. Would you mind? Perhaps you could find a chair at the card table and enjoy the game?"

She looked up at me and lifted one corner of her mouth. "Of course."

As soon as she was out of earshot, I took her seat, trying to appear unaffected by this devious man whose agenda to distract my sister from Sir Ronald had officially crossed the line. I would not allow it. What little confidence Clara had, what bit of armor she wore that protected her from feeling inadequate and undesirable had been long in the making, and I would not allow one man to destroy her dreams nor her attempts to achieve them.

"You and I must have a conversation. Now." My words were clipped, low, but I maintained a strained smile.

Peter sat up straighter to face me directly. "You are angry with me."

"Murderously so," I said.

But Peter's eyes brightened, and he leaned closer. "What have I done now to incite such a rage in you, Amelia? I thought we were becoming friends."

"Friends?" I caught myself fuming on the word and lowered my voice. I could not allow any of our company to overhear what I had to say. "How could you ever imagine that I would desire your friendship? You are the most unamiable, selfish, ill-behaved person I have ever met."

Peter's smile dropped as he raised his chin. Finally. Perhaps now he would take me seriously.

He swallowed, his gaze boring into mine. "Why?"

"Never mind. Only leave my sister alone. You have done enough to draw Sir Ronald's attention away from her, and I can no longer sit idly by. You do everyone in this party a disservice by meddling where you ought not to."

Peter was silent, brows raised. He did not counter me, nor did he seem angry by my response. Whether he contemplated my thoughts or was calculating his own rebuttal, I did not know, nor did I wait before counting more accusations against him in my head.

He took in a long, slow breath before responding. "Georgiana needs me to encourage her."

"Then do you deny it? That you are pushing my sister out of Sir Ronald's company to suit your own ambition for Georgiana's marriage?"

Again he paused, eyes too gentle for the overwhelming fire within mine. "My intention has only been to aid Georgiana in her own endeavor. I have no ambition for the marriage. Only for her happiness."

"At the expense of my sister's? How cruel a person you must be to openly scheme one woman into love by denying another of its possibility. I will ask you again to stop your interference at once."

He let out a disbelieving laugh, rubbing his jaw with a hand. "You do not know me at all, and yet you describe your opinion of me so brashly."

"Do you deny it, Mr. Wood?"

He leaned against the window in his usual carefree manner. "I do not."

I scoffed, shaking my head in disbelief. What surprised me was not that he schemed, but more that he seemed entirely complacent, content even, in his actions.

"Don't look at me like that," Peter said with an edge to his voice. "We are the same."

Immediately I crossed my arms. "We are not—not in the least."

"Really? What of your breathlessness on the hill earlier? And our private picnic away from them?"

I bit my tongue. He was not wrong. But that we were the same in reason? Absolutely not. A man like Peter could never understand the importance of a match like this for Clara, for me. He lived without a care, and Georgiana would too, regardless of whether or not she married Sir Ronald. Their lives would be undisrupted without this match, but for us, it would mean the difference between poverty and freedom. If anyone deserved to nudge her sister nearer to the finish line, it was I.

"You cannot possibly understand my motives. What we *need* from this," I emphasized.

"Do your needs outweigh my sister's desires?"

Huffing, I rubbed my temples. There would be no arguing with a man who had everything, who gave freely to his sister as she desired. Clara and I did not live like that. We were the minority at Lakeshire Park. But I would never admit as much to Peter. Heaven only knew what he might do with that information.

"Spoken like a gentleman who wants for nothing," I said under my breath. No matter what I said, he would never understand. "Just leave my sister alone. Do not engage her again unless she approaches you first."

"Or what?" Peter smiled, and I realized I had no actual threat to back up my demand. "If you want me to step back, Amelia, you will have to give me something in return."

"What is that?" I asked disdainfully, turning my gaze out the window. He knew I likely could not give him what he wanted, yet he baited me with the possibility.

There was a pause, an unexpected hesitation. I drew three steady breaths before he spoke. "Your company. Every afternoon until we leave."

I whipped my head around to meet him. "What? That is preposterous."

"It is the only way I will relent. But you must also keep from scheming."

"You cannot be serious." I shook my head, waiting for him to laugh at his own teasing. What could he possibly want with me? What sort of trick did he have up his sleeve now?

"I am in earnest." He looked intently at me, as though we were discussing a legitimate trade. "Are you in agreement?"

"My company in exchange for you loosening your hold on Sir Ronald?"

"Yes," he said firmly.

I looked away, balling my fists. Who was this man? And why did he live to aggravate me? It mattered not; I had to agree if I wanted to help Clara. Her future depended on this match, and I had no doubt if she was left to her own will, she could secure it. We only needed time.

"Agreed," I said through my clenched jaw, standing. How had this happened? What had I done to deserve such difficulty and trial? Peter could tease and bait and laugh, while I had to plan and pray and hope. Anger at the injustice of my circumstances and the frivolity of his weighed heavily in my chest like molten iron. "But mind, Mr. Wood, if you so much as step out of line, I will make you the most miserable man in all of Hampshire."

To my further irritation, the words only bolstered Peter's grin. "Don't tempt me, Amelia. I am already having so much fun."

Chapter Seven

Mary pulled at my hair, tightening and twisting each curl atop my head.

"Do be kind, Mary." I winced, gripping the handles of my chair.

"Of course, miss. Forgive me for saying so, but you are usually not so tender-headed."

Mary gently pinned a piece of hair, and I relaxed my shoulders. I had not slept well, tossing and turning all night over my conversation with Peter. His ultimatum had soured my mood even this morning. Why, of all the things he could have asked for, would Peter choose my company? There must be some hidden scheme I'd neglected to account for. I would find out soon enough.

The door to my bedchamber swung open, and Clara rushed in.

"Amelia, you are awake. Good." Her eyes were frantic. "I need to borrow your necklace. The flower pendant. Georgiana is also wearing pearls."

Clara reached around her neck to unfasten the pearl

necklace she wore, before yanking open my jewelry box and shuffling through the few items I possessed. Clara hadn't worn much jewelry in London, but clearly she intended to while we were at Lakeshire Park.

"It's in my drawer," I answered as Mary twisted a larger portion of hair at the base of my neck. Her deft fingers were swift and sure. "We cannot have you complementing your rival, can we?"

"Georgiana is not my friend, that is most certain. When I came downstairs, she greeted me by saying my maid had misplaced a pin in my hair and that I should have her adjust it before breakfast."

Mary scoffed.

"The nerve of that girl!" I said. "She and her brother are relentless."

"Do not worry, I told her my maid does not misplace pins, and I played the pianoforte to distract myself." Clara shook her head as she paced to my drawer. "Sir Ronald complimented my talent."

Mary and I caught each other's smile. "How is Sir Ronald this morning?" I asked.

"He is such a thoughtful host. He is taking us through town after breakfast," Clara said over her shoulder as she sorted through my things. "And Mr. Wood asked after you."

"Did he?" I let out a heavy breath. Clearly he meant to waste no time in punishing me.

"I told him you were coming down for breakfast. Are you nearly ready?"

"One more minute," Mary said, holding a pin between her lips.

Clara fastened my necklace around her throat and examined herself in the mirror. "That is better."

"First my gloves, and now my necklace." I shot her an amused smile. "Is there anything else of mine you require?"

"Your wit," Clara said seriously. "Oh, I shall never make it through this day."

If I possessed enough wit, I would not be preparing for an afternoon with Peter. "You do not need it. You need only be yourself."

Clara frowned at her reflection in the mirror. What was it she saw looking back? Why did she care so much about her appearance and distinction? Sir Ronald could not care as greatly as she did. Was love worth such stress?

Mary clapped her hands together, and I looked to my own reflection, meeting light brown eyes like my mother's. Auburn hair framed my face in an elegant, smooth twist.

"Perfect." Clara tugged me up from my chair. "Quickly now. We are late."

Clara and I were the last to arrive for breakfast, and therefore the last to choose seats. She sat at Lady Demsworth's left, while I found a seat by Beatrice, thankfully on the opposite end of the table from Peter.

"What is the town like, Sir Ronald?" Beatrice asked.

"It is small," he answered, peeking at Clara. "The people are kind, and you will find they keep their shops clean and professional. We've a bookseller, a bakery, a milliner—"

"That sounds lovely. We passed by a specialty shop on our way to Lakeshire Park," Georgiana said, chin raised as though she'd built the shop herself. "Hats, shoes, cravats—they sold it all. Their glove maker recently retired, though."

"Yes, that is likely the same shop we stopped at before arriving," Clara said. "Though Amelia did not have a very welcoming experience."

I coughed, choking down a bite of egg, and stole a glance at Peter. He chewed through an unrepentant grin, cutting at something on his plate. At least the desire to keep our secret was mutual.

Sir Ronald glanced at me as though to apologize for my inconvenience. "How unfortunate. It is difficult to keep business afloat so far out in the country. I am sure someone will be filling the position soon. Besides shopping, I shall take you all for a stroll through the park, of course."

"How long do we anticipate being away?" Peter asked, stealing my attention from my plate.

"Likely through the afternoon," Sir Ronald replied casually.

Peter heaved a dramatic sigh, looking to me. "Pity, Miss Moore. You and I shall have to stay behind."

"What's that?" Georgiana looked up at her brother.

"Miss Moore and I have committed ourselves to charity work on the estate this afternoon. We shall have to join you next time." Peter continued eating as though nothing amiss had been said. Our company, however, looked to me.

Wiping my lips with a napkin, I offered a small nod and a most uncomfortable smile. What exactly were Peter's intentions? What on earth had I gotten myself into? I could not refuse him, nor could I question him in front of our entire company. "Indeed, Mr. Wood. I was sure our absence would have gone unnoticed for so *short* a time."

"How thoughtful of you two." Lady Demsworth smiled affectionately. "And now Mrs. Turnball and I have a perfect excuse to stay behind as well."

"Well done, Wood." Sir Ronald nodded in approval. "You always were a generous fellow."

And a schemer and a scoundrel.

Soon after breakfast, Sir Ronald called for the carriage, and the company broke apart to ready themselves. I started up the staircase with no intention of engaging Peter before I had to, but he stole around me.

"Your riding habit, if you please, Miss Moore. I will be waiting down here to see off the carriage."

His smile, curious and confident, dimpled his cheeks. The sight sent a jolt through my chest as I remembered the feeling of that dimple under my fingers during yesterday's game. Blast Peter Wood and his confidence and his cheeky smile. Though I wanted to walk right through him, I had no choice but to nod in agreeance. Satisfied, he stepped aside and let me pass.

Clara tried to be disappointed at my staying behind, until I reminded her that I would be keeping Peter away from Georgiana's influence and Sir Ronald's attention. After changing into my sky-blue riding habit, I filled her reticule with coins of my own before sending her off.

Peter waved as the carriage retreated down the drive, and I rubbed my hands together behind my back. We were not entirely alone as Lady Demsworth and Mrs. Turnball were in the drawing room, but it felt the same, regardless.

"Shall we?" Peter held out his arm, a new easiness to his posture. His bright eyes were full of excitement.

"Where are you taking me, Mr. Wood?" I took his arm, and he tightened his hold. I had little hope his "charity work" was charitable at all.

"It is a surprise. I am certain you will hate it and regret the day you bargained with me."

That much was true. He met my narrowed eyes with a chuckle.

Two horses were saddled just outside the stable. A groom helped me onto the mounting block, setting me easily atop the back of a horse.

"Summer is the gentlest we've got," he said, rubbing her nose. "Aren't you, girl?"

Not that I had enough experience on horseback to know the difference. I hadn't had a real opportunity to ride since childhood. I suppressed my nervousness, rubbing Summer's chestnut mane. She was quite the beauty.

" . . . a mile or so south. You'll find enough there for the entire estate," a man said to Peter, leaving me to wonder what I'd missed. Find enough of what?

"Perfect," Peter said to the man. "Come along, Miss Moore," he called as he led his horse out of the stables and into the morning sunlight.

Anything for Clara. I kicked at Summer, who started lazily toward the gate. At this pace, we wouldn't return until dinner.

With the groom not far behind, we rode side by side without speaking for a time, listening to the birdsong in the treetops. The air warmed as the sun rose above the trees. Enjoying the clopping of horse hooves on the hard dirt path, and the gentle, easy sway of Summer's pace, I relaxed into my own thoughts.

"You are enjoying this too much." Peter's voice was light and amused. "You are supposed to be miserable."

I snapped to attention, catching his contagious smile. "I am horribly miserable, don't you worry."

"Excellent, then some conversation should increase your misery just enough."

I moaned. Why must he ruin my comfortable sunshine? Couldn't we just trudge through our afternoons silently and leave both parties satisfied?

"Do you have any other siblings? Besides Miss Clara?" he asked, as though the question was as intriguing as a hidden chest of treasure.

"I do not. And you?" I asked the question to be polite, before realizing I'd only fueled the conversation.

"It seems we have a commonality. Only Georgiana." He smiled at me, but I looked away. "And what of your parents? How did they meet?"

"Oh no, you're a romantic," I said with a pained expression. He'd be disappointed with Mother and Father's story, and even more so with Lord Gray's. Neither was romantic in the least.

Peter straightened. "Perhaps I am. Most women find the sentiment charming."

"Or unrealistic." I raised a brow at him, and he tilted his head back in jest.

"Amelia Moore does not believe in love?"

"Amelia Moore believes in practicality and sensibility."

"Why?" he asked pointedly, defensively.

I thought for a moment, taken aback by his need for an answer. "Because love cannot be trusted. It comes and goes, and those who have it and lose it suffer most acutely."

I avoided Peter's gaze, though I felt his stare as he spoke. "But they also live more fully than those who do not open their hearts at all."

"I would debate you, but I have a feeling neither of us would win."

Peter chuckled, his eyes lighting up, though he did not press me.

As angry as I was at Peter for all his meddling and coercion, I appreciated the cheerful way he held his opinions. I thought about his words as Summer kept pace with Peter's steed. What experience did Peter have with love? Any at all? To be so confident that love was a strength was an endearing sentiment, but a foolhardy belief. I'd thought Peter more practical than that.

He continued his questioning. "What is your life like in Brighton? What do you do with your days?"

I shifted uncomfortably in my saddle. He likely thought I spent my days on the shore, meeting tourists and entertaining company. What would he think of me if I told him the truth of my situation? No one knew how we really lived. No one ever asked. But what would it hurt to be honest with him? At the very worst he'd think less of me, and then perhaps he'd be tempted to release me from his company.

I cleared my throat. "I play the pianoforte in the mornings, because that is when Lord Gray bathes in the sea, and it would otherwise disturb him. When he arrives home, I see to his comfort, get him his paper, his cigar, his tea. He expects me to stitch and manage the house while he rests. If I am lucky enough for a bit of leisure, I like to read or walk along the shore with Clara."

"I imagine you meet many people there." He stared ahead, and a wave of self-consciousness blew through me. I'd been right. His opinion of me changed in an instant.

"No, actually. We rarely take visitors at Gray House. Though it is fun to watch the beachgoers and imagine their lives and where they are from."

"Careful, Amelia. That is a very romantic sentiment." Peter gave me a half-smile, which I did not return.

"Hardly. What about you? What do you do with all of your leisure?"

"All of my leisure?" He coughed. "You think I mull around taking tea and making calls to all the eligible ladies in Hampshire?"

I imagined Peter with his pinky in the air and suppressed a grin.

"Not that you care, as my money is of little consequence to your highbrow." He sat straighter in his saddle. "But I do have a decent holding, and I manage my tenants and see to their needs. When I am not seeing to the estate, Georgiana is on my heels with a notion or need that she cannot live without and so I see to that as well."

Turning my head away, I pursed my lips. I did not believe for a second that Peter had any idea what Georgiana could or could not live without. Perhaps he required as much extravagance as she did.

"I know you think I overindulge her." Peter's voice had softened, and I met his eyes, surprised at how kind and almost sad they seemed. "But she is my greatest friend. Her happiness means the world to me. What she has suffered from our mother's lack of care, I try to make up for her now. But you may judge me as you wish."

I studied his profile and the confident way he presented himself. Whatever his parents had done or not done, Peter carried much of the consequence. And I could not judge him for *how* he carried it. If I had the means to spoil Clara as he did Georgiana, I could not say that I would not do the same.

"Regardless of what I think, you have done well in your care of her," I offered, and he looked at me questioningly, as though waiting for me to follow my compliment with censure. "I hope the same can be said of Clara, as I feel I have failed her in many ways."

"No." He shook his head. "I doubted any woman at the Season had caught Sir Ronald's attention until you and your sister arrived. Then again, I am surprised he saw her and not you."

What had he just said? Did he mean to compliment me? The cool breeze brushed against my suddenly hot cheeks. "Save your flattery, Mr. Wood. It is lost on me."

"Ah, but your blush says otherwise." Amusement bubbled in his words as he spoke, and I wanted to reach across the space between our horses and shove him straight off. Heavens, he was frustrating.

"Come on, old girl," I said to Summer in a feeble attempt to abandon Peter once and for all. We were nearing the edge of the hill. I leaned forward, and Summer grunted under my weight. "Am I really putting you out so dearly? I cannot be the heaviest load you've carried."

Though she was maddeningly slow, Summer was by far the sweetest, gentlest mare I'd ever met. She would not even bat a fly from her back. In the process of one ride, I had already grown to adore her.

Peter chided her with a tsk, drawing near to me and slapping Summer's rump. She pulled forward in a dash, and I lost my balance, recovering only just in time.

"Peter!" I shrieked as he drew even with me. Every vein in my body pulsed with a lively exhilaration.

Peter laughed unabashedly. "I've been wondering how to convince you to use my Christian name."

I swatted the air at him playfully. "Thank heavens your Christian name will not be the last word out of me." And that no one else was around to have heard my slip.

He bit his lip. "Forgive me, I had no idea she would do that. But you aren't supposed to be having fun anyway, remember?"

"I assure you, I am not having fun," I lied, forcing down a smile.

When we reached the foot of the hill, Peter dismounted first. Summer stopped beside him, and he grasped her reins with one hand, holding her still while I dismounted, and offering his other hand to me for support.

"Where are we?" I asked slowly as I dropped to the soft earth dotted with emerald green bushes.

"A far field." Peter motioned to the groom behind us, who was unlatching two large woven baskets from his horse. "For berry picking. Cook needs two basketfuls to make birthday pies for Mr. Gregory, the butler. Unfortunately, with the house party, no one has had time for the picking. So here we are."

Could Peter see the surprise I felt upon realizing that his intentions had indeed been charitable?

Upon closer observation, the bushes around us sagged with blackberries. Just as we'd had at my childhood home in Kent. My stomach rumbled.

"I imagine you will be very miserable," Peter said, his voice almost a question, handing me a basket. "The bushes are thorny, so—"

"I have experience." I pulled off my gloves without a second thought, reaching into a bush and plucking a plump, ripened berry. I had no need to observe strict propriety out here with only Peter as my companion. His opinion mattered less to me than that of the groom. I popped the berry into my mouth, the tart juice tickling my tongue, and immediately wanted more.

Peter went to work beside me, filling his own basket. For every half dozen berries I picked, I popped another in my mouth. I could not resist.

"If you don't start filling your basket instead of your stomach, we shall be here all day," Peter called from a few bushes down, but I pretended not to hear him. Instead, I sat down in a comfortable, grassy spot at the base of the bush. My basket was fairly full, and my stomach was heavy. Leaning back on my palms, I looked up at the bright blue sky dotted with a few pillowy clouds. Relaxed, I closed my eyes and breathed in fresh air. I let the sun wash over my eyelids, brightening my muted vision with red, and reclined further onto my elbows.

"You are decidedly the worst berry-picker I have ever met," Peter said, much closer than I thought him to be.

My eyes popped open. "Do you meet many? Up there with all your money and prospects?" I withheld a grin.

"Ha ha," he said, frowning half-heartedly. "You are one to talk. The daughter of a baron."

"*Step*daughter. And I see little to none of his money," I said, willing my nerves to remain unaffected by Peter's nearness.

"He gave you a Season, did he not?"

"I am nineteen, and this was my first."

"Oh." Peter cleared his throat. "Did you . . . meet anyone in particular?"

I cast him a glance, before facing the warm sunlight again. Had I even met a dozen different men? Danced more than half a dozen times? "Hardly."

Peter said nothing for a few moments, finishing filling his basket with berries. Then he pulled my basket toward him. I sighed as my guilt compelled me to join him.

"Back for more?" he teased, reaching deeper into the bush beside mine.

I licked my fingers and squinted angrily at him, plucking a few berries for the basket.

"Ouch." Peter recoiled, drawing back his hand.

"Do be careful, Peter," I said lazily through another bite.

He grumbled, eyeing his palm. A thorn.

"Is it stuck?" I straightened, moving closer beside him.

"Quite."

"Here, let me see." I reached for his hand, but he hesitated. "Trust me."

Peter extended his hand, and I took it in mine, surprised

by the roughness of his fingers. I bent over his palm, carefully searching for the source of his pain.

"There. Look away, and you won't expect it." I smiled, thinking of how often I had fixed Clara's ailments. Much more often than our mother had.

Peter looked heavenward, and, holding my breath, I pinched the thorn, which was larger and more deeply set than I'd first thought. He grunted, and I quickly kissed the spot, only realizing what I'd done when he froze.

My wide eyes met his, which were taken aback, and my neck and cheeks burned. This was Peter, not Clara. And he did not require a kiss to seal his wound.

"Pardon me." I cleared my throat, shaking my head as I turned away from him. "Usually when Clara . . . I was not thinking."

He chuckled and continued his harvest. "I appreciate the added touch, nonetheless. I'm quite healed, thank you."

Had I actually just kissed his hand? This had to be a terrible dream. I squeezed my eyes shut, groaning internally. I could never look at Peter again.

After what seemed like an eternity, I picked my bush clean, and together we filled my basket.

"Have you lost your appetite?" he asked when I stood. I willed myself to look at him despite my growing embarrassment. Why had I been so impulsive? "Would it help if I kissed *your* hand before we go?" he said. "Even things up?"

I furrowed my brow at his wicked grin. "You know I was thinking of Clara. Please do not tease me so."

"Were you? Then I swear I shall think of Georgiana the

whole time." He tried to wipe away his smile and waited beside me.

I sucked in a breath, pushing my basket into his chest and heading off toward Summer. Except she was not there. A new, taller horse stood in her stead, and I wondered where she'd been taken. Was something wrong with her?

"Wait," he called, catching up. "I am sorry. Here, have another blackberry."

I took the berry from his outstretched palm as meekly as I could, then turned and threw it right at his perfectly straight nose.

He said nothing as I walked away, but his infuriating chuckle followed behind me.

He'd had his afternoon. And I was quite miserable after all.

Chapter Eight

When the house finally came back into view, Sir Ronald's carriage sat at its front. We'd been gone longer than I expected. Since I'd stubbornly refused to engage Peter in conversation during our return journey, he took it upon himself to detail his recent investments and upcoming tenant house expansion. As much as I tried to be annoyed by him, I found his business well thought out and intelligent. I kept that thought to myself.

I left Peter in the stables, all but running toward the house to find Clara.

She was not in the drawing room, where I found Mr. Bratten and the Turnballs in lazy conversation at the window. Nor in the library, where Lieutenant Rawles paced the shelves. Georgiana and Sir Ronald were nowhere to be found either. Perhaps they'd stayed behind in town? Peter's voice carried from the entryway, and I snuck up the marble stairs to my right, heading for my bedchamber. A muffled cry startled me as I burst through the door.

"Clara?" I ran to her and knelt down by her bed. "What is wrong, my darling?" Had Sir Ronald refused her already?

"Oh, Amelia." She wiped her nose on her sleeve. "It was awful."

"Tell me at once," I pleaded, sitting beside her on the bed and pulling her hands into mine.

Clara shook her head, holding my hands tightly. "She was on his arm all afternoon, making him laugh with old memories. I tried to interject, but she belittled me at every turn. My adorably antique dress, how easily excitable I am, what a great complexion I have for mourning colors."

"How dare she—" I started, but Clara shook her head.

"Georgiana's words were so painted in sugar, Sir Ronald did not catch her true meaning, but I did. She made it perfectly clear that I do not belong with him." Clara buried her face in her hands. "I've been so ridiculous, Amelia. So foolish. How could he ever love me? I am nothing compared to her. You should've seen them together. I do not know what I am doing here."

I wanted to admit that I could relate, that I too felt confused and incapable of staying afloat since we arrived. What *were* we doing here? And what had I been thinking, dealing with a man like Peter Wood? Inept as I was at socializing, I'd sentenced myself to a fortnight of misery in Peter's company. He was proving more intelligent and clever than I first assumed. Huffing, I shook my head. Why had I kissed his hand? Talk about foolish. He'd never take me seriously now. Instead of posing a threat, I'd made Clara and myself a joke.

But feeling sorry for ourselves would not fix our problems. The truth was we were different from this company. We had neither wealth nor social experience, with hardly enough refinement to suit an average gentleman, let alone a baronet.

And yet we were here. *Why?* Sir Ronald must've had a motive to invite us. And unless I was truly daft, that motive was to court Clara. She could not give up.

"You are neither ridiculous nor foolish, Clara. In fact, you are the most intelligent, kind woman I know." I pulled her to my shoulder, kissing her head. "And you underestimate your hold on Sir Ronald by miles. He adores you. We need only give him more time to address his feelings."

"They are friends. Close friends. She knows more about him than I—"

"And? Where is the rule that states one must marry a childhood friend?"

Clara stifled a laugh, lifting her head from my shoulder. "Do you believe he cares for me, then?"

"Very much," I said with fervor. "And Georgiana must see it too if she worked so hard to steal him from you this afternoon."

"What shall I do, Amelia?"

Her voice was soft, afraid, so I strengthened mine.

"We shall have to help him see what he is lacking."

Mary helped Clara into her salmon-colored silk evening dress, which Lord Gray had fumed over for a week when he learned its cost, and I rosied Clara's cheeks and lips with the slightest touch of Liquid Bloom of Roses. Simple, but elegant. Her appearance alone was sure to catch Sir Ronald's attention tonight.

In accordance with my plan, we were the last to arrive for dinner. Clara offered Sir Ronald only a small smile and brief nod as we entered the candlelit drawing room, and we crossed directly toward Mr. Bratten and Lieutenant Rawles, who received us with enthusiasm. Before we'd had time to finish polite greetings to one another, Lady Demsworth called for dinner, and Mr. Bratten offered his arm to Clara without hesitation. To my grand satisfaction, Lieutenant Rawles escorted me into the dining room behind them. Undoubtedly, Sir Ronald would feel Clara's absence now.

I tried not to notice Peter, dressed handsomely in an earthy brown jacket, pulling out a chair for Beatrice. His eyes met mine, and I quickly dropped my gaze. But not before catching Sir Ronald's hesitant glance at Clara.

As I'd hoped, Mr. Bratten set up a card table after dinner, inviting Lieutenant Rawles and me to join him and Clara. The game was uninspiring, but we laughed all the same, teasing each other and praising the winners round after round.

"Three to one," Lieutenant Rawles declared miserably, though perhaps exaggeratedly, when we lost the final game. "They have slaughtered us, have they not, Miss Moore?"

"They have indeed," I answered loudly enough for the room to hear. "Clara and Mr. Bratten are quite the pair."

Mr. Bratten shuffled the cards with enthusiasm. "Your sister is a remarkably skilled player. I am surprised. After our first night here when I witnessed her play, I confess I thought she was the weaker player. But I see now it was Wood all along."

Smirking, I glanced at Peter, but to my grand irritation, he was lost in his book, sitting alone by the fire, minding his own business for once in his life. Exactly as he'd promised. Could Peter's word actually be trusted?

"Miss Clara, if I may," Sir Ronald said, starting toward our table with a half-smile. Clara raised her chin as he approached. "There is a picture I think you'd appreciate in my new book on architecture from the bookshop today. Would you care to see it?"

Clara threw me a glance before smiling shyly at him. "I do love architecture."

Sir Ronald helped her from the table and directed her to a nearby settee. Mr. Bratten and Lieutenant Rawles began a conversation about whist strategy, but my focus stayed with Clara. She blossomed under Sir Ronald's attentions.

The entire room seemed to notice them sitting together, sharing their book under the light of a candle. But only I noticed Georgiana stride to Peter, her eyes fuming and determined. I could not hear their conversation, but he rubbed the back of his neck as she whispered fiercely at him, hovering over his chair.

"What do you think, Miss Moore?" Mr. Bratten asked.

"I'm sorry?" I drew my attention back to the men in front of me. They stared at me, waiting for my response. "Forgive me, gentlemen, the only strategy I entertain in gaming is in chess. Perhaps you should start a match. I'd love to watch."

"Of course." Mr. Bratten, who apparently never turned down a good game, looked hopefully to Lieutenant Rawles.

"Miss Moore, if you are finished, please come and join us," Lady Demsworth called from across the room. She and the Turnballs sat near the hearth, close to where Peter had been, though his chair was now empty.

Weighing my options, I decided conversation with Lady Demsworth would better serve Clara's endeavors than watching a game of chess. I offered my regrets as Lieutenant Rawles pulled out the chessboard and found a seat opposite Georgiana, whose arms were crossed defiantly. She was clearly put out, and I could not blame her. Clara had Sir Ronald's attention for the night.

". . . Mr. Turnball was so surprised I said yes, he couldn't speak for an entire minute. You see, I'd already had seven other offers! He did not think he stood a chance," Mrs. Turnball concluded, and I tried to piece together her words. What sort of conversation had I walked into?

"Poor man," Lady Demsworth hid her laugh behind a gloved hand. "His courage proved worthwhile in the end."

"What about you, Lady Demsworth?" Beatrice asked eagerly. "Surely you had just as many offers of marriage as my mother. However did you choose? Might I ask you to divulge your story as well?"

"Oh, it was not at all interesting, dear. Our marriage was arranged by our parents early on. I am afraid my experience with *choosing* a partner is lacking." Lady Demsworth tilted her head as though an idea had just occurred to her. She clasped her hands, smiling as she gazed around the room. "Might I ask for your help with something? All of you?"

"Of course," Beatrice said seriously, and the rest of us agreed.

Lady Demsworth continued. "Someone to whom I am very close has asked for my help in choosing a marriage partner. Thus far, my advice has yielded no result, and I blame my inexperience. But perhaps with your opinions, I might find the answers I need."

I blinked, looking between the ladies in the room. She

could not be referring to Sir Ronald, could she? Did Lady Demsworth know of Clara's intentions with her son? Or of Georgiana's? Or was there someone else in the room pursuing a romantic endeavor? Judging from the raised brows and anxious, stolen looks, the women beside me had similar questions.

"What advice could we possibly give a stranger?" Georgiana asked curiously. "Perhaps if we knew the person to whom you refer—"

"I am anything but a gossip, Miss Wood." Lady Demsworth smiled coyly. "I am simply curious as to your thoughts on the meaning of marriage. Of course, it is different when you consider the perspective of a woman as opposed to a man, so you may answer for both. I shall open it up to your discussion as you wish."

What a curious topic, and certainly not too broadly debatable. Marriage was something we women thought about every day of our lives. It defined us, our status, and our security. In fact, without it, we were left with little control, if any at all, over our lives. Regardless of what she claimed, Lady Demsworth was not naive of the subject. So why did she care what our opinions were?

"Well," Beatrice started, "to a man, marriage is binding, but to a woman, it is freedom."

"Very good," Lady Demsworth nodded. "Women require marriage to enjoy freedom from the burden of livelihood, while men marry to claim her loyalty."

She raised her chin, glancing between Georgiana and me, as though judging which one of us would speak first. I knew little on the topic of romantic marriage. I was a product of marriage made out of obligation between my own parents and had witnessed marriage made for status after my father died. What advice could I possibly offer that would be of benefit to some hopeful soul?

"Love." Georgiana straightened. "Marriage means love to both a man and a woman. It is a commitment of that love for a lifetime, above all else."

Love? If there was one thing I could not rely upon, it was love.

"I disagree," I said before I could retract my tongue. Every eye in our circle turned to me.

"Go on, Miss Moore," Lady Demsworth encouraged, a renewed interest in her eyes.

Images of my parents flooded my memory. Love had clouded my Father's rational thinking that night at the ball so long ago. It had ruined my mother, changing her into an entirely different person. But worst of all, love had resulted in betrayal, pain, and bitterness for Lord Gray.

Could marriage be enveloped in genuine love? The kind of love that never chipped or faded away with time? My own experience negated the idea, but it was all I had. All I knew. I drew a steady breath, staring at my hands.

"Many marriages find misery when built on the notion that love will be enough to see them through. More often than not, we marry because we have to. Whether for wealth, status, security, or simply adding on to an estate. When the banns are read and the contract is made, we bring our skills and our best efforts to the task. Love is never guaranteed."

Silence filled the air, and I feared I'd said too much. I

should have kept my thoughts to myself, or at least shortened the explanation. I pursed my lips in regret.

"Enlightening." Lady Demsworth seemed satisfied, as though my words were the answer she'd hoped to hear. But why? Surely my opinion was the most unromantic, unpopular, and unoptimistic of all.

"What do you say, Mr. Wood?" Lady Demsworth said. "I know you are eavesdropping as it has been minutes since you turned a page."

I jumped when a chair creaked behind me. Turning slowly, I saw Peter had reclaimed his earlier seat, an open book in his hand. When had he returned? I fought the urge to hide my face in my hands for having been so bold and open with my thoughts. And about marriage. How mortifying!

With an amused smile, he slipped a bookmark into the pages and closed the cover. "I would have a hard time not overhearing with your party so perfectly positioned beside me."

"Well?" Lady Demsworth pressed.

"He will say that marriage is all money and business," Georgiana said knowingly. But that could not be true. Peter, as I knew him, was deeply romantic. Surely he thought love the most important factor in marriage. Yet another subject we disagreed on.

"It can be, and most often is, Georgiana." He narrowed his eyes at her in brotherly annoyance. "But in my interpretation, you are each right," he said. He straightened in his chair, a seriousness in his countenance. "Marriage means companionship. A merging of lives and loyalty. Yes, it is binding, and yes, sometimes it is more beneficial to one party than to the other in terms of monetary or social value. But it is more about what two people can be together than who they are individually."

"And what of love?" Lady Demsworth asked him, glancing to me. I turned forward in my seat, staring at my hands in my lap.

Peter exhaled. "Love is a topic all its own. But I agree with Miss Moore. It is not guaranteed. Only the luckiest among us will have it. And once it is found, it should be most aggressively fought for."

I felt his stare upon my back, but I was unwilling to meet his eyes. If Peter meant to imply that he would not easily relent his scheming to secure Sir Ronald for Georgiana, he did not intimidate me in the least. Though I did not believe that love took precedence over practicality, loyalty most certainly did, and Clara's happiness was my top priority.

"At any rate, I am sure our sex thinks of little else, lest we all become spinsters or governesses," Beatrice interjected with a giggle.

I took no amusement from the thought. The possibility was too real and too clear on my horizon to jest. Why on earth had we chosen a topic about marriage and love in the middle of a house party?

"Thank you all for your thoughts," Lady Demsworth said. "I think I know just what to say to him."

Him? So Lady Demsworth's friend was a man? I turned, finding Sir Ronald and Clara still at their settee at the front of the room. They had abandoned the book entirely, moved even closer together, and were in deep conversation. Clara smiled, giggling about something, which brought an even bigger smile to Sir Ronald's lips. Anyone with eyes could see the two of them were already a pair. The only advice Lady Demsworth's son needed was a push forward. Unless Lady Demsworth disagreed with his choice. Perhaps I would speak to her, try to encourage the union by offering my opinion on *that* matter.

". . . worshipped her. They only knew each other a week before he proposed," Georgiana said. I'd been half-listening enough to know she spoke of her parents. "It was the grandest engagement. He invited everyone he knew to a dinner party the next day."

"How romantic!" Beatrice beamed. "I love these sorts of stories."

Georgiana stared at me with unexpected ice in her eyes, and I was taken aback by the cold feeling between us. Had I missed something? "My mother would never remarry. She has only ever loved my father."

Peter coughed audibly, and Georgiana cast him an equally sharp stare.

Beatrice sat lost in thought, as though contemplating her own engagement, what it would be like, and how she would react.

"Do tell us your parents' story, Miss Moore." Georgiana cleared her throat. "Theirs is the only one we have not yet heard. I am sure it is most intriguing."

I became acutely aware of Peter shifting in his seat behind me. Knowing he was listening made the story even harder to tell. My parents did not have a love story like the Turnballs or even the Demsworths that, though arranged, at least resulted in happiness.

"Oh, no, it is not exciting," I said, sitting straighter and rubbing my hands on my skirts. A pit settled into my stomach, just like it did every time Lord Gray brought up my father. "They met one night at a ball, just like many before them and many since."

"I do love a good ball," Beatrice added dreamily.

"Go on. There must be more," Georgiana pressed. Her voice was too eager. It was as though somehow Georgiana saw my discomfort, knew the words on my tongue were not easily shared, and yet she willed me to speak. Willed me to admit that my parents' marriage did not happen out of love or even arrangement. She couldn't know of something that had happened so long ago and so far away from here. Still, I would not give her the satisfaction of embarrassing me. I could not hide from the truth. One way or another, it would find its way out.

"They shared an accidentally public kiss," I said, staring straight into her eyes. I would not tell her that they'd only just met. That Father barely knew her. That both their hearts were hurting that night, both searching for solace in a friend.

"How scandalous," Georgiana breathed, looking about the room. "How humiliating."

"Georgiana," Peter said low, almost warningly.

It was then that I realized that Lady Demsworth and Mrs. Turnball were watching me with interest. What would they think of my admission? No matter what Lord Gray's position was in society, Clara and I would never be able to escape the truth of our parents' scandal. At least this way, I could control how the story was told.

"Perhaps for them it was. But they married, and I have

much to thank them for, so I find no humiliation in the admission," I said, forcing a smile.

"Of course not." Lady Demsworth's eyes were kind, her voice soft. "It seems to me that whatever scandal resulted was well worth a few months of gossip. You and your sister are a delight."

"Indeed," Mrs. Turnball said with just as much kindness.

Georgiana's sharp gaze grew contemplative as she searched the faces in our circle. "Truly? Is there no consequence for scandal?"

Beatrice fluffed out her skirts. "I find their story to be quite romantic. Two people in love who couldn't help themselves. In the end, what is a few months of gossip compared to a lifetime of happiness?"

Happiness. How I wished that kiss had given my parents some semblance of it.

Georgiana chewed on her lips, quiet and uncommonly reserved. The fire crackled in the hearth, warming me from afar. I couldn't remember the last time talking of my parents had resulted in such a feeling of fullness, of strength. They once had to make impossible choices. If only they were here to guide me now.

Conversation continued as our circle opened to include the remainder of our company. More stories were told of worse scandals than my parents', including embarrassing proposals and courtship stories famously repeated in gossip circles. Lady Demsworth caught my eye, and I wondered how we'd come to have such a strange, casual conversation tonight. Who was her mysterious friend? Was he in this very room?

That night as I lay in bed listening to Clara's even

breathing, I thought of Father's old stories from my childhood. He'd tuck Clara and me in our beds and tell us *his* version of when he first met our mother.

Couples twirled and laughed amongst the crowd that night. He'd asked twenty ladies to dance, but every card was full. Then a brown-haired woman with rosy lips and loose curls wearing a stunning periwinkle dress walked through the open doors. She'd looked like she was searching for someone, but to no avail. He'd walked right up to her, having not even been introduced.

Might I have the next set with you? he'd asked, praying she would not question their lack of acquaintance. She agreed and took his arm, and he'd never felt so perfectly alive. After their first dance, and another, followed by a drink in a cozy corner in the room, Father was smitten. They stole away to an upper balcony where they'd thought themselves quite alone, and he'd kissed her there against the railing.

But they hadn't looked down, and a large party cooling off from the heat of the ballroom bore witness to the scandal. Father was trapped, and Mother was ruined entirely. They'd had no choice but to marry quickly and quietly.

Father's estate was situated far from London in a little town in the country, and Mother had to choose to find her happiness there.

Had they found love, like Father so adamantly insisted they had? Or was their love story one-sided? Lord Gray told an entirely different story of Mother's intentions that night. And I supposed I would never know for sure.

Chapter Nine

I quickly ate my eggs and toast the next morning, hoping to slip from the breakfast room unseen. The ladies planned to gather in the drawing room, but I had no intention of joining them, nor of making myself available for Peter's afternoon call any earlier than necessary. If I abandoned the party and hid myself well enough, he'd never find me, and I could return just in time for a late afternoon walk. Something quick, easy, and that would hopefully keep me free of further embarrassment. We'd not specified that our afternoons need be planned, and even if Peter searched for me early, how could I be to blame for his poor hide-and-seek skills? It was a foolproof plan.

Snatching my bonnet and satchel, I slipped through the entryway and out the front door.

My feet carried me outside beneath the clouds to a mighty oak tree about a half-mile east of the estate. Carefully, I maneuvered around its massive roots that broke free of the earth and surfaced like tentacles.

At last in the comfort of the tree's shade, I sat upon the mossy earth with my back at the trunk, facing away from the house. I could not be more hidden unless I scaled the tree to a higher level. If only I could have reached a limb.

Here was the solitude I craved. When was the last time I'd sat alone with nature as my only companion? I pulled out my sketchbook and pencils, looking around for a subject to draw. I hadn't the skill to draw anything too complex, but I could manage a flower. I chose the bushy yellow weeds that grew along the earthy floor.

After a few pages of sketching, and several attempts to draw a likeness of the birds that perched on the tree's lower branches, my hands grew tired. Securing my book in my satchel, I leaned back against the rough bark. The sun streamed through the leaves, warming my face. I closed my eyes to fully appreciate the moment.

I'd almost dozed off when a rustling sound pulled me to my senses.

"What are you doing all the way out here? Not trying to hide away from me, are you?" Peter's voice spoke in tandem with his footsteps.

Drat. There would be no thwarting Peter today. The man had a sixth sense for finding me. I opened my eyes and grumbled, smoothing my hair.

"Now why would I do that, when I owe *you* my afternoon?" Sarcasm was heavy in my voice.

Peter's eyes were smiling and playful. He held out his hand, which I ignored with a sigh, balancing myself against the tree trunk as I stood.

"Where are you taking me today?"

Peter offered me his arm. "It is a surprise. They've just been moved to a nearby field. We could walk there, if you like." He could not contain his smile, shifting his weight like an eager child awaiting permission.

Curiosity edged its way into my mind. "They?" Who had he invited to join us? Did he intend on humiliating me in front of the entire company this time?

"Come, you will see. And I think you will find yourself very happy." Gently, he tucked my arm into his, as though impatient for me to make up my mind.

Hesitantly, I followed him through the line of trees, back out into the clearing. "You're taking me along the west side of the estate? Were we not here just two days ago?"

"We were, but you'll find a different scene at the top of the hill today." Peter said mysteriously.

I narrowed my gaze at him, but that did not deter Peter. Conversation was his strong suit.

"What is that for?" He gestured to my satchel.

"It carries my things," I said flatly in an effort to dissuade him.

"What sort of things?"

The man could not take a hint. "A sketchbook. Nothing of importance," I said, focusing on my steps.

But of course Peter insisted I show him my drawings, and I had little resolve to deny him. What Peter Wood wanted, Peter Wood always seemed to get. Despite my lack of skill, he praised my efforts, sharing stories about painters he'd met on the streets of Paris. I listened attentively, fascinated by his experience and the lives of the scholars there.

How I envied him. What a privilege it was to observe such culture, to have tutors and opportunities to master talents. Life could be so different. But I would not complain about my circumstances. Without Lord Gray, things might have been much worse. At least Clara and I had a house and a bed and food. Those were the things I worried after now.

"Did you miss your family while you were away?" I asked. The familiarity with which he spoke of France made me wonder how long he'd spent there.

"I missed Georgiana. She wrote to me often. My mother and I have never gotten along, not really. And my father . . . he worked quite a lot. Even at the end." Peter stared ahead, letting out a breath.

Curiosity led me to prod. "Were you close with him?"

Peter glanced at me, hesitating. "I knew him well, and we were close. But my mother's happiness was always his priority. There were many times I wished to know him better. To feel more of his care. His opinion mattered much more to me than my mother's."

"Is she alive, your mother?" By the way he alluded to her, I'd thought she too was gone from his life.

"She is."

I waited for him to continue, but in vain. Stealing a peek, I saw his lips were pursed, eyes set ahead. "Have I silenced you at last?" I jested.

Peter cast me a rueful grin. "Paris is a more appealing subject than my parents."

I understood wanting to avoid something painful, so I did not press him. We walked a few paces in silence, my mind mulling over these new revelations from Peter. He'd known disappointment in his life after all, that much was evident. His mind must have been working as well, for his feet carried him faster, pulling me along at a racing speed.

Before long, we reached the base of the hill. Just in time for me to realize the ache in my feet.

"Slow down, Peter. We are practically at a run already." I panted as he tugged me upward. Nearly there, my lungs heaved, protesting the climb. Whatever the surprise was, at this pace, it had better be worth it.

"Close your eyes." Stopping, he released my arm.

"Why?" I stepped backward, glancing over my shoulder.

"It is a surprise, and I want to see your face precisely when you see it."

"I will not walk blindly like a fool, Peter." I thought of blindman's bluff and how he'd laughed at me. I folded my arms tightly.

"Just close them." Peter tugged my hands loose, and the strangest warmth radiated from his soft grip. "Trust me."

Something about the kindness in his eyes pulled me in, begging me to trust him, to follow his lead. But still, I hesitated. I knew I owed Peter this afternoon, but could I trust him?

Tightening my hold on his hand, I closed my eyes, focusing on each step as Peter led me a few paces upward. I held up my skirts with my other hand, waiting for the moment I would collide with a rock or a tree. But the path was clear, easy, and brief.

Peter steadied me with his strength, the sounds of his excited breaths between us. I was so close to him our legs brushed as we walked, shooting sparks to my toes and my chest. What was this strange feeling? The climb was making me dizzy.

Peter let go of my hand, and I waited, listening for any clue, a rustling, a voice, a smell, to reveal his secret surprise.

"Alright," he said finally. "Open them."

Something was running toward me, a small brown spot on wobbly legs.

"Is that a foal?" My smile grew instantly, and Peter's eyes sparkled.

"Indeed. A colt. He is barely eight weeks old. Curious little one already. Born to that mare there." He pointed to the horse in the distance.

By the time he'd finished his thought, the little foal had reached me. Only he wasn't quite as small as he'd looked before.

I knelt down beside him, taking off my gloves and rubbing his sleek coat. He was a light shade of brown with a blond mane, and within seconds he was nudging his nose all over me.

"Peter." Laughing, I tried to lean back from the colt, but he was so persistent and strong I quickly became pinned beneath him. "Peter!"

"Get off, you," he scowled. "If you are wanting this, you'd best behave yourself." He shook a bag of what I assumed was oats, and the colt jumped and pranced around him. Had Peter planned this adventure for me?

"His name is Winter, and I'm told he'll eat straight out of your hand." He poured a handful of oats into my palm. Feeling his bare fingers brush mine sent another wave of heat to my chest, which allowed Winter to nearly knock me over again in his eagerness.

The feel of Winter's rough, unsteady tongue, and the nearness of chomping teeth was both nerve-racking and thrilling. I petted his smooth mane as he devoured the oats in my hand, until Peter gave me more and more to fill him with.

"Do you like him?" he asked.

Winter nuzzled his nose into my hand, awkwardly trying to taste the oats. It would not be long before he mastered the skill. I gave Peter a full smile. "I like him very much. Thank you for bringing me here."

"Of course. Your smile is worth every effort." He knelt beside me, brushing his hand through Winter's mane.

I swallowed, smoothing my skirts. Surely Peter only meant to be kind. Perhaps we were becoming friends after all.

The colt finished his oats and was laying on the grass, letting me rub his back. His mother was a few paces away, watching over him. Something about the way the sun reflected in her mane looked so familiar.

"Is that—?"

"Summer? Yes."

"Summer just had a *foal*?" My eyes widened.

"Explains a lot, doesn't it?" Peter looked ahead, picking a blade of grass. "The reason Mr. Beckett had to take her back early yesterday was because she needed to feed Winter."

"Well, now I feel absolutely awful for hurrying her like I did." I frowned. Had I known she was a nursing mother, I would have refused to ride her entirely. Summer must still be exhausted.

"Mr. Beckett would not have allowed her out if he did not think both she and Winter were ready," Peter said knowingly.

I nodded, admiring Summer in the close distance she kept.

"That was very kind of you," I said to Peter. "Yesterday—helping Cook pick blackberries for Mr. Gregory."

"You sound surprised." Peter tilted his head. "Am I so incapable of charity in your eyes?"

I smiled shyly at him. Were my opinions that obvious? "I thought you more likely to *buy* blackberries at a market. Not to pick them yourself."

"You think my money defines me," Peter said, his eyes clouded by some new emotion. Sadness, perhaps. Or pain. "I can assure you, at the end of the day, I am only the thoughts in my head and the doings of my hands."

I pondered his words, touched again by the eloquence of his opinion. Could Peter be in earnest? He'd flaunted his money so easily in the glove shop, offering to buy all manner of things for Clara. And he had left us with quite the bag full of ribbons. Then again, I had not heard him speak a word of his fortune since arriving at Lakeshire Park.

"I would guess from your description of Lord Gray you know the burden of work only too well." Peter leaned in, scratching Winter's side.

"Perhaps," I agreed. How I wished money did not define my life, and yet it did. What would it be like to live free of constraint? Free of suffocating circumstances? To choose for myself without thought to society and what I lacked?

Suddenly, Winter stood as though someone had called his name. He jumped around, biting at the wind, chasing after what appeared to be a fly.

Peter and I knelt together, laughing as he played.

"What delight, to be so free."

"Go chase after him, then." Peter smiled mischievously. "Your freedom awaits."

"Do not tempt me." I laughed, half-considering the notion. I thought of Father and Mama and Clara, of our little estate in Kent. Oh, the adventures I'd had. But it was foolish to act like a child at my age. The time for freedom was long past.

"I shall close my eyes, if it will help," he said, covering them with both hands and smiling.

"I cannot." I poked him teasingly, and he rubbed his arm with a playful scowl. "How cruel you are."

"Fine. Then you can watch me." He stood up, grasping my hand and tugging me beside him.

Leaving me standing close by, he darted toward Winter, who leaped wildly as Peter tapped him on the back. Winter retaliated by nipping at Peter's knees. Peter dodged his nips and kicks as though dancing an exotic dance, and I held my waist, laughing, as he reveled in freedom. It became too much to merely watch. The need for a similar carelessness swelled within me.

Timidly, I stepped toward them, and Peter grinned, pushing Winter in my direction. Winter immediately engaged, jumping around me and nipping at my skirts. I gently tugged at his ear in an effort to deter him, but he chased me in circles around Peter.

"Run, Amelia," he called through a laugh, and I pushed Winter toward him.

It was like a game of tag. One minute the colt chased Peter, the next I raced him until I couldn't breathe. On and on and on. Laughing as easily as I breathed, like I hadn't a care in the world.

"He's gone mad." I leaped away from Winter, bouncing him back to Peter like a ball in a game. "Give me something. You must have more food."

Winter nuzzled into my skirts, and I pushed him backward.

Peter was breathing hard, his cheeks flushed from laughter, his wavy brown hair framing his face. He shoved away the colt and linked his arm with mine. "His mother can feed him. Shall we escape?"

"To where?" I swiped a loose curl away from my eyes.

We started down the hill, and I tightened my hold on his arm, bracing myself so as not to slip. Peter didn't seem to mind, pulling me closer. His coat smelled like the woods mixed with soap and oats.

"I can show you the orchard, if you like. You missed it on the tour," he said pointedly, smiling.

I remembered our first picnic together, when he battered me for information on Clara and chased me up this very hill. I did not know who to believe: the glove-stealing, scheming, arrogant man of our first meeting, or the amiable, carefree, kind man I'd witnessed of late. Both were undeniably handsome. But which was the most genuine Peter Wood? I rather liked his friendship this afternoon, but I supposed it did not matter. Either way, I was stuck with him.

"Then shall today's owed afternoon be accounted for?" I teased with feigned exasperation. The truth was, I'd had more fun with Peter today than I'd had in years.

Peter's grin dropped for so slight a moment I thought I imagined it.

"Worried about keeping me at my word?" His voice was

heavier than usual as he gazed across the beautiful, sunlit view that seemed to go on for miles. "The orchard first, and then I shall release you."

We walked a few paces in silence. Had I said something to offend him? I shot him a sideways glance, wondering if he would react to my goading.

"Good. I expect it will take me hours to fix my hair after all this *horseplay* today."

He raised a brow, looking at me with narrowed eyes and a smile on his lips. "Are you attempting humor, Miss Moore?"

I pressed my lips together, trying to remain serious. "I believe it was less of an attempt and more a success. Though I cannot say I find messy hair all that funny."

He chuckled. "For what it's worth, I think *horseplay* looks rather good on you."

I shot him a look of playful derision. At least four curls had loosened from their pins during our escapade with Winter. "Your joke is not as funny as mine, Peter."

"What would Lieutenant Rawles think?" he asked, peering at me through his lashes.

I raised my chin. "I am sure I do not know. Perhaps we should stick to proper conversation on our journey to the orchard." Especially if Peter meant to continue *this* conversation.

"That would not suit me. And I believe I have the final say in our afternoons, do I not?" Peter tilted his head. The orchards were just coming into view, with darkened clouds lulling overhead.

Powerless, I frowned. Was everything a game to Peter? These afternoons were becoming more than I'd bargained for. "I do not remember creating rules. I also do not remember having much choice in the matter at all. You were the one insistent on these afternoons."

He looked straight at the leafy orchard as we approached. "It was necessary, was it not? You cannot have me distracting Sir Ronald. And I cannot have you encouraging your sister." He said the words flatly, without sincerity, and I wondered if he had another motive. Something more personal, perhaps.

"Is that all?" I asked.

He released my arm, thumbing tiny fruit on the apple trees. "What other reason could there be?"

I studied his unreadable expression to no avail. Of course there was no other reason. Peter and I were enemies, two people on opposing sides of a battle. Only sometimes it felt like his compliments were earnest, his attentions given out of care. I shook my head. My inexperience with men made Peter's tiny compliments feel much bigger than they were. It was clearly Peter's nature to smile freely and flatter as he wished. Yet another difference between us.

"We share that priority, then. Loyalty to our sisters." I picked a jagged leaf off the nearest apple tree.

"Indeed." Peter said with as much indifference as though he'd spoken to the wind. That was what I'd wanted to hear, was it not? At least now we were both at an understanding. I wouldn't have to wonder about Peter's intentions with our bargain, for they mirrored my own after all.

Chapter Ten

Thunder rolled threateningly all evening, preceded by sharp lightning. I'd awoken to the storm several times, and now that it was morning, I hoped the sun would soon break through and dry up the ominous rain clouds atop the hill.

Our room was dark and dreary even with the curtains pulled back. I dreaded spending an entire day indoors with little chance of escape, but as I peered out into the darkened morning, my thoughts turned to Lord Gray. I became keenly aware of my breathing, how smoothly my lungs pulled in air and blew it back out again.

How was Lord Gray this morning? Had he slept at all? Many nights I wondered as much, having awoken to his coughing throughout the night. How much time did he have left? His home had been a haven for my mother, but a source of misery and pain for me. Perhaps I should feel grief knowing his illness was worsening, but I felt so little emotion, no hope other than for Clara's future. If she was happy, and we were together, then nothing else mattered.

"Is it morning already?" Clara's voice was hoarse with sleep, her eyes still closed.

"Just barely. It appears it will be a rainy day."

"Good. Then the men will have to stay in," she answered.

I peered out our window, listening to the pitter-patter of rain hitting the glass. She was right. I could hardly avoid Peter today. But at least indoors we would not be alone together. Perhaps then I would not kiss his hand or run wild on a hill or loosen my tongue and tell him even more of my secrets.

"Perhaps I will go down," I whispered. Being up early meant I could excuse myself later. "Will you sleep another hour?"

"Or two." Clara rolled over, tightening her covers around her.

The only person in the drawing room was Lady Demsworth, who looked disheveled with a messy braid and a loose morning coat about her shoulders. I'd known her to be casual in company, but this was quite unusual. What had prompted her to rise so quickly without first dressing?

"You're awake early, Miss Moore. Is everything all right?" she asked as I entered the room. Only a few candles were lit along with the hearth at the back of the room.

"Quite. I fear I've overslept these past few days. I am finally well enough rested. Might I ask you the same question? Are you well?"

Lady Demsworth yawned politely. "A tree was struck by lightning in the night. It felled a fence and loosed a herd of cow. A few of the horses got out as well, likely scared by the storm. Mr. Beckett alerted Ronald a few hours ago. He is fortunate to have so many dear friends staying with us. All four men have gone out to assess the damage. I am sure they will also assist our servants in repairs and in rounding up the animals. Ronald never could sit idly by. As for me, I could not sleep for worry of the cost if he cannot recover the animals and mend the necessary repairs on his own."

"Heavens." But weren't the Demsworths wealthy? Why would Lady Demsworth be so distraught over the cost? At any rate, I had not expected such severe news. "I am terribly sorry to hear it."

"Ronald will get it sorted out. I am sure I worry for nothing, but I am his mother. It is my life to worry over him, being that he is my only child."

"Of course you worry. That is natural. He is fortunate to have you, Lady Demsworth."

She sighed, brushing her skirts and thin coat. "Forgive my appearance. If you are awake, the others will soon be joining you. I should go and be properly dressed."

"Of course," I said as she stood. I wanted to tell her I did not mind one bit if she dressed properly or not. Given the circumstances, there were more important things to worry about. She did not have to pretend or put on a face with me. But before I built up the courage to speak, she'd gone.

Left alone in the drawing room, I moved to a chair facing the window. Raindrops slid down as though racing for a finish line, and for some reason, between the crackling of the hearth and the flashing of lightning, I thought of Peter.

Was he out there in this storm?

Was he safe?

The women gathered in the breakfast room one by one as the storm began to dissipate. More candles were lit to combat the dreary bleakness outside. We ate together without the men, who were taking a stressfully long time to return.

"Should we worry over them?" Beatrice paused before taking another bite of ham.

"I think not," Lady Demsworth replied in a tone that failed to reassure the group.

Mr. Gregory appeared in the doorway. "My lady?"

Everyone at the table turned to the butler.

"Sir Ronald and his company have rounded up a good majority of the herd, though a few head have been lost. And all the horses were found, excepting the colt."

"Oh no." Lady Demsworth lifted a hand to cover her face.

"Summer's colt? Winter?" I blurted without thinking.

"Yes," Lady Demsworth answered, surprised, before turning to the butler. "How long has he been away from his mother? Could he even have survived?"

"There is no way to know for sure, but I think, barring any injury, he could have. Is there anything else, my lady?"

"Please keep me informed. Thank you, Mr. Gregory."

He bowed and retreated from the room.

I scrutinized the faces around the table, each unaffected and relieved. That the losses were few was indeed good news. But what of Summer's colt? Was there nothing to be done? I could not bear to think of Summer having to bear the loss of her son.

No. I had to do something. If there was even a small chance Winter was alive, I had to make my best attempt to find him. Assuming the men had already secured the perimeters, they would give up soon, leaving the fields empty for my search.

"Excuse me," I said, standing from the table. "I am unwell, please forgive me."

"Of course, dear." Lady Demsworth reached out for me, though she was hardly composed herself, but I hurried out of the room and up to my bedchamber. Quickly pulling on my pelisse, I raced down the stairs and toward the entryway.

". . . too gentle and easily upset by such events," Georgiana was saying as I flew past the open doors of the breakfast room and through the front door.

Shutting it behind me, I surveyed the dreary scene. The rain had lessened to a thin mist, hazing my view. *Think, Amelia.* If I hadn't missed Sir Ronald's tour, I might've known where to start. I needed help, but there was only one person I could think of who might actually be able to find Winter. Not a person, actually.

Summer.

The stables were south of the house, and I set off as quickly as I could. My slippers were no substitute for sturdy boots, but they would have to do. With each step, the drenched grass sloshed at my feet, soaking my ankles. I shook my head with a moan. Did I really think I could find Winter without the good sense to properly dress for the excursion?

Pushing the thought aside, I focused on the stable doors until I shoved them open with my own hands.

Summer's stall was the first inside, and I could hear her whinnying and rustling in the hay that should have been a welcome breakfast.

"It's just me," I whispered as I unlocked her door. Hands up, I tried to steady her. I had no idea how to saddle a horse, nor the confidence to ride her bareback. But what choice did I have? My eyes scanned the stall for help of any sort and landed on a stool. On top of it was a small blanket. I looked from the stool to Summer's back, and my stomach knotted.

Summer whinnied again, her hooves restless against the stone floor.

There was no time to think. I spread the small blanket, light enough that it wouldn't slip, on Summer's back and edged the stool parallel with her.

"If we're going to do this, you mustn't run. I'll fall straight off," I lectured as I braced my hands upon the blanket. The stool lifted me high enough that I could swing my leg across, and once I was on, I clung to Summer's mane, wrapping it around my hands. I tried to steady myself before kicking lightly into her side. She took off obediently out of the stables and into the wide-open pasture.

I could feel her spine working beneath the blanket. I had to pull back on her mane slightly to keep her from moving as fast as I knew she wanted to.

Our journey took us up a hill and straight into the woods. Would Winter have been so brave? Drier earth beneath the canopy of trees seemed enticing enough to me, despite its being covered in last winter's coarse needles and leaves. My breath came deep and heavy from exertion, billowing from my mouth like smoke in the chilled air. The bare parts of my legs rubbed uncomfortably against Summer's side as I held fast to her with every muscle I possessed. She weaved through the trees, then stopped to dip her head low to the earth.

I took the opportunity to swing my leg across Summer's back and drop to the ground. If this was where Summer thought her colt was, then perhaps separating would help us find him sooner.

Eyes alert to the smallest movement and ears focused on the smallest sounds, I walked a few paces ahead of her, until at last clouded sunlight led us to another clearing. Something moved just outside the perimeter, stepping forward and then backward. Summer whinnied, and I looked back to find her eyes fixated forward, ears perked at the sound.

She darted past me into the clearing, and I quickened my pace to run behind her. Lifting my skirts, I leaped over sticks and debris from the storm, faster and faster, following behind Summer.

When I broke free of the tree line, I saw him standing right in front of me, swaying in an effort to balance himself, before he collapsed on the grass.

Racing forward, heart in my throat, I screamed, "Winter!"

Summer was pacing back and forth, nudging him with her nose. I fell helplessly to my knees beside him, stunned and afraid. What could I do? Had Winter not been standing just moments ago?

His eyes were closed, his form still. We were too late.

Feet suddenly shuffled around me, and I tried to see through my tears.

"Miss Moore, what are you doing out here?" My blurry eyes focused on Lieutenant Rawles. His voice was kind, but fervent, as he tugged me to my feet. "You must leave at once. This is not for you to see."

How was I moving? I could not feel my feet, and yet Winter seemed farther from me. Looking past Lieutenant Rawles, I saw Sir Ronald holding the colt in his arms while Peter examined its body. All I could hear was Summer's hooves beating the ground and a whine from deep within her throat.

"He is still," Sir Ronald said flatly. "We are too late."

"No," I called around Lieutenant Rawles, his arms wrapped around me like a doctor consoling a patient. My voice was desperate. "I just saw him moving. He is alive."

"Sometimes the eye sees what it wants to see." Mr. Bratten stepped beside Lieutenant Rawles, blocking my view. "You should not be here, Miss Moore. Let us take you back to the house."

Did they not see? Did they not even wish to try? Summer deserved better.

"Get out of my way." I pushed Lieutenant Rawles off, but Mr. Bratten grasped my arm. Despite raising my voice, I was not heard. "You must do something!"

I could see myself in the pity of their eyes. They thought me irrational, desperate. Sir Ronald lowered the colt to the ground. Peter rubbed the back of his neck, and Lieutenant Rawles stood near them, shaking his head in disappointment.

I broke free from Mr. Bratten, stepping toward the colt. My foot hit something hard, rolling me forward and paining my ankle. Looking down, I saw a hard, green ball, and upon closer examination, realized it was actually a tree *nut*. The thought struck me so fast, I had no time to think, no time to explain.

"Check his mouth," I shouted at Peter. "His mouth, now!"

"Miss Moore," Sir Ronald said, and I could tell by his tone he was losing patience. "You need to go back to the house."

"His airway." I barely managed the words as I stepped in front of Peter. Tears ran down my face, their salty taste in the creases of my lips. "Please."

Peter's mournful expression deepened, but he moved to Winter. Sir Ronald scoffed as Peter opened Winter's mouth, reaching inside gently.

"It's blocked," he said breathlessly as he reached deeper. An audible pop sounded, and Peter fell back.

Lieutenant Rawles reacted instantly, rubbing, patting, and shaking the colt's still body. We all watched in silent shock. Three steady raps on his back, then a twitch of a leg, and Winter's eyes flew open.

"There you are." Lieutenant Rawles breathed a laugh, half in shock.

"I cannot believe it." Sir Ronald examined the colt, who was standing, shaking out his tail.

Summer bowled into the men, rubbing her face all over Winter as if checking every inch of him.

I wiped my seeping eyes clear, relief flooding my chest. Summer had led me to this very spot at this very moment, and were it not for Peter's actions, for Peter listening to me, it would have all been for naught.

Peter smiled in awe, watching Winter take awkward steps around the clearing. The men all patted Peter on the back and praised his quick thinking, but he turned to me. His cheeks were reddened as he beamed at me.

"Give your praise to Miss Moore, gentlemen. Did you not hear her?"

"Well done, Miss Moore," Lieutenant Rawles called.

I swallowed the emotion in my throat, nodding.

"Forgive me, sir," Mr. Beckett said to Sir Ronald. "Might I suggest returning both the colt and his mother to the stables? He should eat and regain his strength."

"Indeed, Beckett. If you'll take Summer, I can lead Winter." Sir Ronald held out his arm to me. "Miss Moore, forgive me. I am sure you are cold and exhausted. I should get you home straightway."

"Allow me," Peter said. "As I have no horse, I can see to Winter and accompany Miss Moore on foot as well."

Sir Ronald looked between us, before nodding to Peter. "Very well. See that you do not tarry too long, Peter. I am sure Miss Clara worries over her sister."

Mr. Beckett brought Sir Ronald's horse to him, then secured Summer, while the others found their horses tied to nearby trees. The men mounted their steeds and raced off through the wood.

"Are you all right?" Peter asked me at last, securing a lead around Winter.

"I am still recovering," I said feebly. "But yes, I am well enough."

"You saved him." Peter's eyes searched mine. "And we are all amazed. But what were you doing out here alone? I do not need to tell you how dangerous that is."

I rubbed Winter behind the ears, and we strode toward

the stable together. I would not tell Peter how I'd ridden Summer bareback across the pasture.

"No one would have allowed me to search for him on my own. And I knew what Summer stood to lose if I did not help her."

"I think you two will be bonded forever." Peter rubbed the colt's head.

"Thank you, Peter," I said solemnly. Tears welled in the corners of my eyes, and I fought them back. I wanted Peter to know what his actions had meant to me.

"For what?" he asked, slowing his pace. He looked alarmed, as though I might break. And I felt as though I might.

"For hearing me." I could not contain my emotions. It was so silly, how one small choice influenced me. I rarely cried, and when I did, it was in private. Absolutely not in front of Peter Wood.

Peter stopped, calming Winter before lifting my chin with a finger. He hesitated, and an energy pulsed between us. "Of course I heard you. How could I not pay attention to you, Amelia?"

I wiped my eyes on my sleeve, steadying my breath. "That's not what I mean. You listened when no one else did. You tried when no one else would. You can't know what that means to me."

Peter thumbed away a traitorous tear from my cheek. "I am glad to hear it then. Only please stop crying. I cannot bear to see your tears. You've just saved this colt's life; you should be happy."

"I am," I said weakly. "I fear I am feeling quite a lot of emotions right now."

"Come," he said, wrapping the lead around his hand. "You need to rest before our afternoon together. You still owe me, remember?"

I should have cringed at the reminder, but instead my body calmed. It was an odd feeling that radiated through me, overtaking the rush of shock. For once, I did not feel foolish in Peter's company. On the contrary, I felt seen. Seen and accepted.

Peter let Winter set the pace, and we followed along, unrushed. The wind blew through Peter's hair, and his eyes were more gray under the clouds than green. He had not shaved, nor had he bothered to button his coat, under which he wore a thin nightshirt dampened by rain. It clung to his chest, and I blushed to have been so near him only moments ago and yet so unaware.

When Summer saw Winter again, she nearly broke through her stall to get to him. Peter placed Winter with his mother, who embraced him for a moment with her nuzzled head and neck before pushing him under her to eat.

I held myself perfectly still, taking calming breaths through my nose to keep from crying, though Peter eyed me knowingly. He laced my arm through his, pulling me close, and said nothing as he led me to the house through a drizzle of rain.

This was not the same Peter who hurt Clara with his scheming and attempted to drive a wedge between her and Sir Ronald. This man was real, genuine. My foggy mind could not find the anger and irritation that had so comfortably dwelled there. Instead, I leaned into Peter's arm, letting him bear the weight I struggled to carry. Judging from his small smile, he did not seem to mind.

We entered through the servants' quarters to avoid questioning. Peter was in no mood to relay the event, nor was I. He looked exhausted, as I was sure all the men were from such an early, stressful morning.

At the top of the stairs, he released me. As I walked to my room, I had the oddest desire to glance over my shoulder. My legs were weary, my eyes heavy, but my heart for some reason was alive.

I opened my door as another one closed down the hall. I hadn't realized Peter was staying so close.

"Miss Moore, thank heavens you're safe." Mary pressed her hands to her chest, voice thick with anxiety. "The house has been in fits with you being out with the men this morning. When Sir Ronald burst through the door of the drawing room to tell the story of you saving that colt, Lady Demsworth liked to have had an attack. If anything had happened—"

"Mary." I cut her off, peeling off my damp pelisse and mucky slippers. My arms were suddenly shaking, my hands trembling as though my body knew it could finally rest.

"You know that a lady ought not to interfere—"

"*Mary.*"

Mary's eyes fell, and my shoulders sank. I had not meant to scold her. There was silence save for the water dripping from my skirts.

I sighed, exhausted. "Forgive me. I know you mean well,

and I am sure I have caused you quite the fright. But I *dearly* need a bath."

Mary smiled her motherly smile, though she was hardly older than I, and nodded. "Of course, miss. Never mind my prattle. A bath it is, and a bath you rightly deserve."

"Amelia!" Clara burst through the door and rushed to my side. "Are you hurt? Your dress! It is ruined." Her words were as near a reprimand as any I'd heard from her, yet still as gentle as ever. "What were you thinking going out alone? What would I have done if something had happened to you?"

"I had to help." I shrugged, and she pulled me into an embrace.

"So I've been told. Sir Ronald is very grateful." Clara drew back with a scrunched nose. "You are sopping wet."

"Indeed. How are you, sister?"

"Well enough, though being locked inside has been miserable. I cannot bear Georgiana in the same room for more than a half hour. I fear she is more irksome than her brother." Clara frowned and rubbed my arm. "Are you sure you're all right?"

"Do not worry over me. I shall join you downstairs soon." I tried to nudge her toward the door.

"Take your time to rest and recover," Clara said as I closed the door behind her. After days of oversleeping, this one morning had drained my energy entirely.

Within the hour, Mary had a tub filled with warm water, and every muscle in my body sighed as I fell into it. I was still as tense as if I'd run for miles. I breathed in the freshly cut lavender leaves floating around me, soaked in the water, and let myself relax, closing my eyes and emptying my mind.

Mary let me soak for an hour before returning to help me into a peach-colored muslin dress. She had lit a fire in the hearth to dry my wet clothes and slippers. A tray of meats, cheese, and raspberries, paired with tea sat upon a small table.

I ate in silence, staring out my window at the afternoon sun drying the grass. How very unlike me to interfere in the matters of men. Would Lady Demsworth be angry with me for not only refusing to leave when Sir Ronald asked but also further demanding he oblige me? I did not regret my actions, but I could not bear to have Clara suffer for them.

I pulled on my boots and descended the grand staircase. I needed to see Lady Demsworth. I needed to know how she felt about this morning.

I heard voices from a room toward the back of the house. Instinctively, I followed the sound through an open door into the library. Bookshelves lined the walls and reached nearly to the ceiling. The ladies mingled with the men in close quarters throughout the room.

"Miss Moore!" Lady Demsworth flew across the room, encapsulating me in a suffocating embrace. "You dear, dear girl! I confess I did not even know you'd gone, but Ronald told me everything, and I am without words. What kind of hosts are we to have subjected you to such terrible circumstances?"

"The fault was mine entirely." I drew back, and she loosened her hold. "Forgive me for interfering without permission. I had ridden Summer a few days ago and was quite taken with her. I could not bear to subject her to sorrow without doing something to help."

Lady Demsworth squeezed my shoulders. "We are

indebted to you, Miss Moore. Absolutely indebted. Summer is mine, and I thought I could love no horse greater until I met her colt."

"I am glad I was able to be there at the right time." I had not really done anything worth praising. I'd been most unladylike stealing Summer and riding her bareback in my morning dress, not to mention raising my voice at the man of the house and demanding the attention of four very capable men.

Lady Demsworth leaned closer, and I tilted my head. "I meant what I said, Miss Moore. If there is anything, *anything*, you need. Anything I can do for you or any way I can help. Please do not hesitate to ask me."

I let each kind word sink in, leaning in to embrace her. "Thank you," I whispered into her ear, and she tightened her arms around me.

"Of course, dear. We have grown quite attached to you and your sister here at Lakeshire Park."

"Amelia," Clara called as though on cue. "What rhymes with yellow?"

Lady Demsworth quickly excused me, and I fell into a chair beside Clara. "Hmm . . . cello?"

"Yes." She giggled. "A yellow cello. That will do."

"What game are we playing, now?" I leaned on the arm of the chair.

"We've paired off and must write a poem with words that rhyme with yellow," Clara said. "You should join next round."

After my morning, a game of silly rhymes was as unappealing as eating grass. I tuned my ear to the hushed whispers as the company, most evidently paired off in the room, giggled and scratched on their papers. Clearly, the events of the morning had already blown over, and I had little desire to bring them up again.

Without a second thought, I excused myself. Somewhere in the back of my mind, I'd known staying indoors was not where I wanted to be, and I was grateful I'd already put on my boots. Now all I needed was my bonnet.

Chapter Eleven

The walk to the stable was quick, the air warm and humid after the storm. Instead of entering through the main doors, I ventured around back, which was a more direct path to the horse stalls. The wide door was already opened, its latch broken and dangling, letting sunlight illuminate the otherwise darkened corners. As I entered, the scent of stale hay permeated the air, magnified with the shifting of the animals.

I searched for a groom to no avail. Just so. To be alone for a while would suit my weariness.

Paces away from her stall, a voice drifted toward me.

". . . nice to be taken care of, sometimes. And I think you've earned it with the scare you endured this morning."

I stopped in my tracks. What was Peter doing here? I had not seen him in the library, so I'd assumed he was in his room.

As I crept up to the stall door, I found him crouched by Summer's feet as he brushed her legs carefully. He wore a handsome gray coat—how in the world were his coats always so perfectly fitted?—and a pair of Hessians over equally well-fitting breeches.

I scolded myself silently, blushing. Eyeing a man's breeches in a horse stall when he was completely unaware. How unladylike! Of all the times I should be focused, it was now. At last, I'd caught Peter Wood behaving more foolishly than I.

Summer whinnied, and Peter chuckled. "I understand completely."

"I did not know you could talk to horses," I said, leaning into the half-open stall with the fullest of grins upon my face. Peter had neglected to latch the door behind him, and it hung open freely.

He startled to his feet, brush in hand, and let out a breath when he saw me. "Amelia. What are you doing here?"

I smirked at his rosy cheeks. What would Peter Wood have to be embarrassed about? Surely talking to horses was not the worst thing I had against him. I tugged off my gloves and laid them over the top of the wooden wall. "Escaping games in the library. And you?"

He found a grin to match mine. "I confess I was worried over these two, but Winter has completely forgotten the trauma of this morning, and Summer will indulge in the attention she's getting for the rest of her life, I am sure."

"May I?" I gestured to the brush in his hand, stepping closer.

"Of course," he said, offering it and patting Summer on the nose. "How are you faring?"

"Much better. Did you rest?" I drew the brush across Summer's back, smoothing her coat and cleaning off the dust.

"I slept for a few hours. I thought I was the only one who needed a nap, until I came down and you were nowhere to be found."

"You were looking for me?" I looked up at him.

"I am always looking for you, Amelia," he said, smiling and lowering his chin.

A wave of nervousness stunned my heart, rippling through my chest. It tickled and excited me. Of course, this was only Peter's game, but I could see the fun in it.

"Can we believe him, Summer?" I asked as I brushed her. "He is such a ridiculous tease, with quite the record of persuading and baiting to get what he wants."

"I have no such record." He raised a brow from across Summer's back. "Only a few, small instances of exaggerated loyalty."

"Well, heaven help those who have not yet earned your loyalty, Peter Wood. For they could find themselves made quite the enemy over something as meager as a pair of gloves."

Peter huffed, a determined look in his eyes, his voice harsher than usual. "I wish I'd never entered that shop."

My heart fell to my toes. I stopped brushing Summer as sudden emotion welled in my throat. Was he saying he wished he had never met me?

Peter rubbed the back of his neck, something I was beginning to notice he did when he felt uncomfortable or out of control. "If I'd made Georgiana search for that deuced pair of gloves herself, I could have first met you here. And perhaps you would not look at me like you are now. Disappointed and . . . unaffected."

My brow furrowed, a sudden dryness in my mouth. "What do you mean?"

"Nothing," he said, more to himself than to me. "I only wish you were not angry with me anymore. It would be nice to have a genuine conversation. Not something forced by an absurd bargain."

Is that what he thought? That I was angry with him? That because our friendship was forced by the bargain we'd made, it was therefore disingenuous? I walked slowly around Summer to face Peter, half afraid that I'd read him entirely wrong and was about to make a complete fool of myself for the millionth time.

"I am not angry with you, Peter. Not anymore. I'd venture to say I talk more with you than I do with Clara these days. I've grown fond of our afternoons."

He smiled softly, and I wondered if he believed me, if I was right to be so honest and open with him. He hesitated for a moment, then took the brush from my hand and continued Summer's pampering.

Winter blew out a breath from the corner; he was fast asleep on his belly. Kneeling beside him, I rubbed his nose and petted his mane. He was so peaceful, so perfectly adorable.

Peter was quiet, and I worried I'd said too much.

"What are you thinking about?" I asked before I could stop myself.

"You," he answered, still facing Summer.

I scoffed at his teasing, waiting for him to laugh or cast me his playful grin. Instead, he stayed quiet as he gently attended to Summer. Guilt washed over me; I'd been sure Peter was exaggerating his claim. Regardless, after today, I had to admit he deserved for me to take him more seriously.

Winter stirred, and I coddled him until his eyes closed again.

In truth, I knew so little about Peter, aside from the small clues he gave me about his parents. If we were going to be genuine friends, it was my turn to ask questions. "Where is your estate?"

He stopped brushing for a moment, glancing over his shoulder at me. "About twenty-five miles from here, in northwest Hampshire."

"Did you grow up there?"

Peter's coat stretched handsomely against his back as he reached higher along Summer's mane. It was hard not to notice how naturally handsome he was. My gaze too willingly admired the strength in his arms and shoulders. And those breeches. I bit my lip.

"No. My father spent most of his time in London. He was more interested in the business side of things, which is why I am so well-trained to take over a farming estate."

I sensed his sarcasm to a sobering degree. "Was it a difficult transition, then?"

Peter shifted, brushing toward Summer's rump. I noted the concentration in his profile. "I have a well-trained steward. But no, after I tied up loose ends in London, things have been moving slowly enough that I am not overwhelmed. The choice to move was mine, and I will learn quickly enough. I am simply not interested in upholding my father's business ventures, nor do I think he would have expected me to."

I pondered Peter's words. Since the moment he practically

threw his money at me in the glove shop, I'd assumed Peter relished being rich and loved the society that fed upon status and wealth, but perhaps he truly meant what he'd said a few days ago. His greatest wish, above even wealth, was to be seen for the workings of his hands and the thoughts in his head. Clearly, he could continue his father's work and attain even greater status and wealth, but he did not. Why?

"But you admired him, did you not? Your father?"

"Very much. He was immensely intelligent. He could do math in his head in seconds, and he was an avid reader. But when I think of my father, I do not think of his work or what he accomplished. I think of the few memories I have of when he was *not* working." Peter rubbed his brow on his sleeve.

"You have my full attention," I said, straightening my skirts.

Peter looked curiously over at me. He paused for a moment before resuming his brushing. "Once, when my mother was away visiting her sister, Georgiana begged me to teach her how to shoot an arrow. I must have been thirteen at the time—about to leave for Eton.

"Mother did not allow frivolities like archery or horse racing. Such skills, in her opinion, did nothing to better a person. I knew Father did not have time to teach Georgiana, so we snuck out together to practice." Peter smiled at some distant memory only he could see.

"Georgiana was awful. She could barely hold the bow. When she let her first arrow, she shrieked in terror, and a few moments later, Father appeared on his steed. I thought for sure he'd reprimand me for acting without his permission. Instead, he dismounted, tied his steed to a nearby tree, and stood behind Georgiana to teach her how to hold a bow properly."

I smiled, imagining Peter as a young boy with his father and Georgiana. The protective older brother even then.

He continued. "The three of us rode horses together every day that week. We practiced archery every afternoon, and Father even took us to an opera. Mother never knew. When she returned, things settled back to the way they'd always been.

"I saw in my older years that Father sacrificed a lot to keep order in our house, to keep my mother happy. And to give Georgiana and me as close to a normal home as possible. But it was in those weeks, when it was just the three of us, that I knew who my father wanted to be. And that was enough."

Surprise robbed me of speech. Everything looked so much clearer through this new lens. Peter's carefree nature, his loyalty to Georgiana, and his confidence. He knew what he wanted through experiencing a lack of it in his life.

"I think your father was smart in more ways than one," I said at last. I imagined a man who stood as a cornerstone to an otherwise shaky family foundation. Perhaps even at the cost of his own happiness.

"Those memories led me here," he continued. "There is peace in the solitude. What about you? Could you see yourself in the country?"

"Did I not tell you I grew up in Kent?" I leaned my head against the rough wood wall. "My childhood home was in the middle of several hundred acres. We were quite secluded."

"And you liked it?"

"I loved it. My fondest memories are there. It was the last place that felt like home."

"I wish I knew that feeling," Peter said. He tossed the brush into a wooden bucket and rubbed his hands on a towel. "Some say home is created with your family. That it is more of who you are with, not where you are."

"I am sure that is true. But I think the countryside will always feel like home to me."

Peter turned and took a few steps toward me, sitting down and leaning against the wall, mirroring my position. We were about a foot away from each other, but I still felt a rushing through my veins at his nearness.

"Two questions," he said.

I cast him questioning eyes.

"For your payment to me this afternoon." He let out a breath. "One for fun, the second more serious. You must answer them both sincerely. And you may ask two of your own in the same fashion."

My lips twitched. What was he after? "All right. Go on, then."

"Question number one. What is your favorite color?"

Honestly? Peter bit his lip to keep from smiling, and I found myself doing the same.

"Oh, purple for certain. It is royal, and I look beautiful in it," I said as though I believed the words with all the confidence in my bones.

Peter's laugh echoed off the walls of Summer's stall. "No doubt. I hope you have a purple dress for an evening here, or I shall have to buy you one."

We looked at each other, more comfortable together in a

mucky horse stall than in the most elaborate room in all of England.

"My turn." I shifted closer. I had not before noticed the faintest hint of freckles along his nose. They were a perfectly imperfect asset to his otherwise flawless countenance. "What is your favorite fruit?"

Peter did not hesitate. "Blackberries. As long as you are there to eat more than I do." I playfully shoved his shoulder, and he smirked. "Otherwise, apples. We have thirteen or so rows of trees that span the back of my estate. They are beautiful in the fall, and my cook makes the best apple pie you'll ever taste."

"That sounds wonderful. But I shall have to wait an entire season to try it." I feigned a scowl.

"I'll invite you for the first one, I promise," he said matter-of-factly. A comfortable silence settled between us, and as much as I did not mind it, I also did not want our conversation to end.

"Question number two?" I asked.

Peter looked up, his cheeks dimpling as he pursed his lips in thought. After a moment, he said, "I think if you really want to know a person, you must know their pain, what they hold onto because they cannot let go. And so, I want to know: If you could erase one memory, what would it be?"

I tensed. There were many memories I wished I could erase—most of them containing Lord Gray—but only one replayed in my mind over and over. How I wished I could erase it. How I wished I never knew. Could I trust Peter with the truth? I wanted to. I wanted him to know me, all of me. To tell him my secrets and to see his reaction. Would he continue our afternoons? Would he reject who I was? What I came from? The truth I carried so heavily upon my back?

"Do you really want to know?"

Peter studied me, nodding. "I do."

I sighed, looking up to where Summer stood. My hands were curiously still. But it would not last. It never did. Not when I thought about those words that could never be unspoken nor unheard.

"There was one day, when we lived in London with Lord Gray and Mother . . . I heard them yelling at each other. My own father had never yelled, and so I thought something was very wrong. I went to knock on the door, to see if they were all right, when I heard Lord Gray say my father's name. Jeffrey Moore." I studied the dusty floor, the stray strands of hay and tiny clumps of dirt. I'd never confided the truth of my parents' story to anyone before. Mostly out of fear of their judgment. Then again, I'd never had a friend like Peter.

"He spat something about my grandparents, how they'd come to ruin and the Moore family name was shamed. I never knew them, so it meant little to me that they'd lost their livelihood. But what my mother said has never left me. She said, 'Don't you think I would've done anything to escape him? Do you know how broken I was when you never came for me that night? When you left me, ruined, forced to marry a stranger?'"

"What?" Peter's voice was shocked. "What did she mean?"

I turned to face him, to explain. "She knew Lord Gray, before my father. They were secretly in love in their youth."

Peter's eyes grew wide.

"Lord Gray's family had a summer home in Kent, like Mama's. But he'd been away on a tour of the Continent. The night of the ball was the very day Lord Gray was set to return home. They made plans to find each other. But when he did not attend, Mama's heart was shattered. And so she entertained my father. But Lord Gray *did* attend the ball; he arrived just in time to witness the kiss on the veranda. His heart was equally broken, but his pride even more so. When everything came to light, he would not save her from ruin."

I picked at my fingernails. "My mother claims my father kissed her without her consent. My father, on the other hand, claimed the kiss was mutual and that the evening was like a story in a book. I used to long to have a romance like theirs, to meet a man and fall so instantly, madly, in love."

I shook my head at the thought. Love was not something that came in a day or a week, perhaps not even a year. And if it did come, one could never be sure it would last.

"But now I see it was all a facade. My mother's heart always belonged to Lord Gray. When at last they married all those years later, it was like an entirely new person overtook her body, and I hardly recognized the woman I knew. She was giddy and distracted. She threw parties and hosted lavish dinners. Lord Gray called it his second chance, but he's hated Clara and me ever since my mother died. He once told me that Clara and I are the only part of his life that should never have been."

Peter's voice was low, fierce. "He is an utter cad, Lord Gray. I should duel him for that."

"Duel a dying man? At least challenge someone who can put up a fight for me."

"The next man who looks at you wrong is mine," Peter said, squinting playfully, before softening his voice and dropping his smile. "Is this—your father—the reason you do not believe in love?"

Peter was too perceptive. "I suppose so, yes. If there is anything I learned from my parents' story, it is that love is the greatest risk a person can take. And I simply cannot indulge chance." Not with so much at stake.

Peter leaned toward me, willing me to hear him, to believe his words. "Love is not a risk, Amelia. Love is an inevitable outcome of living. And sometimes it does not make any practical sense at all. But that does not mean we should fear it."

His warm eyes held me there, pulling me closer to him. How was it that Peter could evoke such emotion from me with only words? For all his charm, it was his heart that appealed to me most. I wanted his secrets, all of them, for myself.

"That is a beautiful sentiment," I replied, and he seemed satisfied. I wished I could believe him. I wanted to be brave. "Your turn. Same question."

"Ah, fair enough." Peter took a deep breath and hesitated. "It isn't exactly for gentle ears."

I gestured to the horses in the stall with us. "I think you are safe here."

Peter rubbed his eyes, grimacing. "All right. I'll just . . . get it out then. I have told no one this, not even Georgiana, so I appreciate your discretion."

"Of course," I said. What could Peter have to disclose? Surely it was no worse than what I had just offered.

He shifted in his spot, turning toward me. "My mother . . . perhaps you have guessed. She is not exactly well. It is more of a sickness of the mind than a physical illness." He looked to me, sadness in his eyes.

"When my father died, I rowed at her. On and on and on. I blamed her for his heart attack. She had caused it, I was sure, from her constant bickering at him about his dress, his habits, his expressions . . . nothing was ever good enough for her." Peter's shoulders sunk, and I ached for his weary heart. His parents. For the burden he carried. "I told her he'd worked himself to death trying to please her, to build enough wealth to satiate her, and make our life appealing so she would stay. We barely had him home long enough for a conversation some weeks.

"But of course she rowed back, blaming everything and anyone but herself. I can't remember ever seeing her so angry and terrified all at once." He shook his head. "She did not even cry." He paused. "I have not seen nor spoken to my mother since. It has been almost a year. And it's not that any of it was untrue to say. Only, perhaps some things are better left unsaid."

Peter stared at his hands, lost. How had I never seen this wounded side of him? Bruised and tormented like my own? Without thinking, I reached out to him, my fingers grazing his, and he took my hand, locking us together.

"I'm sorry, Peter. That sounds very unfair," I managed softly, captivated by the warmth of his hand on mine.

"Yes, well. I think unfairness in life is something we have in common, do we not?" He thumbed my fingers, igniting a blaze in my chest. How was this the same Peter I'd met days ago? My enemy and the single most irritating man in existence? Something was changing between us, like a cloud evaporating under the sun.

Winter twitched in his sleep, and Summer looked over her shoulder, quickly satisfied that all was well. But a scraping of wood on stone startled her, and a melody of voices filled the room.

"She's over here," Sir Ronald said loudly.

"What handsome stables, Sir Ronald." Beatrice praised. Most likely paired with Mr. Bratten.

Releasing Peter's hand, I stood, snatched my gloves from their perch, and dusted off my skirts. He rose and opened the door more fully to greet them.

"Wood, there you are. We've been wondering after you," Sir Ronald said, examining the stall door. "Good. Beckett's fixed the latch here."

Winter woke, and though I tried to calm him back into slumber, his curiosity got the better of him. Summer tensed but allowed him to hobble toward the door near her. Georgiana approached him first, taking off her gloves and fingering his mane. Then Beatrice, followed by Clara, took turns admiring him under the watchful eye of Summer.

"And Miss Moore as well, I see." Georgiana eyed her brother pointedly. "Where is the groom?"

"Not far," Peter said, and I wondered if he truly knew.

Clara reached for my hand, pulling me outside the stables. Part of me wanted to stay with Peter, to continue our conversation, but loyalty to Clara won out. When we were alone and out of earshot, she smiled.

"Alone in the stalls with Mr. Wood? You are dedicated to your task to the risk of propriety."

"It was an accident, actually. I had no idea he would be here." An accident resulting in the most real conversation I'd had in years.

"I must ask you to continue your time with Mr. Wood, though I know how he irks you." Clara looked past me, as though assuring herself that no one had followed us. "Sir Ronald is paying me particular attention now. And I mean to encourage him." Clara looked at me shyly, and I drew a breath.

"You are sure?" Could it be true? Had Sir Ronald finally come to his senses? The thought of Clara's heart opened wide for the breaking terrified me.

"I am." She gave me a tremulous smile. "One of us needs to marry with Lord Gray so ill. And if I get a say in whom I shall marry, I'd want it to be Sir Ronald. If he offers for me, would you approve?"

I pulled Clara into a tight hug, feeling confident that should she more fully encourage a match, Sir Ronald would be happy to oblige her. Not to mention that their marriage would help us both immensely when Lord Gray left us. "I approve wholeheartedly."

"Do you? Your opinion, your blessing, means the world to me. I could not accept him without your approval."

"Clara, you have always had it. You do not need my blessing to follow your heart."

Clara's smile touched her eyes. "And what of your heart, sister? I fear your afternoons with Mr. Wood are being noticed by our company. Beatrice asked after him this afternoon, and

Georgiana was sure he was sleeping. And the look on her face when she saw you together just now. I thought she would shoot arrows from her eyes. Are you quite sure your affections are not swayed by the time you've shared with him?"

I scratched my neck, looking away. People were talking? Our arrangement, having been made and kept in secret, might indeed seem confusing from the outside looking in. But Peter knew as well as I did, if not more so, that our afternoons together were only part of a greater scheme for Clara and Georgiana. Admitting our secret arrangement to Clara now would not please her, and we'd just shared such happy news. I would have to feign innocence for a few more days.

"No, of course not. Mr. Wood and I are barely friends." My mind was in agreement, but as I said the words, something else inside me fought against them. A curious feeling. Some hope within me that demanded its voice be heard. In truth, I'd never experienced such a feeling before.

Clara let out a breath. "Good. I confess you had me worried for a moment. Can you imagine being tied to the Wood family after Sir Ronald proposes? How awkward and uncomfortable. Or worse, if he proposed to Georgiana, having to be tied to her. To them together. I couldn't. I never in my life wish to see the Woods again after this trip."

The disgust on Clara's face tightened my chest. Peter was not all *that* bad. True, his presence had not always been one I desired, but something was different these past few afternoons. *He* was different. I'd seen a new piece of Peter, perhaps even a missing piece he kept from the rest of the world. He'd shared some rather personal thoughts with me. Things he likely did not want shared any more than I did the things I'd admitted.

But even still, I could not disagree with Clara. It wouldn't work to be tied to the Woods after Sir Ronald's proposal. There was no way to tell how things would go, and life had taught us not to risk chance. Practicality always seemed the safer bet. It would never be possible to form any sort of relationship with the Woods. We would always be on opposing sides.

The company spilled out of the stables, and Sir Ronald led an examination of the grounds. Much had been ravaged by the storm. Small tree limbs and leaves littered the clearing, with overturned buckets and feed barrels scattered around as well. What a mess. Clara locked arms with Sir Ronald of her own accord, and I nearly fell over at her confidence. It seemed I was not needed here after all. Slowing my pace to separate myself from the group, I saw Peter tossing a stick into a heaping pile by a fence.

Would he notice my absence? Did I want him to? As I trudged back to the house, I could not help but think that secretly I did. And that was a problem indeed.

Chapter Twelve

With nowhere in particular to go, I entered the drawing room, which was lit with afternoon sunlight.

"Miss Moore, what a surprise. Are the others far behind you?" Lady Demsworth asked from the settee she shared with Mrs. Turnball and looked up from her stitching expectantly.

"They continue their walk along the grounds. I fear I have not quite recovered from this morning," I answered, finding a seat nearby.

It wasn't entirely untrue, but after my conversation with Peter in Summer's stall, I could not deny a new feeling also. A lighter, happier feeling that surpassed the lingering exhaustion from this morning. But Clara was right. What place did Peter Wood have in my life? Who knew his intentions for certain? I was here for one purpose, and one purpose only. To secure Clara's match with Sir Ronald.

"Of course, dear, and how could you be? Though I am sure the party misses you." Lady Demsworth returned to her stitching. "Mrs. Turnball and I were just discussing the upcoming ball my dear friends the Levins are hosting at the end of the fortnight. It was so kind of them to extend the invitation to our entire party. They are lavish hosts. I am certain their ball will feel as polished as any in London. Do you not agree, Mrs. Turnball?"

"To be sure," Mrs. Turnball added. "Do you enjoy dancing, Miss Moore?"

"I love it. And I did not dance enough in London. A ball sounds very inviting."

Lady Demsworth clucked, pulling her needle up through canvas. "With your beauty? Were the men blind this Season?"

Mrs. Turnball motioned to the pianoforte in the corner of the room. "Play for us, won't you, Miss Moore?"

I had not played since arriving at Lakeshire Park, but with a nearly empty room, now seemed the perfect time. I knew Lady Demsworth and Mrs. Turnball would forgive my inadequacy. The only song I could play well was Father's. And that did not render me an accomplished lady.

The women sitting next to me made the job of being a proper lady seem effortless, easy, as though the training was ingrained in their bones. They made conversation easy and pleasant. In fact, as I studied their faces, their gentleness and easy comradery, I could not help but wish to be like them. They were so vastly different from the women I'd met in London.

Mrs. Turnball, though quiet and serious, held depth behind her eyes. I truly believed if she was forced into a battle of wits, she would win, and yet her first instinct would not be to battle at all, I was sure of it. Her elegance and grace took precedence. The way she held her head, high and unyielding, confirmed it.

The same was true of Lady Demsworth. Even earlier

while wearing her morning clothes, she exuberated dignity and propriety. In her eyes was a natural kindness, a sympathetic compassion, and yet she fiercely devoted herself to her family. Clara would do well to tie herself to such a mother-in-law. To be among such society.

A Mozart piece spanned the music desk on the pianoforte, and I slid my fingers along the smooth, cool keys to find my place. My eyes studied the notes. I could already tell my playing would be far too slow for what was required.

A knock sounded at the door, drawing my attention, and Mr. Gregory stepped inside, holding a silver platter.

"Pardon me, but a letter has just arrived for you, Miss Moore," he said from the doorway.

Who would write to me here? My stomach rolled as I moved my heavy feet across the room to meet him. The only person who knew my whereabouts, who might need to write to me at all, was Lord Gray.

But as I took the letter from Mr. Gregory, the scrawl was not Lord Gray's. And yet the address was Gray House, Brighton.

"Please summon my maid," I said, hurrying toward the stairs. My intuition told me something was very wrong.

Closing the door to my bedchamber, I stopped in the center of the room, the letter weighing a thousand pounds in my shaking hand.

"Miss Moore, what is it?" Mary burst through the door, breathless. "What is wrong?"

"I have a letter from Gray House. But it is not from Lord Gray."

Mary took the letter from my hand, eyes scrutinizing

the words. "This is Mr. Jones's hand. Why would he write to you?"

My heart sank, fearing the worst. I took the letter back from Mary, slowly pulling the fold and breaking the seal.

Mary stood beside me, waiting for my reaction. Any fate I assumed would also be hers.

Miss Moore,

Forgive me for writing to you while you are away, but I felt it necessary considering the circumstances. Lord Gray's condition has worsened since you left us. He is now bedridden, and the doctor predicts he has but days left before his lungs fail entirely. Because of this, I have penned a letter summoning your cousin, Trenton.

I fear this is finally the end. None of us imagined Lord Gray's illness would progress this quickly. I implore you to find a means of securing yourselves while you have the chance. There will be nothing left for you here when you return.

I have included a letter from Lord Gray, written a few days ago. I am sure he meant to send it.

If I may be of service to you in any way, rest assured I will do everything in my power to help you and your sister.

Ever faithfully,
your servant,
T. Jones

"Miss?" Mary touched my arm, and I realized I was crying.

"It's Lord Gray," I said. "He will die any day. What shall we do, Mary? Our time is running out faster than I imagined. I am not prepared."

Mary squeezed her eyes shut, shaking her head. "I feared it, miss. More than anything, I feared this very thing when we left."

"There is another letter," I said, wiping my tears.

I set Mr. Jones's letter aside and unfolded the second paper. Lord Gray's last letter. What would he have to say to me? One last jab at my family name? I tore at the seal, bracing myself.

Amelia, Clara:

I do not wish to convey regrets, for I am ready to die, and I have been for some time. I only wish to answer for how my death will affect you.

I promised your mother I would see that you both were secured when you came of age. It does not surprise me in the least that you have failed on your own. Since I cannot recommend you to any of my associates for marriage, I have tasked my barrister the burden of finding suitable employment for you so I may meet your mother with a clear conscience.

Upon my death, if you are not married, he will contact you to make arrangements. Your things will be sent for his care until you are ready for them. Do not burden him with your needs until then.

With this letter, I end our association. I do not

need your pity, nor your false appreciation for the life I gave you after your mother died. It was all for her. My only regret is that I did not save her that night after your father ruined her reputation. Had I married her then, I would not have the burden of you now.

Lord Robert Gray

"Miss Amelia?" Mary said quietly.

"We are finally alone," I answered, my sadness hardening into bitterness. "We have nowhere to go."

I wadded the paper into a ball as armor wrapped itself around my throbbing heart. "We will be alright, Mary. Please—speak not a word to Clara."

Mary wiped away a tear of her own. Had she known what was to become of us? "Of course. Not a word."

"And, Mary?"

Her face was red, and I knew she wished to escape, to process the news alone. "Yes, miss?"

"I need an audience with Lady Demsworth right away."

Chapter Thirteen

I stood outside Lady Demsworth's personal sitting room, waiting as her maid introduced me.

"Miss Moore." Lady Demsworth beckoned me to join her by the window. The room was quaint, but bright, with a small chandelier reflecting the sunlight like a thousand tiny stars.

"Thank you for seeing me, Lady Demsworth," I said, sitting beside her. My hands were shaking. "Forgive me for interrupting your time with Mrs. Turnball."

"I am so pleased to have a moment to visit with you privately. I'll confess that I've thought of nothing else but how I can repay you for your determination in saving Winter."

I adjusted my skirts nervously. "Actually, that is precisely why I've called for you. I need your help."

Lady Demsworth clasped her hands in her lap. "Please do not be shy, Miss Moore. I am wholly at your disposal and will be the soul of discretion."

Having known her for so short a time, could I trust Lady Demsworth with my secret? Would I be ruining Clara by admitting my need? Whether we were ruined now or later, we could not change our circumstance, and truth always found a path one way or another.

"Please," I said, before I lost the nerve. "Do not feel in the least obligated toward me. My endeavor with Winter is unequal to a favor of this magnitude. All I ask is for your connections, and if none exist that prove of benefit, I am satisfied solely by you entertaining the thought."

She smiled. "Go on, dear. You have my complete attention."

I stole a glance at the closed door behind me and forced my hands to remain still. Whatever happened next was completely out of my control, but I had to ask.

"I think you know why Clara and I are here. We were so grateful for the invitation, especially Clara, and we've quite enjoyed our time with your company. But there are things that Clara does not know about our future, things that I have only just been told, and I fear we will find ourselves in greater need financially sooner than expected. And so I must ask—do you have any connections that could offer a living or—"

"My dear girl," Lady Demsworth stopped me, grasping my arm with a motherly touch I hadn't felt in years, "will Lord Gray leave you nothing?"

It was the question I feared the most. The answer could cost us everything should Sir Ronald truly prize a wealthy dowry. But I'd already given the truth away. Lady Demsworth merely sought confirmation.

"He will not." I wanted to look at my hands, but forced myself to meet her gaze. "My father's estate was entailed to a distant cousin five years ago who refuses a connection with us. My mother added nothing to the marriage, as she was estranged from her family after the scandal. We are quite literally left with nothing. I would appreciate your discretion. I think you can relate to having undesirable circumstances thrust upon you."

She lowered her chin with evident compassion. "More than you know. I am terribly sorry to hear this, Miss Moore."

"Please, call me Amelia. I cannot tell you the whole of my secrets and have such formality between us."

"Amelia, then," she agreed. "As it happens, I have just the situation for you, and I have longed for the opportunity to speak with you about it." A new excitement entered her voice. "Allow me to elaborate. The person I spoke of two nights ago—the one needing marriage advice. I was referring to my nephew."

I took in a deep breath, blinking, my tongue suddenly numb. I had not expected her to answer so swiftly.

She continued. "He has recently lost his wife, and though he has no desire to remarry for love, he wishes for a wife to help guide his household and see to his young daughters. He is thirty-four, quite wealthy, and very handsome, if I may say so."

My breath caught, my heart racing in my chest. I had not expected marriage. Not like this. Yet, here it was, my opportunity. Practical and sensible. A life of security for myself and, if necessary, Clara as well. Better yet, if she accepted Sir Ronald, we would be able to see each other as often as we wished, with nothing to keep us apart.

"If I may be completely honest," Lady Demsworth said, "I've had you in mind for him since our conversation, but I felt it more prudent to speak to you at the end of the fortnight. His mother was my eldest sister, and I promised her I would help him in any way I could. He and Ronald were not the easiest of friends, but I am sure that could change if reason necessitated it.

"As I said before, he has asked me to undertake the task of finding him a suitable wife. One who sees marriage in a practical light. Who does not expect love as a result. And I am happy to look no further if you accept."

Was this really happening? Must I choose right now? So many questions flooded my senses, I could not keep them all in. "Where does he live? And what does he do? How old are his daughters, exactly, and when does he expect to marry?" I crossed my arms and then uncrossed them again. Did I even have a right to ask such questions? Didn't one simply accept a marriage of convenience based on . . . convenience?

"Might I send word for him today? I could invite him for a day to answer your questions in person. He is a good man, Amelia, and will be a good friend. And perhaps in time you could find a happy companionship together."

I could not argue. She was right. Besides, what choice did I have? Here was an open invitation for companionship, nothing more. A man whose heart had already been taken, who required only friendship in exchange for security. Surely that was what I wanted, wasn't it?

For a reason I could not explain, my memory flashed to Peter crawling out from beneath a rickety table in the dress shop, the carefree manner in which he asked if he could assist me.

Did he feel for me as I did for him? Would it even matter?

I knew my sister; if Clara did not hold Sir Ronald's heart, she would rather me tie her to a cousin Sir Ronald seldom saw than to Georgiana's only sibling. Our life was like a riddle, one that needed solving, and time was running out.

"Of course. Thank you, Lady Demsworth," I said meekly. "Can we not expose the situation just yet? I'd like to meet him and, perhaps, accept him in person."

"Of course, my dear, of course." She clasped her hands together. "How you will admire him; he is such a delight. We were brokenhearted by the loss of his wife, but how wonderful it would be to give him a companion who will treat him as well as Elizabeth did."

I could only nod, lost in thought.

"I shall write to him now. He will wish to meet you and propose to you in person, and I am certain he will come right away."

She left me alone, listening to the sound of my own breathing. This was really happening. I would marry a man for convenience, for security and comfort. Clara and I would be safe. She could have all the time in the world to find a match if Sir Ronald refused her advances. We would be secure once and for all. Was that not all that mattered? I'd assumed the responsibility of practicality over love after Mother died, but now, face to face with the reality of a loveless marriage, the lights in the room seemed to dim.

What was love to me anyway? Pain, disappointment, loss. To have love was to be vulnerable and open to injury. This match would secure my resolve against it. This one choice would take away any hope of love I'd buried all those years ago with Father, and then Mother.

But how could I be sure that love was not worth the risk? I'd never been in love, never kissed a man, never felt that tingling in my chest that Father claimed to feel for Mother when they'd first met.

Or had I? Peter's touch, his smile, laughing with him as we chased Winter in the middle of nowhere. I'd never felt such happiness, such belonging. It had almost felt like . . . home.

Chapter Fourteen

Mr. Pendleton was his name. David Pendleton. I rolled the name around on my tongue and tried to focus on Lady Demsworth's words. She had me cornered in the hallway, barely out of the breakfast room, excitement in her voice as she told me the whole of his life. But I could hardly get past the sound of his name on my lips.

"He is as tall as my Ronald," she said. "And he loves horse racing, so you'll have to indulge him in those endeavors now and then." It was as if she'd forgotten the despair of my circumstances and the engagement was as good as done in her mind.

"I expect we shall receive his response directly; he is fortunately staying in his country house for the summer. I imagine we will have him for dinner within the next few days." Her eyes were bright as she anticipated my response.

"How wonderful." My voice cracked at the end. I thought of Peter and felt as hollowed out as an old tree. Thankfully, Lady Demsworth rushed away to tell Cook we would be receiving another guest.

I'd taken a tray in my room the evening before, claiming a headache, and fallen fast asleep. I had few thoughts for Lord Gray other than pity and anger at his neglect. There was no use fighting against a circumstance that stood as tall and immovable as a mountain. Just as I'd done when Mama died, I'd have to take a breath and keep moving. At least I had Mr. Pendleton to save me this time. His family had to be more welcoming than Lord Gray.

Apparently, the night had continued rather late for Clara and the others, as I heard not a sound even long after breakfast. Sunshine beamed brightly through a front window, and despite rain-sodden grounds, nature called to me. Clarity seemed to come in its presence, and I was in dire need of clearing my thoughts, of realigning my priorities and finally facing my own future.

Not to mention avoiding Peter. Our conversation in the stalls yesterday had left me feeling vulnerable. I'd grabbed his hand on an impulse, knowing full well that our afternoons together were no more than casual meetings to protect our sisters. And yet, I'd felt something. Something surprising. Something real. Had he felt it too?

No. Peter was invested in his duty to his sister. He kept me entertained to keep me away from Clara just as I'd done to him during our first few days here. How mortifying to have been so bold and forward. I rubbed my temples. If only I could cancel our bargain and flee from these feelings that only seemed to confuse me more, especially with an engagement on my horizon. But, now more than ever, Clara needed me to keep Peter at a distance. This time was crucial for her and Sir Ronald to make their match. Like it or not, I would have to be available later this afternoon.

"Do be careful not to muddy this," Mary pleaded as she laid out my light-blue riding habit. "There are only so many remedies for mud stains, and I would hate for you to ruin such a lovely color."

I offered my thanks for her concern, promising to ride only through the driest edges of the estate. Mary pinned my hair tightly in curls beneath my most fashionable hat, and I tugged on an old pair of leather riding gloves.

When I arrived at the stable house, Mr. Beckett was leading a beautiful filly back into a nearby stall.

"Excuse me, sir," I called as I approached. "I hoped for a ride this morning."

He looked up. "Of course, Miss Moore. I saddled Grace for Lady Demsworth, but she made other arrangements this morning. Would you care to ride her?"

"Actually, I am quite attached to Summer. Is she well?"

"A quick ride will suit her today. Just let me finish with Grace, and I shall have Summer ready for you directly."

"I shall ride Grace." Peter's voice sent a tickling shock through me, and I hastily turned to meet him. He wore a brown coat and a soft smile, moving toward the filly. "That is, if Miss Moore does not mind a companion."

Before I could speak, Mr. Beckett stepped forward. "Oh, no, not Grace, Mr. Wood. She is not keen on male riders—"

"Is that so?" Peter rubbed Grace's nose. Obviously, he liked the idea of a challenge. "Surely *I* can change her mind on the matter."

"I would not recommend it, sir." Mr. Beckett's face grew serious. "She's known to buck and cause injury."

Peter stole the reins from Mr. Beckett's hands, a look of confidence in his eyes. "Perhaps Grace has yet to meet her match."

Mr. Beckett saddled Summer while Peter switched the sidesaddle on Grace.

"Does this account for our afternoon, then?" I raised a brow at him.

"I intend to keep you out all afternoon, so yes," he said as he tightened the leather straps.

I sighed. This was exactly why people were beginning to talk. How would it look if Peter and I were found on a long ride together? Would they assume we pined after each other? That we held a shared affection? The idea was absurd. And yet . . . Peter's voice, his very presence reeled me in like a fish caught on a hook. I wanted to be near him. What did that mean?

More, what did it matter? I stopped, waiting by Mr. Beckett and the mounting block. I could not entertain this feeling growing within me, whatever it was. I was as good as engaged to Mr. Pendleton. I *needed* to be. Besides, Peter had said himself the only reason he desired my company was to ensure I kept from encouraging my sister. Regardless of his persistence, that was all he cared about.

Settling atop Summer, I brushed through her golden mane with my fingers. I grasped the leather reins and patted her neck before urging her into a slow walk beside Peter and Grace.

A few moments passed, and the stables shrank behind us.

"Were you sneaking away again?" Peter asked.

I shrugged. "Sometimes I prefer the solitude." Especially when I needed time to think.

"I can relate to that. I quite enjoy getting lost in the middle of nowhere."

Summer whinnied her agreement, and Peter and I laughed.

I took a deep breath of grass and earth and wind.

"What a lovely view," Peter observed, expressing my very thought. His appreciation for nature, the way his eyes soaked up the scene before us, enticed me to relax and enjoy it as well. The afternoon was too good to waste on thoughts of my future. I would push all thoughts of Mr. Pendleton and Lord Gray out of my mind. Here, now, I would live in the present.

Unbelievably, Grace rode calm and neutral under Peter's hand; even Mr. Beckett registered shock at the miracle as he followed behind us as chaperone.

Peter and I rode along the west pasture where green grass and weeds with tiny yellow and purple flowers painted the scene. The earth sank beneath the horse's hooves, the ground still damp and muddy from the storm. I caught my breath at the beauty of the sky above the open fields. The clear blue vastness opened my chest, liberating my heart from the constricting weight of my circumstances. Oh, to be as free as the wind, as limitless as the sky, as luxurious as the sun! I felt so complete in the open pasture beyond Sir Ronald's estate, and I never wanted it to end.

Peter swerved right, nearly knocking into Summer and me.

"Whoa, girl," he said to Grace, pulling back on the reins. "Don't turn on me now."

A tinge of anxiety pinched my brow. We'd only been riding for a quarter hour. How long would Grace last? "Perhaps she is bored. Shall we try it at a run?" I asked.

"Yes, thank you." Peter gave Grace her head, glancing nervously at Summer, who, to my great surprise, bolted right after her.

The wind rushed past me with Summer in full gallop, and I imagined at any moment the breeze would lift me up and carry me away. The further we escaped, the greener the landscape became. Suddenly, I understood Peter's earlier sentiment of being lost in the middle of nowhere.

Slowing, I dropped Summer's reins and reached toward the clouds. Out here, nothing mattered. Out here, I was free. Peter slowed beside me, and I hugged Summer's neck, my cheeks warm with a new energy pulsing through my veins.

Peter stared at me, a strange hitch in his own breath, as if air had been caught in his lungs.

"What is it?" I sat up, searching his brightened eyes.

"You." He locked his eyes on mine. "You are the most beautiful woman I have ever seen, Amelia Moore." Sincerity laced his words, and a tingling spread within my chest.

I nervously patted Summer's mane. Peter could not mean to compliment me so greatly. My emotions of late must be exaggerating his words. "What are you after with such flattery, Peter Wood?"

His smile broke free. "What might it earn me?"

"Nothing but trouble, I am sure."

"Perfect. As long as it involves you."

I flashed him a feigned scowl, nerves fluttering wildly in my stomach. We needed a new subject, and quick.

"Is this not a perfect day?" Peter asked, as if he knew my thoughts.

"In every way." I turned my face to the sky. "I love the way the grass smells, and the sound of the wind blowing through the trees. And the birds flying freely, soaring even. Brighton is an entirely different environment."

"But do you not love the ocean? It is vast and mysterious, much more so than the farmlands here."

"The ocean is the only part of Brighton I do like. But it is just another place I cannot explore. I don't want to merely imagine what it might feel like to have a wave wash over me. I want to jump in. Here, at least, I can roam wherever I please, and experience all the beauty right at my fingertips."

"I see." A smile touched his eyes. "I am pleased to hear it."

At that moment, Grace leaped into a run, bucking wildly and running far off our grassy path and into the sludge of mud in the middle of the pasture.

Time stopped as I watched Peter pulling feverishly at the reins, tightening his grip and trying to recover his hold.

"Grace!" I yelled, following as close as I dared with Summer. "It's all right, girl! Grace!"

Peter steadied her for a split second, just long enough to jump down into the mud, boots slopping noisily. He slapped Grace on the rump, and she took off at a run. "She will have to find her own way home." After feeling through his pockets for something, he frowned. "Blast. I've lost my fob watch."

I stopped beside him and started to dismount. "What does it look like?"

"Stay up, Amelia. This mud is deep," Peter said with a tightened jaw. Every step he took required great effort, his boots rising from the thick mud with a sucking sound.

"I am not afraid of a little mud," I said, balancing on Summer and searching the brown slog for any semblance of a watch. The sun hit a glimmer a few paces away. "But I can see that you are not as comfortable with it as I."

"I love it." Peter frowned with heavy sarcasm. "I would sleep in a bed of mud every night, given the chance."

"Would you?" I snorted, and he glanced up at me in mirth. I lifted my skirts and hopped down, and my boots instantly sank to my calves in mud. I did not want to disappoint Peter if I was wrong in what I'd seen, and I was just as capable as he to wade through mud.

He started toward me, obviously coming to rescue me from the same sticky situation he'd found himself in. I put every ounce of energy I had into my legs, pulling up my feet from their grasping holes.

"Do not attend me, Peter. I am fine."

He threw his hands in the air and muttered something about "audacious" and "stubborn" under his breath.

I made my way closer to the glimmering piece until I was close enough to see that it was in fact the watch.

Several feet away, Peter bent over the ground and poked at what appeared to be a rock. He tossed it over his shoulder, barely getting his hands dirty, and missing Summer by an inch.

He thought me audacious, did he? I pulled off my gloves

and tucked them neatly into the pocket of my riding habit. I plucked the watch from the mud, the dirt coating my hands as I examined it. My lips pursed, and I thought of the promise I'd made to Mary about staying out of the mud. I'd have to clean my hands somehow before they muddied my dress.

"Here. Your stubborn, audacious friend has recovered your fob watch."

"Have you really?" He straightened up, hurrying toward me.

I placed the watch in his outstretched hand. "You're welcome. But if you call me audacious again, you'll have this to answer to." Holding my muddy palms up for him to see, I gave him a serious look. "If you were an honorable gentleman, you'd offer me a napkin."

"It is occupied," he said as he pulled out a handkerchief to wipe his watch clean. Honestly? Did his watch take precedence over me? First gloves, and now this? "Is that so?"

He grunted, clearly too busy in his examination to bother with my current need. Perhaps I should make my problems more of his. I moved beside him, then hesitated. How would Peter react to *my* aggravating *him*? Would he be angry with me? This was my chance to find out.

"Peter, you've something on your cheek," I said nonchalantly.

"Hmm? Where?" His brow constricted, and he looked to me.

Before he could blink, I swiped my muddy fingertips along his cheek. It was hardly more than a few streaks of mud; still, I had to suppress a laugh as his face registered shock.

I could see his mind working behind his eyes. Slowly, he

tucked his watch back into his fob pocket. My instincts told me to run.

Before I could turn around, Peter had my wrist and forced my other hand to my face, smearing mud along my ear. I whipped my head around and yanked my wrist from his grasp, but Peter merely grinned, clearly pleased with himself.

This wouldn't do. But I was out of mud.

Dipping low, I let my hands sink just far enough into the muck for one last coating.

"Amelia . . ." Peter straightened as I stood to meet him, his face suddenly fearful. "We are square now. An eye for an eye, you know."

"Did you not say only moments ago that you wanted this, Peter? What was it you said? You did not mind trouble as long as it was with me?"

Peter stepped sideways, eyeing my hands. "Let's have a truce, shall we? I will give you your ransom, whatever it may be."

I took a step closer, and Peter dashed behind Summer, pulling her along with him.

"Are you *really* hiding behind a horse?" I jested.

"Name your price, I beg of you." Peter's voice was laughing, terrified.

"Anything I want?"

"Anything. I swear it."

"All right, Peter. Come out."

His eyes peeked above Summer's back.

Hands held innocently in the air—though I remained undecided as to whether or not I would relent—I moved with effort around Summer to meet Peter. Just as I reached out to him, my right foot got stuck in the mud, and before I could find my balance, I was falling, face first. I grasped the lapel of his coat in an effort to save myself. But it wasn't enough. I shrieked as we fell, a splattering sound welcoming us. Peter was laughing, breathless, as I tried to use his neck to pull myself up out of the sinkhole.

"Let me help you," he said, and for a moment, I thought he meant it. But staring into those clear, bright eyes meant I paid little attention to his hand digging beside me. He coated his fingers with mud and drew lines along my cheek, dabbing my nose for a final touch.

I sucked in a breath.

"Shall I continue? Or do you officially forfeit?" He laughed, dimpling his cheeks.

I felt a sudden urge to pull him toward me and kiss that smiling face. I steadied my voice. "I will accept your payment," I said, a bit breathless.

"Agreed. Anything you want. I wish you could see yourself. I'm afraid my handkerchief cannot fix you now." He rocked himself onto his heels. He wrapped my arms around his neck and lifted me effortlessly from the muck. My dress, my boots, and especially my hat were caked in heavy mud. Mary was going to murder me.

"What are you doing?" Never had a gentleman carried me before, or been so close to me. With shallow breaths, I tried not to notice the feel of Peter's strong arms wrapped around me, nor the smell of his freshly shaved jaw despite the mud.

"I am rescuing you." He winked. "Should we visit the

creek next? I think you're in need of a little washing up before Demsworth throws me out of the house for ruining you."

"Good idea." I agreed as he lowered me to my feet on dry ground.

Peter turned to Mr. Beckett, who'd continued ahead before circling back to us. "Winter will be missing his mother. Miss Moore and I shall return on foot directly."

"Of course, Mr. Wood." With a nod, Mr. Beckett moved toward Summer.

Peter tucked my arm into his, muddy and filthy as we both were, and we headed toward the trees.

Chapter Fifteen

The cool water rose to my calves as I stepped in it. Mud dissolved from my boots and the hem of my dress into the flow of the creek that rushed over its rocky path down the bend. Low branches from sagging trees hung over, mirrored by the water, shading us in a great canopy of green. I bent down, glancing at my reflection. Sure enough, Peter had painted my cheeks and dotted my nose with mud.

"Perhaps I shall try my hand with a brush and paints next. I have talent, do I not?" Peter stepped toward me, grinning.

I splashed him with a flick of water before untying my hat and tossing it onto the bank. Lifting a handful of water to my face, I washed away the dried mud.

After helping me pick off the thickest coating of mud from the back of my dress and hair, Peter pulled out his watch and carefully wet the silver cover. There was a gentleness to his touch that signified value and worth.

"It's lovely." I stepped out along the bank of the creek and retrieved my hat.

"It was my father's," he answered solemnly, following me onto land. "He gave it to me a few weeks before his chest pains started. I'd just returned from Paris. And I've worn it every day since."

My heart swelled for him, knowing loss as I did. Except I had none of my parents' belongings. Not even a string of pearls from my mother. Lord Gray kept a box of her things locked away; I could only hope to recover the items after his death.

"It is a very handsome watch."

"There is an inscription on the back. My father had it done." He turned the watch over in his hand. "It says, 'Time is not guaranteed.'"

We looked at each other, and I had a distinct feeling that something was indeed growing between us, a pull that grew stronger cords, tying knots that would not easily come undone. "How very true."

"Before he died, he told me to remember that some things aren't worth being angry over, but plenty of things are worth fighting for. It is a motto I try to live by." A look of sadness briefly crossed his face.

"I love it." I leaned in, peering at the watch. That explained both Peter's carefree nature and his loyalty to his sister. "Your father's words are beautiful. It's something my father would have said."

"Forgive me, but did you lose your father as suddenly as I lost mine?" Curiosity laced his voice, though his eyes were filled with compassion.

"Pneumonia," I said before I lost the nerve. I had not spoken of Father's death in a long while. Why did I want

Peter to know? It was as though my heart needed to tell him everything. We'd shared so much with each other already. "Sometimes I fear I am forgetting his face."

Peter interlocked my hand in his, sending a tingling sensation through me. His gaze was serious and sweet. "I am so sorry, Amelia."

"Thank you." I nodded, swallowing back my rising emotion. "I miss him very much. As I'm sure you miss your father."

"What is this wretched lot we've been cast? There must be happiness ahead." Peter offered a gentle, easy smile.

I thought of Lord Gray and my impending engagement, how everything would be changing soon. In Peter's presence, I'd nearly forgotten what awaited me. "There must."

Peter walked me to the clearing, our hands locked together.

"What would you choose for your future?" I asked. "If you could create your own happiness."

Peter stopped his pace as though he was surprised by my question, but he did not hesitate. He hardly blinked. He simply said, "Time. I want those moments where time stands still, where you're aching from laughter and everything is right in the world and you are surrounded by the people you love. That is happiness to me. I refuse to work as hard as my father did. I refuse to sacrifice time for the sake of greater wealth or status. For at the end of the day, what I wish for now is not his money, but his time."

Peter's words filled me like new breath, and my fingers tightened around his. His thumb traced mine, and he pulled me alongside him, forward.

In truth, I felt a similar desire for my future, especially since meeting Peter, and I envied the ease with which he admitted his hopes. Time was not something I had control over. Would I find such happiness with Mr. Pendleton?

Walking back to the house must've taken hours, for our clothes were nearly dried, but I found myself wanting more time, more conversation, and more of Peter's hand holding mine.

As we stepped around the tree line, Peter pulled my arm through his, and I peeked up at him. Though the creek had washed away much of the mud on our clothes, there were traces of our adventure evident in every crease of us.

"Perhaps we can sneak through the servants' quarters," I suggested as we approached.

"I think it is too late for that." Peter gestured to the terrace.

"Miss Moore, what on earth has happened to you?" Lady Demsworth stood in the entryway with Georgiana.

"Peter!" Georgiana said aghast, covering her mouth with a gloved hand. "What have you done?"

I racked my mind for an explanation. We'd been so caught up in conversation, neither of us had come up with a story that might soften the blow of our muddied clothes and hair. We were surely a sight to behold. Perhaps I could tell them the truth—while somehow omitting the fact I'd started a mud fight that ended with me wanting to kiss Peter Wood.

"Miss Moore was bucked from her horse, and I managed to save her from getting trampled," Peter lied. "Unfortunately, the dirt in the pastures was soaked from rainwater, so we stand before you alive, but very much filthy."

"Is that true, Miss Moore?" Lady Demsworth asked, aghast.

I glared at Peter's smug expression. Some nerve he had, painting me as a damsel in distress. If he thought I would agree to his story, he was entirely mistaken. Even if the tale had been spun in my favor, I could not lie to Lady Demsworth.

"You are every bit the tease," Georgiana said to Peter, then whispered something to Lady Demsworth.

"Miss Moore?" Lady Demsworth pressed, suppressing a smile.

"Peter lost his watch in the mud trying to prove he could ride Grace. He couldn't find the watch on his own, but with my help, we found it." It was mostly true, with a few omissions.

"Fortunately, Miss Moore has the eyes of a hawk," Peter said.

Nudging him in the ribs for that last remark, I moved toward Lady Demsworth. "I am sorry, Lady Demsworth. Please forgive me. I swear it will not happen again."

"You are forgiven. But it is nearly five o'clock. You must be famished. Dinner will be ready in the dining room in an hour."

"Thank you, Lady Demsworth." Shrinking as I passed into the foyer, I winced as my footsteps echoed across her immaculate marble floors, my boots spreading mud and creek filth behind me.

Mary managed to draw me a bath, though she scowled the entire time. I did not complain about the biting cold water, nor the roughness as she brushed dried mud from my hair. Instead I thought of Peter and this new, blazing feeling in my chest that warmed every bit of me. What did it mean? And did he feel it too?

After drying off, I chose a blue silk gown, and Mary salvaged my hair, pinning it into a loose bun at the base of my neck. Before leaving my room, I retreated to my trunk, pulling out a small, secondhand vial of perfume my cousin Caroline had given me in London. It smelled like lilacs, and I rubbed a few drops along my neck and in my hair before descending the stairs for the evening.

At dinner, Sir Ronald announced that the men would be attending a fencing exhibition the following day. Beatrice swooned at the mere thought of it, likely imagining Mr. Bratten with a sword, until Lady Demsworth demanded that none of the four men fight but only attend as spectators. Peter grimaced, clearly put out by the request.

For some reason, the gentlemen took longer than usual with their port. Clara picked at her gloves beside me on the settee, eyeing the open doors twice a minute.

When she stiffened beside me, I looked to the door.

"No cards for me tonight," Sir Ronald said to Mr. Bratten, but his eyes found Clara.

I squeezed her hand, and she stood, walking toward him. His happy smile was effortless, and she followed him to the pianoforte.

That was easy enough.

Until Georgiana swooped in, curls bouncing as she placed her hand lightly on Sir Ronald's arm. Perfectly in the way. How could I get rid of her? I could steal her attention with private conversation like Peter had done with Clara. Ugh, I was no better than he.

"That's a scowl if I've ever seen one," Peter said, taking Clara's vacated spot beside me on the settee. "What is wrong?"

Glancing again to Clara, I frowned. Admitting my frustration to Peter would not do, though he knew the feeling as well as I. "Nothing at all."

Peter traced the path of my gaze. "Georgiana?"

I flicked my eyes to his. He couldn't truly want me to answer.

His eyes took on a pained expression, like he was torn between paths and didn't know which to choose. "I am afraid I cannot intervene."

Clara was lifting sheets of music, while Sir Ronald opened the keys. Was she going to play? Had he asked to hear her?

"Could you not invite her to join us? Just for the evening?"

Peter crossed his arms. "Would you do the same for Georgiana tomorrow?"

"Perhaps if the occasion presented itself."

"And if it didn't? Would you remove Clara just for the sake of creating time for Georgiana?"

I could barely entertain the idea. "No. I would not."

"You have my answer."

I sighed, neither angry nor content. I understood him completely, actually. Peter, who I'd once thought to be the greatest schemer of all, was more of an honest player than I.

"You were quiet at dinner," I said. In truth, he had hardly spoken two words of conversation.

Peter shifted his knees toward me, relaxing. "I am exhausted from chasing after you all day."

I chose to ignore his baiting, for surely he only sought to aggravate me. "You should go to bed," I said matter-of-factly, and he smiled.

"If I did, then how would you bear to be without me tomorrow? I shall be gone all day at the fencing exhibition." He raised his chin, and his eyes brightened. "You will owe me an extra afternoon for missing tomorrow."

Did Peter truly care to miss *one*? I turned my shoulder, facing him. "We made no arrangements for such a circumstance. You lose your afternoon by choice."

Peter pursed his lips playfully, leaning his elbow alongside the back of the settee and resting his head on his hand lazily. "That is mean."

I grinned at his displeasure. "It is fair. You look like you could fall asleep. Go to bed this instant."

"You shall have to take me. I am too tired to climb the stairs alone." He leaned in, a smug smile on his lips.

"Peter Wood," I chided, pinching his arm. "Where is your honor?"

"I have none. But you keep insisting that I acquire it."

"Why do you say that so often? It is very derogatory to claim one has no honor. Surely it is untrue."

My question seemed to sober him, as he took a deep breath and rubbed his face with his palm. "What does it even mean to be honorable? I think it is ridiculous to claim a word that no one in his right mind can live up to."

How could I refute that? No person was perfect, nor would they ever be. Yet many claimed the word. "I suppose it means you are trying, and succeeding more often than not. Do you have principles? Are you virtuous? When one is honest, trustworthy, loyal, and acts with compassion, then I think the word is deserved."

Peter shrugged contemplatively. "Then perhaps I shall try a bit harder. When you ask me next, I'll have made up my mind if I am capable of distinguishing myself."

"You are capable." I shot him a sideways glance. "It is very admirable to be honorable, you know."

Peter sat up straighter. "Admirable to you?"

"Loyalty and trust are very important to me." I glanced to Clara, who'd just finished playing a Mozart piece rather beautifully.

"I can see why they would be." Peter smiled kindly. "I hope you do not think I take any of this lightly. I do consider myself an honest man. Perhaps only a little more selfish than the rest."

"What makes you say that?"

"Because I only want what will make *me* happy. I do not care enough for the rest of the world like you do. Still, when I think of how you journeyed out alone to save Winter . . ." Peter shook his head. "You acted out of compassion. I cannot think of the last time I did something solely for another person, without thought of myself."

"Peter, you are here with your sister right now. Is that not solely for her?"

"I suppose. But I want her to be happy. And Demsworth is a good friend, so the visit is not at all a sacrifice."

"Just because you are getting something good in return does not mean you are not sacrificing a great deal in the effort. My racing out to find Winter was not solely for Summer. Her heartache would have been mine also had we lost him."

"That is because your heart is so good." Peter's eyes softened.

I looked down. I did not want to talk about my heart, or his for that matter. I'd be better off remaining as impartial as possible with Peter. My heart would thank me for it when I took Mr. Pendleton's hand in a few days' time.

"I think I shall find a book to pass the evening before I retire." I stood, heading to the small bookshelf by the hearth. Most of the books were poems or academics, and I chose an English and French dictionary. Never had I been allowed such an extensive education with more than the proper English language, and I wanted to take every advantage possible.

Peter gave me an easy smile when I returned, though I refused to give him more than a quick glance.

"French, hmm? Interesting choice. *Êtes-vous couramment?*"

I did not understand his words, but I would not admit as much to him. I opened the book to a page, skimming until I found what I needed. Completely unaware of how to enunciate beyond having heard tourists use their native tongue, I practiced in my head before saying, "*Couchez-vous.*" *Go to bed.*

Peter laughed out loud, and I grinned. Eyes looked our direction, and I blushed feverishly to have drawn such attention over nothing more than a joke.

"Well done," Peter praised, glowing. "Though I think

what you meant to say in English was 'teach me French,' and I would love to."

"That is not—" I started, but Peter raised a finger to stop me.

"Just a simple phrase tonight, I think. And then I shall retire and leave you be." His eyes were as green as the sea, their depths just as intriguing.

"Fair enough," I agreed, closing my book on my lap. "Go ahead."

"Watch my lips," he said, staring at my own. He waited only a moment before saying, "*Tout est plus lumineux.*"

Peter's full lips were as inviting as the depths of his eyes, so much so that I hardly heard the sentence. He watched me, waiting, but I was frozen to my seat.

"A-again. Please."

Peter smiled, and this time I looked into his eyes as he spoke. "*Tout est plus lumineux.*"

"*Tout est plus lumineux,*" I repeated. "What does it mean?" My neck flushed at his nearness and the serious gaze he gave me from underneath his lashes.

Peter dipped his head toward mine. "Look it up." He stood to bid our company good night and, after one last glance, sauntered away.

I lifted my book, flipping through pages to translate the phrase. I was both excited and hesitant to know what Peter had said. I scanned the papers slowly, running my finger down the lines, then up to the next page and halfway down again until I found what I was looking for.

Tout. All, everything. Everything *est plus lumineux.*

What on earth had he said? This was going to take me all night. My eyes were heavy, but my mind was curious.

"Mr. Bratten, do you know French? Could you translate something simple for me?"

"Of course, Miss Moore, what is it?" He raised his brow in anticipation.

I repeated the phrase, hoping he would forgive my pronunciation.

"Ah. To what are we referring?" he asked, serious. "As in, what is the subject?"

"Oh, I . . . I am not sure." My cheeks grew warm, and I felt rather foolish. I hadn't considered that I was asking Mr. Bratten to repeat something completely foreign to me. What was I making him say aloud?

"It matters not. I was merely curious. The phrase translated literally is 'all is more bright.'"

Offering my gratitude, I sank back into my chair, warmth spreading through me like melting butter on bread. There was depth, beauty in the sentiment, but the phrase itself was a bit mysterious. I was sure tonight Peter's voice had betrayed a note of seriousness, of kindness. Whatever could he mean with such a phrase? I could hardly wait to ask.

Which, I was sure, was precisely what Peter wanted.

Chapter Sixteen

The men were gone the next morning, having taken an early leave for the exhibition, which was a few hours' drive away, so Clara and I headed for the stables after breakfast. We'd not had more than a few minutes together in days.

We stopped by the stalls first so I could check on Winter, who was feasting on a pile of oats in a small bucket.

This time I rode Grace. Her gray coat was smooth with hints of black, and I could not help but think of Peter as I settled atop her saddle. Was it only yesterday we rode together through the mud?

Clara rode a mare of equal hands, and together we set out. Mr. Beckett rode with us, leading us around the estate a few paces ahead.

"Tell me everything," I said to Clara when I was certain Mr. Beckett was out of earshot. "How are things faring with Sir Ronald?"

Clara's happy grin was immediate. "Oh, Amelia. I never want to leave. I do not know what I shall do if I must."

"Has he said anything to you? Hinted at all of his feelings?"

Clara's eyes met mine shyly. "Not exactly. But he said last evening how he'd missed me since London."

My jaw slacked. "Clara. What did you say?"

She shrugged and laughed. "I agreed. I told him that the Season was the happiest I have been in some time. And not for the balls or society, but for his company. He seemed encouraged, but that was that. I hope I did not scare him away. If the men do not come back soon, I shall go mad with worry."

Grace huffed as we climbed a hill, and I scratched her mane soothingly. Staring at my sister, her open smile and kind heart so vulnerable and free, my own heart blanched and fought for its freedom. But only one of us could have that opportunity. One of us had to be realistic, practical. And love was not practical; it was the biggest gamble of all. Clara could take that risk, as long as I developed a plan should she fail.

"And what of Georgiana? How does he behave toward her?"

"Friendly. I can tell he cares for her, but I'm not sure how seriously." Clara brushed away a loose strand of golden hair. "Is it very wrong of me to feel pleased at her jealousy? Georgiana's eyes were raging at me all of yesterday."

I could not help but smile. "Not at all. She will have to get used to the sight, I daresay."

Clara scrunched her nose. "I should hope not. If Sir Ronald and I marry, Georgiana will not be invited to an event for years if I have anything to say about it. I've quite had my fill of her. Haven't you?"

I swallowed. I could not blame Clara for desiring a separation of the two families. As much as I admired Peter, Clara was my sister, and I would do anything for her. "I would not blame you in the least."

We rode a few paces, alone in our thoughts, when Clara sucked in a small breath. "Oh, look! There it is."

Mr. Beckett had led us to a beautiful greenish-blue pond, a hidden gem in the middle of an expanse. We dismounted, and he pulled a large bag from his saddlebag.

"Would you like to feed them?" he asked in his gruff voice. "The fish."

Clara's eyes sparkled, and she tugged off her gloves. "Yes, thank you."

He opened the bag, filling our hands with bread crumbs, and we threw out handfuls as far as we could, laughing when Clara's farthest throw barely exceeded three feet.

"You must work on your arm, Clara, if you plan to marry a countryman," I teased.

"Hush. I am merely encouraging the fish to swim closer to land. For visual purposes."

Mr. Beckett laughed politely beside us, filling our hands again and again as we ventured around the perimeter of the pond. The fish bubbled up to the surface of the water, flicking their tails as they fought for a bite.

We spent the afternoon along the bank watching the fish until Mr. Beckett's bag was empty and the water stilled. Birds chirped in the trees, dipping down to steal worms and bugs from the earth. Being with Clara like this reminded me of

Father. I could almost believe he would pull up on his steed, fishing poles in hand, and join us on our afternoon adventures.

Nothing about Brighton reminded me of Father or Mother. Brighton was filled with sickness and chaos. A house that had never been a home. A shell of a life that kept us living.

Sitting beside Clara, I considered telling her about Lord Gray, to share the burden of his inevitable death and of my plan to save us with Mr. Pendleton. Would she be angry with me for keeping these secrets? If all went as planned and Sir Ronald declared himself, none of it would matter to her anyway.

Clara watched the clouds pass by slowly in the sky, her gaze contemplative and serene. I studied the curve of her nose, the blue in her eyes, and the soft, natural curls that framed her face. My little sister. She deserved the world.

"I love him," Clara said softly, arms around her knees. "I love him, Amelia."

"I know you do." I pulled her close, kissing her hair. "And he's a fool if he does not love you back."

That night, we gathered in the drawing room, and Beatrice played the pianoforte while we waited for the men to descend for dinner. Lieutenant Rawles was first to enter, then Mr. Bratten, followed shortly by Sir Ronald, who walked straight to Clara, beaming to tell her the news of the exhibition.

"The fencing was incredible. You would not believe how fast their footwork was, how powerful their swordsmanship."

Clara matched his enthusiasm with ease. I left them alone on the window seat, watching the door.

Where was Peter? And why was I looking for him? His was the only company I should not be seeking. The afternoon was long past, which meant I owed him none of my time, but still my thoughts were filled with nothing but him.

I smoothed my skirts as I paced the room, feeling my hair for any loose pins. Last evening had been different. His attention felt personal and more . . . meaningful. What exactly had he meant by that phrase "all is more bright"?

Just then, Lady Demsworth stood. "Good, we are all here. Shall we, Ronald?"

I looked to the door and found Peter's eyes waiting for mine, curious and warm. Crossing the room, he bowed to me, offering his arm. "Might I escort you in, Miss Moore?"

I bit back a smile, remembering our conversation about trying to be honorable. Perhaps Peter had taken it a touch too seriously. "Why, thank you, Mr. Wood. How dashing you are this evening."

His grin grew full then, on the brink of laughter. "If I'd known good manners granted me your flattery, I would have long since abandoned my ill repute."

I took his arm and freed my smile, acutely aware of Peter tightening his hold and slowing our steps behind the others. My heart was much too happy to be near him, thrashing around in my chest like a long-abandoned puppy.

Dinner was casual and brief, though at one point, Beatrice giggled so hard at Mr. Bratten's reenactment of a winning fencing blow, she tipped her cup over, spilling her drink over my dress. Fortunately, no one seemed to notice, and I patted down the worst of it with a linen napkin.

We finished eating, and as Lady Demsworth rose to lead the ladies to the drawing room, I snuck away to my bedchamber to change. As I turned up the stairs, I heard Sir Ronald ask the gentlemen if they minded skipping port.

Mary helped me change into a pink evening gown, and I quickly returned to the drawing room.

Lady Demsworth and Mrs. Turnball greeted me as I entered. The rest of our company was clustered together in the back corner around a small table and two chairs. The men stood on one side and the ladies on the other, and they appeared to be rivaling teams. Laughter filled the air.

"Miss Moore!" Beatrice broke away and grasped my arm, pulling me to the table. "Thank goodness, we need you."

"Amelia!" Clara clapped her hands. "We've found her. Gentlemen, we have one more player."

"Who are we missing?" Mr. Bratten eagerly searched the faces of the men.

"Wood," Sir Ronald announced loudly, and everyone craned their necks to look for him.

"Yes?" Peter looked up lazily from his seat near the hearth, book in hand. He looked warm and comfortable, and I'd have much preferred to join him there instead of playing whatever game I was now caught in the middle of. Peter's eyes met mine, and he closed his book, standing.

"We need you," Lieutenant Rawles called as Peter strode toward us.

"We're at a standoff," Sir Ronald added.

Peter tilted his head. "How so?"

"We each have two points," Georgiana said to me. "Men versus women. Mr. Bratten and Miss Turnball tied on the third round."

"What is the game?" A new nervousness heightened my senses.

Peter sided with the men, who encompassed him in what looked like a huddle. A very secretive huddle.

"The first one to smile loses. You must win, Amelia. For all women." Clara shot me a hopeful expression.

I broke a smile then, and three serious faces chided me. Apparently smiling at all was unacceptable.

"What must I do? I do not know how to make Mr. Wood smile on my best day."

"Pishposh," Georgiana said. "I've seen you with my brother. Now is not the time for modesty. Now is the time to pull out your best weapons."

"Which are?"

The ladies stared at me, and I realized we were in just as close a huddle as the men were.

Beatrice leaned in. "Flirt."

"Flirt? With Mr. Wood?" I almost laughed outright but caught myself before anyone could reprimand me.

Georgiana's face grew serious, and she stepped forward. "He is good, Miss Moore. I've seen him turn the heads of women who live like queens. You cannot let him flatter you, or it will be over before it even begins. You must take charge and dominate the conversation, turn it back on him. Use body language to intimidate him."

"You are serious." My voice came out shocked, horrified.

Flirting with Peter would be the grandest embarrassment of all.

"Yes," Beatrice added. "But you cannot smile. If you feel the urge, you must look away immediately and clench your teeth together. Bite your tongue, anything. We cannot lose!"

"Thirty seconds," Mr. Bratten called.

Georgiana stepped forward, eyes focused on mine. "He is wickedly ticklish on his neck, near his collarbone. Get close to him and . . . fiddle with his cravat or something. Whatever comes to mind."

"His cravat? That is terribly improper." My chest tightened, nerves seizing my breath at the mere thought of intentionally being so close to Peter. There had to be a way out of this.

"That is the name of the game, apparently." Beatrice pursed her lips. "Besides, they are surely telling him to do worse to you."

"Please, Amelia," Clara begged. "This cannot be worse than how you fashioned a guess at blindman's bluff. Mr. Wood knows it is only in jest."

"All right." I felt a terrible urge to laugh at the ridiculousness of this game, but the girls were already adjusting my dress, smoothing my hair and pinching my cheeks.

"Are you ready?" Sir Ronald asked.

"Just," Clara responded.

All I had to do was make Peter smile. And quickly. Except I could not so much as twitch in the attempt for fear of smiling myself. Perhaps if I thought back on how irksome and infuriating he'd been among the first days of our acquaintance, I could maintain a frown. His confidence, the way he threw his money at me, and how he schemed so arrogantly to oust my sister from the party. Oh, yes, he would lose this game. And I would make him miserable for every time he'd ever teased me.

Peter sat at the table, facing me. He had a look of forced contempt on his face, not unlike my own I was sure. But I did not sit. Smoothly, I held his gaze as I moved around the table toward him. He took a steady breath through his nose as I leaned back against the table in front of him.

"What are you up to, Miss Moore?" He raised a brow, tightening his lips.

I had to look away for a moment, clearing my throat of the tickling urge to laugh. Could I do this? Flirting was not my forte. I did not even know how to properly bat my lashes.

"Mr. Wood," I said tantalizingly, as though casting a net for prey. "My, don't you look handsome tonight."

Clara giggled behind me, and Beatrice hushed her.

Peter straightened in his chair. "That is the second time you've told me so tonight. I am beginning to think you are in earnest. Tell me, Miss Moore. What is it about me that you find so attractive?"

Heat rose into my cheeks, and Peter swallowed back his own humor. He was making fun of me, I knew it, but I had to stay serious. I would have the last laugh. Not the first.

"Without question, I am most affected by your smile." And he almost gave it to me. Heart pounding in my chest, I reached for his cravat, tugging it loose. "But you really should teach your man to tie better. This knot is atrocious."

Peter stole my blush, lifting a hand to his neck. "I knot my own cravat, thank you."

"Perhaps you'd like a woman's touch." I reached out again, but Peter took my hand, stopping me.

"You've told her, haven't you, Georgiana?" His eyes flashed amused daggers to his sister behind me.

"Oh, no, I'd never," Georgiana said. "Just like you'd never tell Lieutenant Rawles of my ticklish wrists."

Peter looked to me, shaking his head and releasing my hand. "I've outgrown it anyway."

"Have you?" I wanted to smile so badly, but I couldn't, not yet. I lifted my hands to the sides of his neck, surprised when he let me touch his skin. He stayed painfully still, breathing through his nose steadily, like a guard standing at attention. Loosening his cravat further, I studied his jaw, set and determined, and his eyes that searched mine with more seriousness than humor.

As I retied the knot in an ugly oversized bow, he raised his chin to aid my view and handling of the cloth, though his eyes never left mine. Puffing out the loops, I let my fingers linger near his collarbone. His skin was smooth, warmth radiating through my fingers and sending tickling waves to my chest. Peter's shoulders twitched, and his jaw tightened. I wondered if he'd bitten down hard on his tongue.

"Well done." I grumbled. The bow was done, and it had been a glorious failure on my part. Apparently, Georgiana had been wrong about his ticklishness. What next? What other weakness did Peter Wood possess?

"Don't pout, Miss Moore. It is maddeningly attractive." Peter's eyes were teasing, smiling when his lips couldn't.

I cast him a scowl, drawing a heavy breath. I'd played my best card too early.

"You've changed your dress," he said, leaning in and resting his elbow on the table inches from my skirts. Much too close.

"I fell victim to an unattended drink at dinner."

"You were gone quite a long time," he said, tilting his head at me. His eyes were searching, questioning, but for what I could not tell.

Why did Peter care? What kind of cards were up his sleeve? Perhaps I could turn the conversation on him. I rested my hand on the table even closer to his elbow, leaning in. "Are you counting the minutes we are apart, Mr. Wood?"

I swore I saw a twitch in his cheek, a deepening of the crease just to the left of his mouth. Peter cleared his throat loudly, sitting up from his relaxed position.

"He smiled!" Georgiana shrieked.

"No, no, no, he recovered," Sir Ronald argued, followed by voices in varying degrees of agreement.

"Keep going, this is getting good," Beatrice said with a hint of pleasure in her voice.

Blast it all, I'd nearly had him. Now it seemed we were at a stalemate. I racked my brain trying to remember anything Georgiana might have said that could help me outwit Peter. She'd said to compliment him, to get closer. To intimidate him. What more could I do?

Peter fiddled with his newly tied cravat. "You have quite the talent, Miss Moore."

Why did he sound so sincere? He looked like an overgrown child, proud at having just tied his first neckcloth. "Thank you, sir. I shall charge by the minute, should you need my services in the future."

"The future, hmm?" Peter studied me, an idea forming clearly in his eyes. "Since you have so openly displayed your talents, perhaps it is my turn. Shall I read your palm? Discover the secrets of what is to come?"

Palmistry? Like a vagabond on the streets of London? "You want me to give you my palm for a reading?" My voice was unconvinced.

Peter's lips parted. He nodded. "May I?"

My hands tingled at the thought of his touch. Any other time I would've laughed and walked away, but the gentlemen behind Peter bore enthusiastic grins, confident of victory. This game meant something to Clara and to the other girls, so I needed to put my own feelings aside. I would not forfeit. Somehow, Peter managed to skim by without smiling during my attempt. Maybe I could turn his fortune-telling against him.

I cast Peter a hard stare. What was I so afraid of? "As you wish, Mr. Wood."

I slid off my gloves, placing them on the table. My heart fluttered in my chest, and I crossed my arms tightly.

"Are you right- or left-handed?" Peter asked. He was playing the part, looking serious and professional.

"Right," I said.

"Your hand, please."

I took a calming breath, then exhaled slowly. Where had Peter gotten this idea anyway? Palmistry was even more ridiculous than a woman tying a man's cravat. I held out my right hand, palm up, looking away to the dark window across the room.

Before he'd even touched me, I felt a tingling in my skin.

Was that why Peter had taken such steady breaths through his nose? Because he felt the same way? This dizzy, this excited, this . . . affected?

His warm hand took mine, and immediately my senses came alive. This was unlike the time we'd held hands in the stalls, or even in the pasture. The way his fingers brushed against my skin as they felt every groove in my palm was mesmerizing. I felt the sensation all the way to my toes.

"And?" I said in an effort to hurry him.

"This is most interesting, Miss Moore. Most interesting, indeed." Peter pulled my hand closer, and I leaned in. "You have a very square hand," he said, pressing my hand between both of his, as though measuring its size. "That tells me you are a practical thinker. Stubborn, perhaps, and strong-willed."

I squinted at Peter. "Tread carefully, Mr. Wood."

He pressed his lips together, staring at my palm. "This line here"—he drew his pointer finger along the center of my palm—"is long, indicating that you are an inward thinker. Smart and sensible, but perhaps not as good at sharing?"

"Has he studied this art?" Clara asked from behind me. The answer was no, but Peter had apparently been studying me.

"Both hands, if you will, Miss Moore." I lifted my left hand, and Peter held them side by side, searching.

"Ah, here it is. The love line."

My eyes widened. "The what?"

"Your future, of course. It all begins with marriage, does it not?"

Someone snorted, and a man blew out a laugh.

Peter brushed his fingers across my palms, circling, tracing, and likely formulating more ridiculous things to say. Watching his resolve crack under pressure was worth my embarrassment. He would not last, I was sure of it.

He sniffed, looking up at me and feigning serious concern. "You will be disappointed, I'm afraid. As I know you are anything but a romantic."

I nearly pulled my hands away, but he caught them, lifting them higher.

"This line here"—he traced a curvy, longer line—"is strong and determined. Just like the man in your future. I see happiness here and prosperity. And a very clever, very handsome man to share it with." Peter looked up at me. "That stubborn, practical side of you will not stand a chance against his charms."

I bit down on my tongue hard, making my eyes water. He was teasing me. And it hurt so bad not to smile. I had to say something. Anything. "And how will I know when I've met him?"

Peter scrunched his nose. "I am a palmist, Miss Moore, not Cupid. But I might suggest encouraging him when you find him. So he knows his intentions will be well-received."

"Men do not need encouragement," I argued.

"Oh, yes. Especially when the lady is particularly wonderful and intimidating." He raised his eyebrows playfully. "It does not have to be a grand gesture. Just enough to prove your affection matches his. That is, if you wish for his proposal."

Something was coming. I knew he prepared to humiliate me in some form. I needed to take control, so I said, "I shall need a demonstration."

The men behind him were shaking with silent laughter.

"Oh, there are many ways to encourage a man, Miss Moore. You could flutter your lashes, for example." Peter's cheeks dimpled but not with a full smile. He batted his lashes up at me.

I pressed my lips hard together. My chin was quivering, but so was his. "That is not enough. I'd want him to really know." My voice was shaking, eyes filling with tears at holding it all in.

"Then after you've fluttered your lashes at him, warmed him up, so to speak, you should . . ." Peter cleared his throat. "You should wink at him, so he knows how dearly you wish for his proposal."

"Wink at him?" I repeated in astonishment, nearly on a laugh. "That is the worst advice I have ever been given. You are a terrible fortune-teller."

"Try it." He folded his arms and stood. "You will have every man in this room at your feet."

"I will do no such thing." I stared at him. His chin wavered at the terrified sound in my voice.

"Then do you concede?"

"Of course not."

Peter waited. As did everyone in the room.

I turned to the girls, who nodded in encouragement.

Huffing, I mimicked Peter's folded arms, shaking my head. If I was going to do this, I would do it right. I stepped around him, and Peter mirrored my movement until we had switched places. I was sitting in his chair, and he was leaning against the table.

My cheeks flushed. I'd never been so embarrassed in all

my life. Tilting my head, I looked up at him and fluttered my lashes ridiculously.

The men stepped closer. Peter's lips twitched. How was he not smiling?

I licked my lips, and Peter's gaze dropped. He was suddenly still, watching. This was utterly absurd. Completely mortifying. I thought to wink, but my lips started to curl—oh, how it hurt to force my mouth into a line!—and Peter was as near to smiling as I. A small breath escaped me, and I thought of Clara.

It is only a wink, Amelia, for heaven's sake.

Chin raised, I met Peter's gaze and *winked.*

Peter's eyes widened, his cheeks flushed scarlet, and his own lips parted as though he had never been so surprised. Desperately, I released my smile, it broke across my face, and I bent over, laughing.

"Champions!" Sir Ronald yelled, pumping a fist into the air as Mr. Bratten punched Lieutenant Rawles in the arm.

Peter smiled fully then, breathing hard.

As the men cheered, we huffed, the anger of four women intensifying with each happy smile from the opposing team.

Beatrice frowned. "Georgiana, I think I would like to see your dress for the ball after all."

"As would I." Clara took Beatrice's arm.

"Amelia?" Georgiana raised a brow, beckoning me to follow suit. "Shall we?"

I seized on the opportunity to leave Peter and this ridiculous game behind me. "I am dying to see it."

"Wait, no." Sir Ronald lifted a hand. "It is not even

eleven. You cannot retire just yet. Let's play another round of blindman's bluff."

"Come, ladies," Georgiana called as she moved toward the door, ignoring Sir Ronald's pleas. I had to give her credit for holding a decent grudge for once. We followed after her, despite complaining and calling from the men behind us.

I'd reached the doorway when Peter called, "A moment, Miss Moore?"

I thought to run from him, that man whose dimpled cheeks had been my undoing, but his strides were too quick. Peter crossed to me, out of earshot from the rest of the party, and I glanced toward the stairs where the other ladies had reached the top.

"I won fair and square," he whispered.

I poked his chest with my finger. "You are a horrible flirt, and I shall never forgive you. And you absolutely smiled before I did."

"I did not," he said only half seriously. "But I'd be willing to play again if you'd like."

I scowled at his teasing, and he chuckled. "Go to bed, Peter Wood."

"One thing more, and I shall. Did you decipher your French like a good pupil?"

I crossed my arms confidently, "I did. It is 'all is more bright.' Though I am not sure what it means."

"Yes. More succinctly in English, 'everything is brighter.'"

"And what does it mean?" I searched his face for an answer.

Peter hesitated, shifting his weight. "Have you ever met someone who enters a room and the whole of the atmosphere changes? The feel, the temperature, the very air you breathe? An angry person could silence a room, intensifying the energy there, while a soft-spoken person could set that same room entirely at ease in the next moment." He rested a hand on the doorframe as he took a slow, long breath. "With you, Amelia, everything is brighter."

I'd forgotten to breathe, my heart slowing from its earlier excitement. Peter was not teasing me. Not now. He was quite serious, quite honest. And that was the most beautiful thing anyone had ever said to me.

"I will see you tomorrow afternoon. Do not think I will go easy on you just because your pride was wounded tonight." He winked and turned away.

What a teasing, irritating man. Wasn't he? My words were beginning to feel insincere in my head, as though they smiled in their own knowing way. Even I wasn't so sure I meant them anymore.

Chapter Seventeen

Georgiana closed the door behind her after the four of us entered her bedchamber.

"You did well, Miss Moore," she said. "I told you he is good."

"He was most improper," Beatrice said. "No matter how entertaining it was to watch. I applaud you for lasting as long as you did."

"Thank you," I said from where I stood by the small window across the room. My mind was still whirling from what Peter had said about me. His words were the loveliest I had ever heard, even now as they echoed in my memory.

"They will never let us live it down." Clara frowned. "Mr. Wood will be infamous."

Georgiana sat on her bed, letting down her hair. "In a party as small as this, perhaps. Usually, Peter will do anything to stay out of the line of gossip."

Beatrice sat in a chair by Georgiana's desk. "Won't we all?"

"Are Sir Ronald's parties usually much larger?" Clara asked.

Georgiana brushed her fingers through her curls. "Yes, the Demsworths are nothing if not extravagant with house parties. But when Sir Ronald's father died, and everything came to light, the guest list was the first thing to go."

"So it's true?" Beatrice sat up straighter, eyes questioning.

Georgiana smiled a cat-like smile.

"I did wonder why things were so casual," Beatrice said.

Clara looked to me, confused, but I had no idea what they were talking about.

"What is true?" I asked. "Is something wrong with Sir Ronald?"

Beatrice turned to me. "Surely you've heard. His father was a terrible gambler. No one had any idea until his death, but of course by then it was too late. He left Sir Ronald with mountains of debt, and after he paid them all off, there was nothing left. I hear they barely keep the estate running. A portion of money remains untouchable in the bank until Sir Ronald marries. Or so I've heard."

"It is true," Georgiana agreed, almost happily. "But I imagine that money will not be untouchable for much longer."

Her meaning was clear, her words pounding in my ears.

Beatrice added in a hushed voice, "My mother says that is precisely why he held this party. They stayed with family over the Season, on a very frugal budget. Now, he means to choose a wife, have a small wedding, and live comfortably again with the sum his father locked away."

"He is . . . poor?" My tongue felt numb.

"Quite. Which is why not many women from the Season suited his fancy. Too many were only interested in him because they thought he held a *fortune*." Georgiana emphasized the word as she looked pointedly at Clara. "But he needs only a few good years of farming to replenish his holding."

A few good years. The walls in the room constricted, and my hands grew clammy. This was not the security I'd imagined. Did he know Clara came with nothing? Surely he planned on a dowry increasing his income. A dowry like Georgiana most certainly held. Would our poverty change his favor? We'd come this far, and I was so close to giving Clara her heart's desire. But the risk was more severe than I'd anticipated. Even if Clara secured Sir Ronald, could he provide her with stability? Would Father have allowed a match based on such a gamble? Frustration beat upon me like the pelting of hard rain in a storm.

Clara rubbed her temples. What did she think of all this?

"My brother and Sir Ronald are a lot alike, you know." Georgiana looked to me. Her eyes were sharp, almost unfeeling, and I wanted to turn away.

She continued, "Peter will need a considerable dowry from his wife to replenish the amount mine will cost him. Otherwise, he will have to go back to London and work for more income like my father did for my mother. In truth, Peter is *expecting* wealth in his marriage."

She spoke the words to the room, but I knew they were intended for me. Her lips curled upward, and I swallowed, looking down to my hands, gloved in secondhand rags. I felt as worthless as a grain of sand.

Somewhere deep down, I'd been harboring hope.

Dreaming of a place and time where Peter would save me from my circumstances. The vision had become so clear. I'd tasted it in the small moments we'd shared and in the beautiful words he'd spoken.

But money was something I did not have. I could never meet his needs.

"Are you well, Amelia? You look rather pale," Beatrice said.

"I am well. Perhaps a little tired from these late evenings. Clara, dear, should we retire?" I stood, reminding myself that my focus was on Clara and her future.

She forced a smile, though her eyes were filled with worry over Georgiana's attempt to dishearten her. "Of course, sister, as you wish."

When we were safe in our room a few doors down, I locked the door behind us. The room was quiet as Mary had retired for the night.

Leaning against the wood frame, I took three deep breaths. Georgiana was right. Peter would never think of me as anything more than a friend to tease for a fortnight. He came from a wealthy, established family name, and I came from scandal. That he would need a dowry to bolster his estate was not surprising. Sir Ronald, more so. What would they say when they discovered Clara and I had nothing?

For the first time since arriving at Lakeshire Park, I realized fully the impossible nature of our endeavors. Men did not often marry penniless women, even for love. Perhaps Lord Gray had known all along that we would fail this close to the finish line. This entire trip might have all been a joke to him.

Then again, Sir Ronald knew misfortune. And misfortune often led to compassion. He of all people should understand our reasons for staying quiet.

I turned to Clara. "Did you know of Sir Ronald's debts?"

Clara shook her head. "He has said nothing of debts. Only that he and his family live modestly and do not often travel, which has never bothered me. I've never questioned it."

"Have you told him of Lord Gray? That we likely will get very little, if anything at all, as a dowry?"

"Are you certain Mother and Father accounted for nothing?"

"I am sure. I've spoken with the solicitor myself several times." I groaned inwardly, loosening Clara's dress as she let down her hair. Why had no one thought of our futures?

Clara sighed. "No, I have not spoken with Sir Ronald. How terribly awkward. To speak of it would assume that he is thinking of a match, and I can make no such assumption yet. But to be honest, if it is true that he is poor, at least he and I have one more thing in common."

My sweet Clara. I gave her much less credit for handling bad news than she deserved. But if she stood any chance against Georgiana's dowry, we needed to try a different approach. "Perhaps you should find a moment to tell him. I think it is time he knew our circumstances fully. Then we shall see how he reacts."

"Very well," Clara said dejectedly as we dressed in our nightclothes. When our hair was finally in curling papers, we settled into bed. My mind instantly turned to Peter and a crushing pain replaced the glow that had been in my chest.

Though nothing had passed between us, I could not shake the feeling that I'd already been rejected by him.

Thank heavens I had Mr. Pendleton. I should have sent my acceptance of him right away. Even if Clara did make a match with Sir Ronald, we'd need another source of security.

What would happen in these next few days? We had less than a week to sway Sir Ronald fully into Clara's favor and to secure my match with Mr. Pendleton.

I curled into myself. We were running out of time.

Chapter Eighteen

When I descended the staircase the next morning, company was lacking.

"Miss Moore," Beatrice said with a kind smile, embroidery in hand. "Your sister is out, and the men gone. It appears it is just you and I until the others awake."

I sat across from her in the drawing room, sighing as I searched out the window. It was a beautiful morning, and I wondered where Clara was, and if she planned to speak to Sir Ronald today.

"How is your morning?" My hands were still compared to hers, so I fingered through a book of architecture on the side table.

"It is well. I am more rested than I thought after our late evening. I suppose the men retired early. I am told Mr. Bratten, Sir Ronald, and Lieutenant Rawles left early with the gamekeeper to set traps this morning."

"Well, I hope they felt our absence last night," I said, shooting her a laughing grin, which she returned.

"It is clear they did, as well they should've. Have you seen

Mr. Wood yet today?" Beatrice broke from her stitching, raising a playful eyebrow at me.

"I have not." And I was not sure I wanted to.

Beatrice studied my face. "Do not tell Georgiana I said this, but you two Moore sisters have given the men here quite a stir. She wouldn't admit as much, but I have never seen Mr. Wood pay more attention to a lady than he has paid to you this past fortnight."

A strange laugh bubbled out of me. "No, no. Mr. Wood and I are good friends, but we are ill-suited for anything more than that."

Beatrice suppressed a smile. "Your secret is safe with me, Miss Moore." She took back up her stitching, and I sat in stunned silence.

Did I have a secret about Peter? He was handsome and charming and delightfully funny. And I'd been thinking of him much too often. Certainly more than Mr. Pendleton, and he was as good as my intended. More than I thought about Sir Ronald or Mr. Bratten or Lieutenant Rawles, and those men were my friends. But I did not wish to spend all day with them like I did with Peter. Our time together was never enough. And those moments I'd imagined kissing him . . .

Oh, no. I did have a secret about Peter.

A knock sounded on the door, and Mr. Gregory stepped in. "Miss Moore, Lady Demsworth would like to see you in her sitting room."

"Of course," I said, rising and following him from the room. How could I have opened my heart so willingly to Peter? If he had any intention of courting me, his mind would be swayed by my lack of dowry. Indeed, it was only a matter of time before he found out the dire truth of my circumstances.

Moments later I stood in Lady Demsworth's doorway, and she ushered me in with a girlish squeal.

"Miss Moore, I've received a response from David! He is eager to meet you and will arrive in four days' time. Business nearby requires his attention, so unfortunately we will only have him for dinner, but before he leaves, I am confident you will have your engagement and the security you need."

My mouth fell open, and I quickly closed it. "Th-that is . . . wonderful news. I . . . hardly know what to say. Thank you." The last was nearly a question. Why was I surprised? Of course Mr. Pendleton would come. That had been the plan all along.

"I am so pleased. So very pleased," she continued. "I just know the two of you will be a perfect match."

"Yes," I breathed. A perfect match.

Loveless.

Risk-free.

Easy.

Chapter Nineteen

Closed away in my room, I successfully avoided the company for the rest of the afternoon, knowing Peter would be after me to claim my indebted time. His words from last night filled my thoughts, fighting against those spoken by Georgiana. What would he say if he knew I had no dowry? Would he think me a fortune hunter? Would he look at me differently? Would he look at me at all? I could not bear to see a change in him. I could never tell him. Especially since I would be meeting David Pendleton in a few days' time. Soon, it wouldn't matter if Peter loved me, dowry or not, at all.

Mary begged some lavender vinaigrette from Lady Demsworth's maid, and I stayed in bed for an hour sniffing it in hopes it would bring relief from what I assumed were the early symptoms of a heart attack.

"Are you in pain? Shall I call a doctor?" Mary asked, fanning me with the biggest fan she could find.

"No pain," I said on an exhale.

"I think I should call on Miss Clara," Mary said.

"You musn't. She cannot know." I tried to stand, but Mary held my shoulders down.

"Has something more happened since the letters?" Mary looked at me, worried.

If I did not tell someone my secret, I feared I might burst. Mary listened intently as I relayed my conversation with Lady Demsworth and explained that Mr. Pendleton was actually coming to meet *me* for an arrangement of marriage.

"Oh, Miss Moore." She shook her head. "How can you keep all of this to yourself?" She fanned harder. "For what it's worth, belowstairs I hear Lady Demsworth's nephew is quite the catch. Amiable, kind, wealthy. You could do far worse."

"It's not that." I waved away her fan, sitting up. "This is all so fast, Mary. Before, I thought we had weeks, not days. I hoped for a month before Lord Gray died. Then I made this arrangement, because what choice did I have? And yes, I'd felt rushed, but not entirely so. Now I am days from engagement . . . to a stranger . . ." I clutched my chest, and Mary hastily started fanning again.

"Do not think of it as only marriage, Miss Moore. Think of it as a saving grace. This match will give you everything you need."

Yes, but what will I lose?

The door creaked open, and Clara stepped in. "There you are. Where have you been all day, Amelia? We've all wondered after you. Beatrice said something about Lady Demsworth needing to see you?"

Clara strode to the armoire, fingering through her evening gowns. Mary and I exchanged a worried glance. I knew I should tell Clara the whole of it. But how would she respond?

Would it devastate her beyond repair to hear how close we truly were to poverty? Or that I'd spoken in secret with Lady Demsworth and agreed to marry a stranger? Her knowledge of either of those things would change nothing, only cause more pain. I could bear it all for us for a few days more.

"Oh, that was nothing. She was only being a good hostess. Checking on our stay." I motioned to Mary to help me change for dinner.

Clara looked over her shoulder at me. "Thank heavens. I had the strangest idea that Lord Gray was calling us home early."

"No, of course not," I said quickly. The truth was just the opposite. I bit at my finger, hating to keep the truth from my sister. "Never mind. What shall you wear tonight?"

Clara chose a pretty pink gown, and I wore lavender. I had Mary let my hair down, rearranging it to hang softly down my back. I feared a headache was coming on despite my vinaigrette.

At dinner, Lady Demsworth shot me a knowing smile, which I returned with as much gratitude as my nerves would allow.

"Miss Moore," Peter called from the opposite end of the table. His attention stung, now that I knew how incompatible we really were. "Your absence was noted this afternoon. Are you quite well?"

His hint at our bargain was as subtle as a yellow rose. Lady Demsworth looked at me curiously, as though anticipating my answer with equal interest. I knew she'd judge my response as a reaction to our earlier conversation. I needed to choose my words carefully. "Quite. I trust this evening will make up for this afternoon's lost time."

Peter smiled through a bite of beefsteak. "Indeed."

"Will you play this evening, Miss Moore?" Beatrice asked.

Clara straightened. "Forgive me, Amelia. I did not have a chance to tell you. Sir Ronald requested a display of our talents this evening. Each of the ladies are to pick a song to play or sing."

My gaze flicked to Sir Ronald, who smiled and said, "I'm afraid you have no choice. A musicale is a tradition at my house."

"To play or to sing?" Peter tilted his head. "Which will you choose?"

"Neither will fall well on your ears," I warned seriously. "But I suppose I shall embarrass myself less on the pianoforte."

"So modest," Georgiana goaded. "That is what all women say when their confidence is lacking."

"Indeed," I replied without hesitation. "I hope it is very clear that I know my own capabilities well."

"She speaks such only because she compares herself so harshly to Mozart himself," Clara said defensively. She pursed her lips and shot Georgiana a fiery look as though she desired nothing more than to wring the girl's neck.

Plates of baked custard distracted us, and all too soon Lady Demsworth rose, leading us to the music room on the second floor.

I had peeked into the room a few times during our stay, but tonight the space was lit with dozens of candles, their light reflecting in mirrors that lined each wall. In the middle of the large, open room was a grand mahogany pianoforte, glossy and detailed with beautiful craftsmanship. Four tall windows behind it spanned nearly the entire length of the front wall, their curtains drawn open to reveal a breathtaking view of the moon and stars.

Gliding my hand along the ornate carvings on the grand pianoforte, I found myself twirling from wall to wall, taking in the grandeur of the vaulted ceiling and floating along the smooth tile floor beneath my shoes.

"I think I want this room all to myself," Clara said beside me, breathless. "This pianoforte, and this chair."

I squeezed the arm of a cushiony purple velvet chair as I walked toward the windows. "And this view."

Servants had lined chairs in rows a few paces away from the pianoforte, facing the windows. Georgiana fingered a harp. Beatrice presented two separate pieces of piano music to her mother to choose between, and Clara looked over her own sheet music. Was she going to sing? And then I realized I had nothing that would display what little musical talent I possessed. Not to mention the fact that I'd scarcely played the pianoforte since arriving here.

I knew only one song from memory. One song I'd forced myself to learn by heart.

Father brought the pages home after a weekend in London. He said he'd bought them from a poor composer on the streets. When at first I attempted to play the song, the notes did not make sense. Half of them looked partially erased, and I was sure Father had been swindled by the composer. But he forced me to practice the pages hours on end to make sense of the music he was sure was a masterpiece.

It took me weeks to riddle out the chords, until one afternoon, I realized the partially erased notes were not meant to be erased at all. Played in tandem with the others, the music fell into place, like an orchestra of the most heavenly sounds.

The first time I played it, I wept at its beauty. Whoever this composer was, he was a genius. And Father, when he heard it, could not speak for an entire minute. He made me play it multiple times a day. He tried going back to find the composer, but to no avail.

After Father died, I took to the pianoforte to play his song. But Mama could not abide it. She stole the pages from their ledge and cast them into the fire. The change in her had already begun to surface.

Since that day, I copied down Father's song from notes in my memory and played it as often as I could at Gray House. Now more than ever I needed to free the notes, the music that both uplifted and broke me.

Settling on the bench, I loosened my fingers with a few scales, stretching out the joints and muscles that had grown stiff from the absence of practice. Pushing all thoughts of marriage aside, I let myself feel. Music had a way of healing, and I was in desperate need of it.

The men arrived too soon. I knew I was not ready, and thankfully Georgiana offered to play first, so I took a seat beside Mr. Bratten in the back of the room. She held the harp delicately but firmly, and despite our disagreements, I could not help but admire her. Her flawless performance earned great applause from the room.

Clara stood next, accompanied by Lady Demsworth on the pianoforte. She sang an angelic rendition of a French song from our youth. My courageous sister had blossomed here at Lakeshire Park. Sir Ronald hardly blinked as he watched her in clear admiration.

Clara curtseyed when she finished, and Lady Demsworth beckoned me. It was my turn. As I made my way empty-handed toward the pianoforte, I heard Georgiana remark disdainfully to Peter about my playing from memory.

Performing for a small group was almost worse than for a crowd. Knowing each of member of the audience personally, I felt self-conscious playing something so meaningful in front of them. But Clara would know the piece, so I would play for her.

I closed my eyes, picturing the music before me, and slowly struck the first soft note.

The immediate rise and fall of the notes lifted me from the room, a melody that transcended the stars, and I escaped reality as I always did when playing Father's song. One scale followed by another lifted me higher, until my chest was on fire, and I felt a yearning within my soul to never land.

As my fingers flew across the keys, I thought of Peter and how it felt to be so close to freedom and yet so confined to circumstance. I let the notes speak my sorrows and pains, feelings that no words could describe. To have so much in front of me, but to be so afraid, so alone, and so inept at reaching for it raged like an old familiar storm within my soul. Why could life not be like this song? Inspiring, hopeful, brave? I wanted to be as consumed by life, by love, as I was by the notes I played. I wanted my heart to burst with longing. I wanted my soul to sing.

But as the notes softened and descended, rising again

only briefly and then slowing, falling, I felt my feet upon the floor again. Grounded, where I belonged. My breath caught, and tears pricked my eyes.

The air was alive with clapping and hushed praise. I rose, and my eyes found Peter, his cheeks flushed, his gaze serious. Lady Demsworth and Mrs. Turnball were standing in appreciation beside the men, and Clara stood off to the side with a hand to her chest. Only she could truly understand.

I suddenly felt very exposed, pushed into a corner like a museum display, and shut the lid of the pianoforte.

Lady Demsworth reached out to me. "That was the loveliest sound I have ever heard, dear girl."

"It was beautiful, Miss Moore." Mrs. Turnball breathed with feeling. "So beautiful."

I looked to Peter, whose expression was unreadable. He studied me, much like he had last night, only now I felt like he was seeing me for the very first time. I needed to escape, to take a moment to recover.

When Beatrice took my seat on the bench and all eyes were on her, I slipped out through the back door, tiptoeing down the stairs and out into the darkness of night.

Chapter Twenty

Two glowing lanterns lit the veranda. I stole one from its perch, using it to light the stone stairs leading to the darkened expanse in front of me. Sitting on the lowest step, I set the lantern beside me as I took in three deep breaths, clasping my shaking hands together. I focused on the open fields that surrounded the estate, painted black and hilly and lush with crops.

I could not calm my mind, the melody of Father's song haunting the silence of night. Rubbing my eyes with my palms, I pressed hard against my face as though to eradicate all feeling with sheer will.

"There you are."

I froze as Peter's steps stopped beside me.

I watched him settle beside me on the step, torn between the necessity of his absence and longing for him to move closer. "Peter, you should not have followed me."

"Your music . . ." he said earnestly. "Why did you never tell me you could play so well?"

His voice alone calmed my tensed muscles, easing my

fears. “I have played that song no fewer than a thousand times, but put a page of any other music in front of me and I assure you I will disappoint.”

Peter laughed softly, leaning near enough to radiate warmth. We sat together in amiable silence, two friends on a stone step lit by a lantern’s glow.

I gazed up into the golden-spotted sky, so serene and magnificent. And so very far away.

When Peter finally spoke again, his voice was soft, full of compassion. “Tell me what has you so out of sorts.”

I swallowed. How could he know me so well? Were my secrets written so plainly in my countenance? “It is nothing. I am only worried for my sister. I fear I am not doing a very good job at securing a future for her.”

“I do not understand. Why must you be responsible for your sister’s match? Is that not your stepfather’s responsibility? You should be free to live as you wish.”

Should be. Yes, he was right, I should be free. But I was not. This fortnight was about securing our futures, and the surest way to do that was for me to marry Mr. Pendleton. The deed was nearly done. “You cannot possibly understand.” My words were weak, flat.

“Then tell me, and I shall.”

I gave him a half-hearted smile. “My circumstances are not your concern.”

Peter shook his head, his voice low. “What if I want them to be?”

I wanted to reach out to him, to let him wrap his arms around me and fall into his warmth, but as much as my heart ached for it, my mind knew it was neither practical nor sensible to let my emotions take precedence now. Peter did not know how great my needs were. And I could never ask him to work as hard as his father had for his mother. To sacrifice time and memories at home for financial security when he had everything sorted out so perfectly to match his dreams.

I huffed, narrowing my gaze at him, and he drew a deep breath. For once, he did not press me on my silence.

"I have something that might cheer you up."

He moved the lantern to the step above us, and I saw his face more clearly. Those gentle eyes that smiled into mine. In his hands, he held a small package.

"For you," Peter said, placing the package between us. "A bit overdue, I'm afraid."

He looked pleased, almost smug, as I untied the string. Had I ever been given a gift before? Not that I could remember, and certainly not from a gentleman. What had Peter thought to get me? And why? I removed the lid of the box and unfolded the thin paper wrapping.

Gloves. Ivory gloves.

Emotion welled up in my throat, and I swallowed, words eluding me. I looked to Peter, whose smug expression transformed into something new. His eyes were soft, yet serious, and if I hadn't known him to be so shameless, I'd have almost thought him shy.

"Do you like them?" he asked.

I pulled the gloves out as delicately as though they were made of actual ivory. They were pristine, so bright and smooth. But what shocked me was the mustard pair also sitting inside the box. And the burgundy pair beneath them. Three pairs of new, perfectly sized, beautiful gloves.

"Peter," I breathed. "This is too much. And far too kind. I cannot—"

"They are for you. I ordered them that first night. After you ran into me outside the drawing room." Peter's lips twitched. "I had to track down a retired glove maker, an old friend of the Demsworth family."

I shook my head, too stunned to speak.

He took the ivory pair from my hands, placing it gently on the stair between us. His eyes met mine with a question, a hesitation, before he took my hand in his, loosening the glove from each of my fingers.

My heart pounded with every soft touch, every tender caress of his fingers on mine. At last, he pulled my gloves free and held out the new ones for me. I pulled them on. A perfect fit.

"How?" I asked incredulously. How had he figured the perfect size without my hands for a fitting?

"You truly share hands with my sister. I stole a pair of her gloves to replicate."

"Thank you, Peter," I managed. I hadn't been allowed new gloves in years. Lord Gray had barely spared the expense for new dresses for the Season.

"Of course," he replied. "Luckily, you were already here. Otherwise I might have spent the entire fortnight trying to find you."

"I should confess I'd hoped to never see you again." I raised my brow at him in jest.

Peter feigned a gasp. "You wound me, Amelia."

"I am glad you've changed my mind on the matter," I said, before realizing how forward, how flirtatious the words sounded. I bit my tongue, cheeks ablaze. I should not tease Peter. Not anymore.

Peter leaned his elbows back on the step above us. "As am I."

Fuzziness clouded my thinking. The space between us smelled like the woods mixed with leather and soap. Peter. My deep breath felt like a saving grace; I feared I had stopped breathing altogether. Could it be that Peter cared? That he too felt this tingling, fuzzy pull?

"What are you thinking?" he asked timidly.

I wanted to tell him that I felt it too, that I wanted to spend another afternoon with him, to ask him about his childhood, his adventures, his travels. But I had too many secrets now. No matter what Peter thought of me or how I thought of him, there were too many reasons against us now. My lack of dowry, his family name, and perhaps greatest of all, our sisters' opposition to each other. Clara especially would despise the connection. I could not create something new with Peter if it meant destroying my relationship with Clara.

Besides, I'd already settled on Mr. Pendleton. He was not a risk in the least, but a sure means for security and comfort. He knew all of my secrets, and he needed me as much as I needed him.

"We should go back inside," I said. What if we were seen out here, alone in the dark? I could hear the pianoforte, which meant someone was playing and the musicale continued on, unaware of our absence. Perhaps Mrs. Turnball played. Or Georgiana.

"Indeed," Peter agreed, sighing. But neither of us moved.

Peter still held my old gloves, brushing the fabric with his fingers as though the touch connected us. He turned his gaze to the stars, lost in thought.

If only things were different. If only I was free. I knew I should go back inside—nothing good would come from sitting on this stair with Peter—but I wanted one more minute.

"If you could be anywhere right now, where would you go?" I leaned on my hand nearest him. "And do not say something to tease me."

Peter looked at me with a grin, his full lashes hiding the smile in his eyes. "You asking me not to tease you is a tease in itself. But I have my answer, actually. I've been thinking about going back to Paris. It is a beautiful time of year for it."

"I've never been," I admitted as a breeze blew through the shadowy trees.

"You would love the food." Peter winked, and I slapped him playfully on the shoulder. He ducked, grinning. "And the flowers, and the views of the Seine."

"I've always wanted to go."

"Where *have* you been?"

"London," I answered with disdain. Clara and I had seen most of the city during the Season, but the busy chaos of town did not entice me to return.

"Ah, yes. Your Season. Was it not all you'd dreamt?" He shot me amused eyes, still thumbing my gloves absentmindedly.

"Not exactly."

"That is because I was not there for you to tease. Imagine this fun multiplied exponentially."

"Ah, yes." I laughed, leaning closer to his twinkling eyes. "I can see you now, clad in your fancy tails with a colored cravat and a wicked grin on your face, trying to decide what to do with yourself."

Peter laughed alongside me, then leaned back and met my gaze. His eyes grew distant, thoughtful. An owl hooted above us in the trees. "I would steal your first dance."

My heart rattled and regained a faster beat. I had not yet imagined what it would be like to dance with Peter. Pulled close, only the two of us. My eyes dropped to his lips, and I took a shallow breath. I grew tired of fighting the pull between us. Why did I try to deny what my heart so clearly wanted? If I had to marry a stranger, didn't I deserve to enjoy one evening with Peter? I could worry about forgetting him later.

"I would ruin you for all other women." I nudged his shoulder softly with mine. "Where I lack in socializing, I excel in dancing. You wouldn't be able to let me go, and we'd dance set after set. Everyone would stare at us. Think of the talk."

"Oh, yes, everyone would talk." Peter looked heavenward. His jawline was smooth, squared, though a smile danced across his lips. "We would be banished from the assembly rooms for months. It would be delightful."

I could think of nothing better. "There is a ball at the end of the week. We can outrage the poor people of Hampshire all evening if you wish."

I reached for his arm to tug into mine. But instead of

lacing arms, he pulled me up from the stair, grasping my right hand in his and placing my left atop his shoulder.

"And dance we shall." He grinned, holding my waist close with his left hand.

"Peter!" I sucked in a breath as he waltzed me along the grass under the light of the moon. "If anyone sees us—"

"You were not lying. You are quite a good dancer, even with no music."

We danced to the music made up in Peter's head, and I laughed as he twirled us under the stars, lifting me up and twirling me again. His green eyes smiled into mine, and for a moment I felt like nothing bad in the world could ever happen again. Like I finally belonged, right there, with Peter.

When our silent music ceased, Peter slowed, swaying me back and forth in his arms. I rested my head on his shoulder, breathing in pine and soap, and he released my hand to brush a curl from my face. I ran my hand up his arm and to his shoulder, my heart pounding against my chest.

I loved Peter Wood. I could see that now. As clearly as I could see each star in the sky.

But would my love be enough when he was expecting a dowry? Would he be forced to continue his father's legacy despite his own personal dreams? I could not bear the thought of his rejection if he knew the truth of my circumstances. Neither could I endure our love turning into bitterness or resentment or pain. How could I know that choosing Peter would not end as tragically as Father's choice with my mother had? Days, weeks, even sometimes a year was not enough to know if love would last. I could not risk it.

Mr. Pendleton was the safer choice. His was a match

where both companions knew what they would receive. Where neither party was in danger of disappointment. He was a companion who could protect me, keep Clara from pain, and provide security for us both.

All I had to do was reject my heart.

I pushed back from Peter and retreated a few steps. "We are both here for our sisters. We should go inside and focus on them."

Peter frowned, his hand gripping air as though he still held a part of me. I turned back to the stairs to retrieve my lantern.

"What if we weren't?" Peter's voice, soft and inviting, stopped me in my tracks, and I turned to face him. "If you were here alone, would we still be outside, dancing under the stars together?"

He stared intently at me, as though my answer meant everything to him. His question filled the corners of my mind. Why did he persist? It was cruel, really, to imagine anything other than the bleak future ahead of me. But he asked the very question I'd been aching to answer for days. What if Peter was only Peter, and I was only Amelia? What if I was not nearly destitute nor controlled by circumstance?

When Peter walked in a room, would my heart still chase after him? Would I let it?

I did not know how to respond. This was no longer a question I could tease my way out of answering.

"Amelia?" he asked softly, waiting.

I turned away from him. "We should not be talking like this, Peter."

"How else should we be talking? Would you like me to go first? I have plenty to say if you'd let me."

"No." I spun around, but I was not prepared for the look in his eyes. It was hopeful and sweet, captivatingly handsome in a new way. A light only Peter could shine. A hope I did not want to dull. But I had to. "Please. This trip has always been for Clara. I must give her heart this chance. If Sir Ronald offers for Georgiana, Clara will be devastated, and any connection to your family will only cause pain. I am sure Georgiana will feel the same. We must maintain our distance. It is better this way. We are better as friends."

"I disagree entirely." He frowned, and my heart crumbled, hopeless and brooding.

But I had to speak the words. I had to cut the last tie that connected us. "I must cancel our bargain, Peter."

"What?" He reared back. "Why?"

"My life is more complicated than what you know. I do not think you would be dancing with me under the stars if you knew the whole of it." Of Mr. Pendleton, of Lord Gray, of our pending homelessness and poverty.

"I do not understand." Peter shook his head, his voice breaking. "I know you. I have told you more about myself than I've divulged to anyone else. You must give me a better explanation, a better reason than that if you wish to dismiss me so easily."

Easily? This was the hardest thing I'd ever done. I steeled my resolve. This was for the best. For everyone. "We've only known each other a fortnight. You do not know me—not really. Anything you have to say is not based on rational thinking." I thought of my parents, of the choice they made after one night. I took a step back.

Peter stepped forward, focused, pleading. "I assure you I have thought of everything—"

"I shall have to beg your forgiveness." I wiped away a tear, clearing my throat. "At present, I cannot offer more of an explanation. I think in time you will see I have made the right choice."

I grabbed the lantern and Peter's gift from the step and walked alone into the house.

Chapter Twenty-One

I'd trained my heart against pain too well. Too easily it retreated to its cage, like an animal too beaten down to stand. I slept in the next morning, having no good reason to wake.

When I entered the drawing room, Mr. Gregory approached Lady Demsworth, bowing. "Sir Ronald and the men are anxiously awaiting your arrival in order to begin the competition, my lady."

What competition? Had I missed something?

"Of course. Now that Amelia is here, we shall depart directly. Inform Miss Turnball, if you would, please, Mr. Gregory." Lady Demsworth turned to me. "It appears Ronald cannot wait another moment. Shall we?"

"Forgive me, I must have missed an explanation—"

"Of course you did, what with your mind on other things," Lady Demsworth said as she led me out onto the veranda. "The men have organized a fishing competition. The biggest fish wins a prize."

"Oh. That sounds . . . diverting." What sort of prize were they competing for? And would Peter be there?

Beatrice and I accompanied Lady Demsworth to the pond, which was as serene and beautiful as I remembered it being, to find Mrs. Turnball, Clara, and Georgiana already there. A small group of chairs had been placed a short distance away from the men.

Poles in hand, the men looked serious, having each secured a spot along with a servant to assist them with their tackle. Peter stood near the pond, and I leaned back in my chair, watching him. Waiting. But he would not meet my gaze. It seemed that even our friendship was ruined. I tried to tell myself I did not mind, that the distance between us was all for the best.

"Welcome, ladies." Sir Ronald waved. "I have decided that the biggest catch will win tickets to a symphony at the concert hall this evening with the lady of his choice. The competition will last two hours. After which, the largest fish will be weighed, a winner declared, and then Cook will prepare a delicious feast for us all."

"Huzzah!" Lieutenant Rawles cheered, nearly dropping his pole.

Peter wiped his brow with a handkerchief, looking rather worn already. He was fiercely competitive, but was he a good fisherman? I'd yet to see him fail at anything.

"On my count," Sir Ronald called. "Three. Two. One!"

At the mark, the poles were cast, zipping through the air like invisible arms reaching out for prey. The men were silent, eyes focused on tiny ripples in the water.

"Where did they get their poles?" I asked behind a gloved hand.

"Sir Ronald bought them from a tradesman," Clara

replied. "They are bamboo rods imported from India, but the gamekeeper made the line and flies himself."

"That is impressive." Try as I might to remain impartial, my eyes flicked to Peter. Though he stood far enough away I could not determine his expression, the tenseness in his shoulders and curve in his back told me he awaited a bite. Could he want the prize as greatly as Mr. Bratten or Sir Ronald did?

"Mr. Bratten's creel is a bit presumptuous, is it not?" Georgiana snickered at the rather large and bulky basket hanging from the man's side.

"He had it custom-made," Beatrice said, biting her lip. "He picked it up at the market last week, when we all went to town together. I pray he catches at least one fish."

"Oh, look!" Clara pointed in the distance. "Lieutenant Rawles's line is jolting!"

"He's got one." Lady Demsworth lifted a hand to shield her eyes from the piercing sun.

A flopping tail broke the surface of the shiny water. Lieutenant Rawles's man hurried forward with a net, scooping up the fish after the lieutenant had reeled it in close enough. The fish was large, but not as meaty as some I'd seen with Clara. There were certainly bigger fish to be caught.

Beatrice jumped from her chair in applause when Mr. Bratten proved as much a few minutes later, followed by Sir Ronald, and then Peter. I clapped with the ladies as Peter reeled in what seemed to be the largest fish yet. I watched for his reaction, but Peter seemed despondent as his man rolled the fish inside his creel. It was as though the sport held no real competition. Or perhaps winning meant nothing to him.

Leaning back in my chair, I sipped a glass of lemonade brought to me by a servant girl. The sun beat like fire upon us, despite our constant fanning.

"Where were you this morning?" I leaned toward Clara, decidedly avoiding watching Peter as he reeled in another fish.

"Out." She smirked.

"With Sir Ronald?"

"Of course. Until Georgiana found us in the gardens with that brother of hers," Clara responded from behind her fan. "We spent the morning together, the four of us. I'd almost forgotten how distasteful it is to have Mr. Wood's opinions thrust upon me."

Had Peter already reverted to his scheming? "That is most unfortunate. Though I think by now Sir Ronald knows his own mind."

"I should hope. But Georgiana can be very convincing. I worry she has more than one ace left to play."

"Did I hear my name?" Georgiana asked, a false sweetness to her voice as she stared pointedly at Clara.

"From me? What would I have to say about you, Miss Wood?" Clara matched Georgiana's tone so well I hardly recognized her voice. It was unlike Clara to be confrontational and rude.

I felt uncomfortable and uneasy to be seated in the middle of their exchange. Tension filled the air, negative and uninviting.

"I only heard Sir Ronald's name and mine together." Georgiana's smile was bitter, tempting.

"You must hear only what you wish to hear," I said before

Clara could respond. "Clara and I speak of everyone here today. Your name is nothing special in our conversation, I assure you."

Georgiana looked taken aback, and I felt a twinge of guilt. What would she say to Peter? And how would he react upon hearing how I'd spoken to his sister?

"Thank you," Clara whispered to me. "I cannot stand her, not even for a moment anymore. She is like an unwelcome fly that cannot be squished."

I let my shoulders fall, torn between the loyalty I felt for my sister in that moment and a sudden rush of emotion for Georgiana. Protectiveness? Compassion? Whatever it was, it opposed my natural instinct.

Georgiana traded seats with Beatrice a few minutes later, laughing with Lady Demsworth to Clara's further annoyance. The afternoon grew hotter, both in temperature and temperament. My fan was nearly a blur.

"Time!" called an attendant, holding a large watch high above his head.

Each man handed his pole to the servant assisting him and brought forth his creel to be sorted through. One by one, the fish were placed on a table scale and measured in length.

Finally, the attendant brought a paper to Sir Ronald, who stood in a half circle with the other men around us. He unfolded it; the wait was unbearable.

"Weighing in at thirteen-and-a-half pounds, the prize goes to . . . Wood." Sir Ronald wiped sweat from his brow from the unrelenting heat. "A night at the symphony. Name your companion."

Applause filled the air, and Peter nodded with a

half-smile. He rubbed the back of his neck, looking almost hesitant at the decision before him.

Who would he choose? How I wished things could be different between us. That he could choose me, and we could go as friends. I found myself studying the faces of the women around me, holding my breath. Distance was better. I had a plan, and I had to see it through.

"Miss Moore," Peter said, squinting up through the bright sunlight at Sir Ronald. "If she agrees, of course."

Me? My face grew warm despite my vigorous fanning, and Sir Ronald looked to me for my answer. I could not decline the invitation surrounded by the entire party, and Peter knew as much. He knew I meant to focus on Clara's future. I had all but refused him last night, and yet still he chose me. Should I be angry at his blatant disregard for my wishes? Or moved that he cared enough to overlook them? My mind argued the former, but my heart . . . my heart felt only relief.

"I should be delighted." I tried to sound nonchalant, and Peter looked curiously at me, as though to measure my sincerity.

"Wonderful," he said. "We shall leave directly after dinner. Georgiana will join us as chaperone."

At that, the party dispersed, some looking more dejected than others. No one could've been more displeased than Georgiana, who nearly stomped forward to confront Peter. Glancing over my shoulder, I could've sworn she was giving him quite a row. But he only smiled, kind and easy, as though he had not a care in the world.

Chapter Twenty-Two

After dinner, Mary readjusted my hair and freshened my dress with a misting of rose water. For the first time since we'd arrived at Lakeshire Park, I'd had little to eat for dinner and even less to drink. Mary forced me to eat a cold sandwich to keep from getting a headache. But all I could think about was Peter. If I was careful tonight, perhaps I could convince him that despite what I'd said, despite what I had to do, we could still maintain our friendship.

Peter and Georgiana waited for me in the foyer, and as I stepped forward to meet them, Peter took my hand.

"You look lovely," he said softly.

"Thank you." I allowed myself one glance at his fine fitted coat and wavy hair.

"You were absolutely right about purple. You wear it like a queen." Peter took my arm in his, and Georgiana cleared her throat as we passed her. I winced in embarrassment to have her so close to us, but Peter did not seem to mind.

"I was joking about that, Peter," I said in a low voice.

"I am not." He helped me into the carriage, papered in

shades of blues and golds. I cast him a pointed glance, and he merely smiled. The man was determined.

I sat on one side with Georgiana and him opposite me.

"How far is the drive?" I asked, shifting in my seat. Hopefully not far; I was already tired of Georgiana's pursed lips.

"Less than a half hour. Further north of town toward Winchester," Peter said, leaning back in his seat. "Relax, Georgiana. You love the symphony."

"I do," she muttered. "But I had different companions in mind."

"You do not have to speak so mysteriously in front of Miss Moore. It is no secret that you and Miss Clara are vying for the same man." Peter lowered his chin at her, and Georgiana cast him a horrified glance. What in the world was Peter thinking? Georgiana looked ready to leap from the carriage.

"It is true." I cleared my throat. What was *I* thinking? The words spilled from my lips on an exhale, with not a single thought to control them. "Allow me to apologize for what I said earlier. Clara was indeed talking about you."

"I knew it!" Georgiana pointed at Peter. "She hates me, and she means to ruin my life."

In a flash, I realized Peter's motive for the evening. He wanted to bridge the gap between his sister and me. Did he think that would make a difference? Would it?

"She does not hate you," I said, capturing her attention. "Nor do I. But circumstances require us to be enemies for the time being."

"You see?" Peter said as though to prove a point. "It is

exactly as I've told you. Miss Clara could likely be your friend if Sir Ronald was not in the way."

"But he is." She crossed her arms. "And you've given Clara an entire evening alone with him, while I am stuck here with you."

Peter's gaze flashed to me in a moment of worry, before he turned to her. "Only for the first part of the evening. Miss Clara will likely go to bed with her sister when we return."

Georgiana looked to me, and a familiar emotional pull resurfaced. A weighted force that begged for attention, cried for action, no matter how impractical and nonsensical. For truly, I had never wanted Georgiana to like me more than I did at that moment.

"Peter is right," I said. "I shall make sure of it tonight."

Georgiana's grin bolstered, and she turned to Peter. "But I shall still find a way to make you pay for this. The night is young yet."

Her words reminded me of Peter's owed favor from our quarrel in the mud, and I glanced between the two of them.

"Indeed, the fun has only just begun," I said. "Mr. Wood has to make good on his promise to me."

Peter raised a brow, but the corners of Georgiana's mouth twitched.

"What promise is that?" she asked.

"He owes me one very generalized ransom, a duty or whatever I wish of him, for which I have yet to make him answer. I thought perhaps you could assist me in choosing his fate this evening."

"Ooh, the intrigue. To have such advantage over him.

That does sound like fun. What shall we have him do?" Georgiana reached out to Peter and straightened his cravat.

Peter's lips were pursed as he flicked a look of betrayal at me.

"Perhaps he could cater to our every need, like a butler?" Georgiana laughed.

Her sudden change in mood encouraged me. "Or we could make him stand with applause after every piece?"

"Humiliating." She beamed. "And brilliant."

"Need I remind you that this 'favor' you are sharing with my sister was meant as a gift, Miss Moore." Peter lowered his chin at me.

"Never fear. I am sure you will owe me another soon enough."

Georgiana and I schemed for the duration of the ride while Peter wavered between laughter and sulking. The drive took about twenty minutes, but it felt like five in conversation.

The carriage stopped outside a large, tan brick building with two pillars on either side of the entryway, and Peter hopped out immediately. He helped me down, but held fast to my hand, assisting Georgiana with his left hand.

When she was out of earshot, he pulled me close and wrapped my arm through his.

"I am trying to be angry with you," he said, his voice light. "But my sister is actually smiling, which is worth more than my pride."

"I promise to keep you from ruin, Peter." Nudging him in the side, his full grin surfaced, and it was as though our conversation the night before had never occurred.

"Hardly. Though I had hoped you'd use the favor for something more . . . mutually beneficial."

I nearly tripped over my shoes. "Peter Wood."

A servant opened the door to the theatre for us. Georgiana had already found friends, conversing near a wide, red carpeted staircase that led to seating higher up. Georgiana stepped beside us as we started up the stairs, her eyes alive with excitement. I'd never attended a symphony orchestra, but Georgiana's enthusiasm was contagious.

Peter led us upward to the balcony seats along the left side. Hordes of people were already taking their seats around us. The area was decorated with red cushioned chairs overlooking the broad black stage. Walking toward the edge of the balcony, I was struck by the size of the audience below us, and even above us higher along a back balcony. The ceiling was crowned in ornate carvings of flowers and vines, and the walls were papered in hues of red and brown.

I took an empty seat beside Peter, settling in just as the curtains drew back and the symphony orchestra appeared. Each member was dressed in black, their sleek instruments gleaming in the stage lights. We were close enough that I could see the musicians tightening their strings and shuffling pages at the last-minute as the conductor stood to greet the audience.

"Amelia," Georgiana whispered from Peter's other side, "perhaps we should force Peter to play his viola when we return. He is quite accomplished."

"I would rather fall over this balcony." Peter crossed his arms regally, and Georgiana scrunched her nose in a suppressed fit of laughter.

An older woman turned around and shushed him, furthering Georgiana's fit, until at last the conductor spoke. A hush came over the room.

"Look at the carvings," Georgiana said quietly to Peter. "I've never seen them from this view."

Peter's hand brushed my skirts as he balanced himself, looking up at the ornately carved ceiling. "Fascinating. Grecian, I believe."

I loved his appreciation for architecture and culture. As I watched him studying the room, his chin lowered slowly, and he found me, a seriousness expression on his face.

"What do you think of it all?" he asked.

"I love it. All of it. The lighting, the wallpaper, the carpets . . . even the musty smell."

Peter breathed a laugh. He set his hand on his leg, near to mine in my lap. "All part of the experience, is it not?"

I looked away, forcing myself to remember my place and my goals. We could be friends, but that was all. Any affection Peter thought he held for me was fleeting. I willed the music to begin.

"Georgiana knows about the gloves," Peter said softly beside me. "I told her this morning."

My gaze sharpened. "Why? What did she say?"

"I am tired of secrets. I hate them, actually. Georgiana thought the story funny but has not said a word about it since. I should have told her that first day at Demsworth's. I should have told everyone."

"No," I said, shaking my head. "It is better this way."

"Why?" Peter looked at me fiercely. "What is the benefit of keeping a secret from someone you care about?"

I had a feeling his question was more pointed than innocent. "For fear of losing that person's good opinion. Or being seen differently in their eyes."

"That is exactly the thing I appreciate most about love, Miss Moore. Its opinion is not easily swayed by status or money or flaws. Unless it is betrayed, it is most forgiving. And it holds steadfast in any weather."

I closed my eyes, letting out a breath. I felt like a feather tossed in the wind—dizzy and floating and high. Did Peter mean his words? That money, or a lack thereof, could not sway love? My secret was not as small as a pair of gloves. My secret would be shocking to discover. No matter how Peter tried to convince me, I knew the truth. At best, love was a double-edged sword.

Music filled the air like a tidal wave rushing upon us. A perfect harmony of notes, loud but soothing, reverberated off the walls. The musicians played one song after another, some fast and merry, others somber and slow.

Peter tilted his head, closing his eyes in appreciation.

Regardless of what the future held, I was glad to share this moment with him. This memory. Where music changed us.

I leaned closer to his ear. "Can you feel it?"

Immediately his eyes snapped to mine. "What do you mean?"

"The music. It's as though the notes are tickling my skin."

Peter shifted toward me, his leg brushing mine. "I can feel it," he whispered in my ear, sending a shiver through me. "And I never want it to end."

A standing ovation for the superb performances of the night lifted us from our seats when the final song ended.

Peter spoke to me over the applause. "There is someone here I want you to meet. An old friend of mine from Eton."

I opened my mouth to protest, but the excitement on his face stopped me. Georgiana stifled a yawn, looking as tired as I felt.

But as we made our way through the crowd, it was my name that was called. And from a voice I'd tried to forget.

"Amelia? Amelia Moore!"

"Who is that?" Georgiana stopped with a hand on her hip.

"It *is* you," Evelyn said haughtily, breaking through the crowd. Her resemblance to Lord Gray was astounding, and I felt like I was in London again, pushed aside like a wilting flower. "Why are you not at home with Robert?" Her squeaky voice was full of disdain, and I blushed to be spoken to as though my name was dirt in her mouth.

I tore my arm from Peter's before her narrowed eyes could take note of the connection. "Clara and I were invited as guests to Lakeshire Park for a fortnight. We will be returning to Brighton shortly." Though she had to know the lie. Why else would she be here, so far away from her home in Bath, yet so close to Brighton?

I scanned the room for my cousin. If Trenton was here, it meant he'd wasted no time making his way to claim Gray House.

"To think of all my brother has done for you. Even after your mother died. And here you are." Evelyn frowned in distaste, shaking her head. "No matter. Trenton has been summoned. Your time amongst the *ton* is over."

Peter stepped forward, his chest rising. "You will mind your tongue, ma'am."

"And who are you?" A slow, hateful smile curved Evelyn's lips.

"Clearly, we need not be introduced." Peter laced my arm through his, and I found Georgiana, who looked at me with both interest and pity.

"Watch yourself," Evelyn crooned as Peter steered us away. "Her family is as low as they come."

Peter clenched a fist, and I had to half run to keep up with his pace. Tears pooled in the corners of my eyes. Guilt, anger, sorrow, pity, pain, embarrassment. All at once and all-encompassing. If Peter had not seen me clearly enough before, certainly now he could piece the puzzle together.

I forced myself to keep my composure as we waited for the carriage, and when it arrived, I nearly threw myself inside, huddling in the corner of the bench with my face in my hands. I told myself not to cry.

I heard Georgiana adjusting her skirts across from me.

Peter heaved a heavy sigh as the door closed behind him, and I longed to run away. To hide beneath the deepest rock. What must he think of me?

I sunk lower, sniffing back the emotion that wanted to burst from me. Then the carriage jolted forward, and I could not contain it any longer.

"Who was that woman?" Georgiana's voice was soft, betraying interest.

"Georgiana," Peter's voice was clipped in warning.

She reached out a hand to me and rubbed my arm. "She was very rude, whoever she was. You did not deserve that, Amelia."

My heart burst, and I sobbed freely. Peter started to move toward me, but Georgiana stopped him. And she was right. Comforting me was not his place, nor proper by any means, no matter how badly I wanted to fall into his arms.

Instead, Georgiana took me into her own arms and patted my hair with her gloved hand. "We shall forget about that horrible woman and her porky neck, and get you and your sister straight to bed."

Georgiana's voice was thick with humor on the last word, and I let out a small laugh through my tears, choking back another sob. This was why the heart could not be trusted. It only ever caused pain. Tuning my ears to the comforting sound of the horses' hooves, I closed my eyes and breathed deeply as Georgiana stroked my arm.

Misery had found me yet again. To run from it was as foolish as running from age. And yet, I always tried.

When the carriage pulled up to the drive, my cheeks were dried and stiff. I could not bear to see Peter's pained expression as he helped me down. I nearly ran up the stairs to my room.

Mary helped me out of my dress and into my nightclothes. As I sat in front of the mirror unpinning my hair, the door flew open, and Clara ran in frantically. At the sight of her, I fell apart all over again.

"Amelia! Mr. Wood insisted that I see to you immediately." Clara knelt beside me, staring desperately into my eyes. "He said someone found you at the concert hall?"

"Tomorrow," I begged, wiping my tears and composing myself. I could not bear to tell her the truth tonight. Tomorrow I would tell her everything. "Would you sing to me until I sleep?"

"Of course I will. Mary, will you help me with my dress? The night is nearly over anyway." Clara smiled at me before helping me under the covers of my bed. She had so much strength, so much courage. Would she be angry with me for keeping Lord Gray's secrets for so long? I'd only meant to protect her heart, to give her a chance at happiness without carrying the burden of our fate.

Listening to the melody of Clara's soprano, my mind filled with thoughts of home and of happiness, and, just before I drifted off into sleep, a pair of curious green eyes.

Chapter Twenty-Three

There exists a peaceful moment when one first opens one's eyes, when all the world is just as it should be. And then you blink, and just like that the moment vanishes like smoke in the wind.

"Good morning, miss." Mary clasped her hands in front of her and offered a curtsey. "Mr. Wood asked that I bring this tray up to you. Most of the party has already dispersed for the day, and Lady Demsworth expects Mr. Pendleton to arrive sometime this afternoon."

Rubbing my eyes, I grimaced. "Thank you, Mary."

She propped the curtains open, revealing a clearer view of the small tray of tea surrounded by biscuits and fresh blackberries. Instantly, I thought of Peter, and my heart sank, remembering how terribly our evening had ended last night. I pressed a hand to my forehead. I'd never been so embarrassed.

A folded note with my name scrawled in a gentleman's hand propped up against the teacup caught my attention. The paper was smooth as I unfolded it.

Amelia—

I hope sleep found you in overabundance last night. I hope it served to erase cruel memories of our evening prior, and I hope you have awakened refreshed and just as lovely as I always find you.

I wanted to tell you how much I enjoyed taking you to the symphony last night. Your company is, simply put, my favorite luxury. In case any discomfort still exists in your memory, I offer you tea the way I like it, biscuits, and the sweetest blackberries Cook could find to start your day.

I have taken Clara and Georgiana to town to pick out flowers for the ball. Away from Demsworth to ease your worries. I thought an afternoon away might do us all some good.

If I come back in one piece, I hope to see you later this afternoon.

Yours, etc.

Peter

"You are smiling, so I hope it is good news," Mary said as she laid out a white dress on the edge of my bed.

"Is Clara still out?" I exchanged Peter's note for the cup of tea, which was delightfully delicious. Sweet with a touch of bitter.

"With Mr. Wood and Georgiana, yes. They left an hour ago." Mary fussed with the sleeves of my dress, and I took her hint to hurry with my morning preparations.

After dressing and savoring my blackberries and Peter's

tea, all while Mary managed my hair, I tugged on slippers and swiped my bonnet from its perch.

I'd reached the top of the grand staircase when voices reached me. When I rounded down to the second floor, I recognized Lady Demsworth's voice, but it wasn't until I was in full view of the foyer that I saw who she was speaking to.

"Miss Moore, what perfect timing! Mr. Pendleton has arrived for the day and was expressing his excitement to meet you." Lady Demsworth's smile could've reached her ears.

I'd stopped halfway down the staircase, looking between Lady Demsworth and a thin, smart-looking gentleman with a topper hanging loosely in a hand at his side. His smile was full of effort, and though his eyes were kind, they were weary and exhausted. I measured my heart, which was still and unaffected, and took the remaining steps to greet him.

"Mr. Pendleton, I am pleased you could make the journey so soon." I curtseyed. "It is wonderful to meet you after hearing such compliments on your character from your aunt."

Mr. Pendleton bowed. "Likewise, Miss Moore." His voice was deep, firm. Not nearly as carefree or lively as Peter's.

Lady Demsworth clasped her hands together. "Your things have been sent to your room, David. Might I suggest a walk to stretch your legs after your ride? I can have tea set out for when you return."

I dared not tell her I'd just had a late cup.

"Thank you, Aunt. That will do." Mr. Pendleton said, a more genuine smile touching his lips.

Lady Demsworth turned to leave, and I felt the full awkwardness of the situation before me. A man and woman meeting for the first time to determine if they could force a marriage and make it amiable enough for both parties. A business transaction, I told myself. This was not like my afternoons with Peter. This was different. This was practical.

"Shall we?" Mr. Pendleton held out his arm to me, and I took it gently.

He was nearly a foot taller than I, and I noted the squareness of his jaw, the point to his nose, and the hazel in his eyes. He was, as Lady Demsworth had said, quite handsome. But something was missing. A brightness, it seemed. I wondered what he saw in me.

"How was your journey?" I asked as he led me along a gravel path at the southern end of the house.

"Not terribly long," he answered. "My country house is about a day's drive from here."

"You are right then, that is not terribly long." I bit my lip. Unlike Peter, conversation was not my strong suit.

"And your stay so far? How is it measuring up?"

"Quite well. My sister is enjoying herself very much, and the Demsworths have been excellent hosts in keeping us all busy and entertained." I smiled up at him, but he only looked forward, moving at a steady pace.

"Demsworth has always been a playful fellow. Easily agreeable."

"And you? Are you playful, Mr. Pendleton, or more of a quiet sort?" I asked. He should know right away that I wanted to waste no time in getting to know him. If we were going to make this work, he needed to know me as much as I him.

He glanced at me with a look of surprise, before

half-smiling as he'd done earlier. "Depends on the day, I suppose. You, though, I would guess are more playful."

"Depends on the day," I agreed.

"My aunt tells me that your family is . . . broken." Mr. Pendleton surveyed the scene before us.

"Quite. As is yours, I'm told."

"Yes." His voice was full of regret. "In a different way."

"I am sorry for your loss," I said, pausing briefly. "I understand you have two daughters?"

His eyes lit up then, if only for a moment. "Margaret and Annalise. This is the first time I've left them since . . ."

"Of course," I said quickly, to keep him from having to discuss a painful topic. "How hard that must be for all three of you."

Mr. Pendleton nodded. "Do you only have the one sister, then?"

"Clara, yes. She and I come as a set. At least until she is married." I earned a full smile from Mr. Pendleton then, but not a response. We walked together in silence for a long moment, and I feared I'd said too much. Surely he would speak, if nothing else but to relieve me from my obvious discomfort.

I counted my steps as we walked. I'd reached twenty-three before he spoke again.

Mr. Pendleton cleared his throat, slowing his pace. "You are prettier than I imagined. And easier to talk to. I'm having a hard time believing a woman like yourself is in need of the arrangement I am offering."

I stopped, staring up at him. "That is kind to say, but also accusatory, sir."

"I only mean I would not put it past my aunt to try her hand at matchmaking." He raised a brow at me.

I released his arm, crossing my own. "I shall take that as a compliment, but I assure you my circumstances are dire. In all honesty, my stepfather will die any day. He has abandoned us both in home and in financial security, and unless Clara or I find a match by the end of the fortnight, we will both be homeless and destitute."

Mr. Pendleton reared back his head. "Surely not."

"Are you trying to convince me to look elsewhere? I think both of us could do far worse than each other."

Mr. Pendleton looked thoughtful. "You are a force to be reckoned with, Miss Moore."

"You may call me Amelia. We haven't much time to get to know one another."

Mr. Pendleton studied my face, and I lifted my chin to give him a full view of me. Speaking my secrets aloud to a man felt entirely liberating. Here I stood, completely vulnerable before him, and yet I did not care in the least what he thought of me.

"David," he replied. "I am happy to meet you, Amelia."

David and I finished our tea, enjoying the light breeze that blew across the veranda. We talked easily, and I felt comfortable enough in his presence. He was quiet, soft-spoken, but held his opinions firmly. I liked that he cared enough to speak his mind, but only when he deemed it necessary. He liked to talk about current affairs, and I listened with interest, though I had little to say in return. He did not tease me, though, and he rarely laughed or joked.

Dust grew above the trees, signaling the arrival of horses. A carriage perhaps. Peter. I straightened in my chair, suddenly nervous and feeling painfully exposed. What would Peter think, seeing me with David? Did Peter know to expect him? Of course not. Peter had no idea of this secret.

"Perhaps we should go for a ride?" I turned to David. I needed an escape, and fast.

"It looks as though your party has returned." David motioned for a servant to take away our trays. "I have not seen my cousin in some time. We are not especially close, I'm afraid."

I licked my lips. Why had I not been more forthcoming with Clara? I'd not thought any of this through. Any ounce of control I thought I had was seeping like honey through my fingers. I followed David to the drive, where Mr. Gregory opened the door to the carriage.

Peter stepped out with a frown, helping Clara out first, then Georgiana. Another carriage followed, carrying the rest of the company. Had they left together after all?

"David!" Sir Ronald called. They clasped hands as the party enveloped them.

I felt Peter's eyes before I found them. "How was your morning?" he asked, drawing me away from the company.

Already, I missed the easy tones in Peter's voice, the gentle smile that never seemed to leave his lips when we were together, and the light in his eyes. I remembered his letter from this morning and smoothed the curls framing my face.

"I am well rested, to be sure," I said, captivated by the

sudden seriousness in his gaze. "Thank you for the tea, and the blackberries."

"And the note?" Peter stepped forward. He held a pink flower in his hand.

My gaze dropped to his cravat. The note. Was I wrong to allow my heart to leap at the thought? Even now, with David only a few paces away? Try as I might to push Peter away, he only ever seemed to move closer.

I cleared my throat. "The note was . . ."

I could not look at him. We were too exposed, too vulnerable standing there in our secret conversation, surrounded by people. I felt as backed into a wall as I'd ever been. "The note was very thoughtful, Mr. Wood, thank you."

"Amelia!" Clara walked toward us, away from David. She was not smiling. "What is the meaning of this?"

I couldn't remember the last time I'd seen Clara so angry. "Please, lower your voice, Clara, my dear."

She stopped in front of me, and Peter took a few steps back, frowning. "This gentleman told Sir Ronald he is here for you."

My gaze flicked to Peter. If he'd heard anything, he made no indication of it. "I will explain, but later."

"Whatever does he mean? Do you know this man?"

"I only just know of him. Please. I promise to tell you everything tonight," I whispered fiercely, begging.

"Miss Moore," David said, approaching our small group.

I felt dizzy, my eyes darting from Peter to Clara to David. What should I do? What should I say? I knew what I wanted, but what I wanted was not practical. What I wanted would only cause more pain and rejection.

Clara turned, including David in our company.

"Mr. Pendleton," I said, willing my voice to steady. "Allow me to introduce my sister, Clara. Clara, this Mr. Pendleton."

"I am pleased to meet you, Miss Clara," David said with a bow.

Clara curtseyed, drawing David into polite conversation about his visit, and I glanced at Peter. He beckoned me with a nod of his head, but I could not move. I'd barely known Peter a fortnight. If what Georgiana said was true, he would question everything when he learned of my poverty. How could I trust my feelings for him? Or his feelings for me? How could I risk my future, Clara's future, on something so fickle as love? Especially when Clara detested Georgiana and, by extension, Peter.

If I stayed by David, I could for certain share amiable companionship, knowing security and comfort for the rest of my days, and Clara's as well. He knew the truth of my situation, and he accepted me. He did not seek love, so he would never expect more from me, and I would not risk losing his affection, for I would never have it.

"Shall we go for that ride?" David's voice pulled my attention back to him.

Peter stared at me with a furrowed brow.

"Of course." I took his arm. This was the path of least pain, the path of most surety. Clara glanced between us, shaking her head. But she did not know how necessary this match was. I walked beside David into the house to put on my riding habit.

Grace seemed exceptionally slothful today, likely due to the rising heat of the late afternoon. I was accustomed to Summer's slow pace, so I did not mind. Though I missed Summer, Winter needed her more than I at present. David drew even with us, though his lips pursed. I wondered if he wished we were riding faster.

"Do you have many horses?" I asked.

David shifted in his seat. "We typically sell our common foals. I breed mostly racehorses in my stables."

Ah, that accounted for his pursed lips. I'd been right. He was likely not accustomed to riding this slow.

Grace, responding to the depth of his masculine voice, veered right and chomped at David's leg. He hurried his horse just in time to avoid her.

"Forgive me," I said, pulling hard on Grace's reins. "She has a mind of her own."

"Indeed," he said with a frown. "I do not think she likes me."

"Grace does better at a run, but for some reason she is more ornery than usual today."

"Not to worry. I can maintain my distance for now. I am set to leave after dinner, but there is more we must discuss."

I glanced to Mr. Beckett, riding a few paces behind us. "Of course."

"Forgive my awkwardness," David said. "I have not entertained the idea of a wife for long, and with how sudden my aunt recommended you, I'm afraid I had little time to think on what to say.

"I am not sure what my aunt told you of my situation, but I want to be clear, before we speak any further." David's deep voice was solemn. "I lost the love of my life, the mother of my children. I will never find another woman I cherish more. My heart is forever full of her." He looked out into the distance with purpose. "But I do need a companion. Someone to oversee the affairs within the house, and to care for my girls and their upbringing. We have lived simply since my wife died, but my girls need a lady of the house to guide them in example. And I need help."

Grace whinnied beneath me, shaking her head and readjusting the bit in her mouth.

David continued, "You and I need only be friends. I am not looking for"—he hesitated—"romance. But I can promise security. For you and your sister."

I swallowed when he finished, nodding my head. "I understand. And I think that is all very reasonable."

David looked to me, a curiousness in his hazel eyes that reminded me of Peter.

How I would miss Peter's playfulness.

"And you? Surely you think of more than just my money."

I forced a laugh. "No, actually I am quite set on your money." I remembered how I'd refused Peter's offerings at every turn, how I'd wanted nothing from him, yet here I was asking for so much from a stranger. "But more so for my sister than for myself. You see, Clara is here for Sir Ronald. If he does not return her affection, we must keep from his family until she is recovered. And I want her to have another Season, if necessary, and every opportunity for a happy match.

"If they *do* wed, they may need support, and I want to be in a position to offer it. I do not need love as she does. But I cannot bear her unhappiness."

David nodded, completely unaffected by my forwardness. "That is fair. And an easy price to pay for my family's needs."

My family. He said the phrase as though they would always be separate from me. Separate from us. Clara and I against the world, as usual.

"I would need it written into our contract," I said with as much pride as I could muster. "An unbreakable arrangement, unable to be abandoned."

"My word is as good a deed."

"I'm afraid I will not relent on the matter." I pulled back on Grace's leads, halting her.

"Why?" The creases of David's eyes wrinkled, scrutinizing my stance.

"Because I am tired of living without certainty. I will not endure it again."

He hesitated, then agreed with a firm nod of his head. "I am sure it can be done."

We returned to the house without another word, both lost within our thoughts. Was this how my mother felt before marrying my father? Had she been this scared? If only Lord Gray had saved her then. Perhaps, as he'd said, we'd all have been better for it.

Chapter Twenty-Four

"Not now," Clara said when I entered our bedchamber. "I do not want your secrets to ruin my dinner. But afterward, when *he* is gone, you owe me an explanation."

I nodded. She looked exactly like my mother had when she was cross. Clara did not speak a word to me as Mary finished fastening her dress, and I could not blame her. We did not keep secrets from one another, and I would be just as angry, just as hurt, if our roles were reversed.

Clara's shiny blue dress shuffled as she descended the stairs. I wore yellow, with my hair pinned high atop my head. We were the last to arrive in the drawing room, and Clara left my side without a backward glance.

David met me at the door, but my eyes found Peter standing with his hands on his hips, his eyes shooting daggers, just behind him.

"Good evening, Miss Moore." David bowed, then took my arm, barely giving my appearance note.

"Mr. Pendleton."

He led me into the dining room, seating me beside Sir

Ronald, across from Georgiana. Peter sat next to his sister, sawing the food on his plate with precise force.

Instead of the usual casual evening, an air of formality overtook the drawing room after dinner. The gentlemen took longer with their port and did not settle in as quickly with cards or other games. It felt like an evening during the Season, where the ladies held their tongues and batted their lashes while the gentleman discussed important topics.

When the hour struck nine, David stood. "Thank you for this afternoon, Demsworth, Aunt Violet. I should be on my way. I have business to attend to in the morning."

"Of course," Lady Demsworth said, casting me a worried glance. "We've quite enjoyed your visit."

David turned to me. "Miss Moore, might I have a private audience with you on my way out?"

I felt the weight of every eye staring at me as I nodded slowly, taking David's arm. Peter stood, but Georgiana grabbed his arm, pulling him back down beside her.

"Good night to you all," David said, his voice distantly ringing in my ears.

In the entryway, Mr. Gregory handed him his coat and top hat, opening the door for us. Our feet crunched upon gravel as we walked toward David's coach, arm in arm in the cool evening air.

"I do not want your answer right away," David said when we reached the door, his face darkened by night. "But I would be most pleased to ask for your hand. I am happy to fulfill all your requests, and I think in time we shall become good friends."

Not knowing how to respond, I cleared my throat awkwardly, swallowing the bitter taste in my mouth.

David continued, "Take a few days, be sure this is what you want, and what you need, then send me word. You and your sister are welcome to join me at any time. My younger brother and his wife have offered their home nearby should you need a place to stay." David took my hand, hesitating for a moment before kissing my knuckles. His gentle touch felt odd after hearing him so fervently declare that ours would be a friendly companionship, nothing more. Could such a thing be? Would it always feel so awkward, so forced between us?

"Thank you, David," I said evenly. My hand had never been kissed before, even gloved as it was now, but still I felt nothing. Nothing at all.

I snuck past the drawing room, back up the stairs to my bedchamber. It took me half an hour to wiggle free from my dress alone, but I did not want to speak to a soul, not even Mary. I feared I would either cry or scream for the raging of emotions I felt within me. Some from frustration at having such a terrible fate in life, and others at being unable to choose what I wanted. Did I even have a choice to begin with? No one else had asked for my hand.

I'd just climbed onto the wide window seat when Clara opened the door.

"There you are," she said, breathless. "Why did you not come back? Everyone was waiting for you. Have you accepted him, then?"

Was it the shadows from outside that darkened Clara's amber eyes? Or just my imagination?

"He offered, but I have yet to answer," I said, turning to gaze at the moon high in the night sky.

"You're sacrificing for me, and I will not have it."

"I do not have a choice, Clara. I am doing this for us."

"For us?" She stood above me. "No, thank you. I will not be responsible for your poor decision. Our happiness does not rely on money alone. I refuse to believe that."

"And what if Sir Ronald chooses Georgiana? What then, Clara?"

She said nothing, but looked away. How could I have foreseen everything falling apart like this? I had to tell her everything. To make her understand why this match with David was necessary, whether I wanted it or not. Clara did not deserve for her world to be torn apart. But we were out of time.

I pressed my palms to my eyes, forcing back the emotion that rose in my throat. My voice came out soft, pained. "Lord Gray is dying. He told me so himself before we left. And the letter I just received from Mr. Jones confirms that Lord Gray will leave us any day. Evelyn was at the concert hall with Trenton, which means our cousin has been summoned. I thought to return, to beg for mercy, for any sort of livelihood, but Mr. Jones informed me that Lord Gray has forbidden it. He wishes to never see us again."

"What?" Clara's jaw opened in shock.

I reached out to her. "This arrangement with Mr. Pendleton is the only way I know we will be safe."

"We will work. Together." Clara was erratic, disbelieving as she tried to make sense of everything I'd kept secret.

I shook my head. "You do not understand, and I am glad you do not. Clara, one of us must be able to support the other or we will be separated. And I cannot lose you. I won't."

"Sir Ronald will offer for me," Clara said willfully, holding herself in her arms.

"Even if he does, do you honestly think he can support the both of us?" The question stung, but it needed to be asked.

"It would take some sacrifice, but yes."

"I do not wish to be sacrificed for either. David will provide a home for me, and it is a path I choose for myself as much as for you. If things do not work out here, he lives more than a day's travel from them. He is not close friends with Sir Ronald. You need never see them if you wish."

Clara shook her head, disappointed. "Is there no one else you admire? No one you could make an arrangement with, someone who is not a complete stranger?"

I said his name before thinking, "Mr. Wood."

Clara sighed. "This is not a time to joke, Amelia. I am in earnest. A connection with the Woods would be worse than servitude." Her words were tiny needles pricking at my heart.

"Mr. Pendleton asked me to consider carefully his offer and send word when I have come to a decision. I mean to do that tomorrow. And you shall be the first to know."

Clara let out a small huff, clearly dissatisfied. "Fine."

"Can you ever forgive me?" I asked. "I only wanted to give you a fortnight here without worry. I'd hoped we'd have more time to plan than this."

"I forgive you," she whispered, emotion thickening her voice. "And I am sorry, Amelia. You should not have carried this burden alone. And you should not have to marry a stranger."

Clara pulled me into an embrace, and I felt her shoulders shake with emotion.

This will all be a memory one day, I thought. *We will yet grow stronger for it.*

"There must be happiness ahead," I replied, more to myself than to Clara. I thought of Peter and the conversation we'd had in the creek about our families and our hopes. What I wouldn't give to go back to that day.

To stay in that moment.

To be free.

Chapter Twenty-Five

I skipped breakfast and stayed in my room all afternoon, having no desire to face Peter. I knew any conversation with him would result in misery. If he was unaffected by the news of my impending engagement, my heart would ache to have lost his favor. If he was upset by it, I'd endure hope that we would continue on as before.

Amid the struggle, I could not silence the voice in my head that told me I'd made a grand mistake, that I needed to give Peter a chance to react to my circumstances, knowing them fully. Perhaps nothing would change. But what if, together, we could find a solution to all our problems?

I sighed, pulling out a book of poems from my table drawer. Admitting my circumstances was a risk not only for me, but for Clara as well.

Try as I might to hide away, a knock on my door interrupted my late afternoon reading.

"You'll have to forgive my intrusion," Georgiana said, stepping over my threshold uninvited. "But you've stirred up quite the gossip downstairs. Only no one will come up to claim your company. No one who is able, that is. I've had to stifle Peter more than once to keep him from ruining himself." Georgiana sniffed as she took a chair by my unlit hearth. "You look awful."

Touching my hair, loosely pinned and frizzled from a day of neglect, I guffawed at Georgiana's blatant honesty. "Thank you, Georgiana. For your surprising visit, and your humble compliment."

She returned my smile, but without warmth. "Let's get right to it, shall we? Have you accepted Mr. Pendleton?"

So Clara hadn't told all. "That is my business, and mine alone."

"Not when it affects my brother, it is not."

"How could my engagement to Mr. Pendleton affect your brother?"

"Don't be daft, Amelia. He follows you around like you are royalty, and though it has taken me some time to notice, it is clear he admires you greatly."

I dropped my gaze to the floor. "Admires me, perhaps. But he does not know my circumstances. He would not love me, if he knew."

"I am in no mood to be mysterious," Georgiana snapped. "You are a fool if you reject Mr. Pendleton."

"You speak with such certainty. Forgive me if I do not trust the tongue of a serpent." My words were brash, but I'd had quite enough of Georgiana's interference today.

A slow smile curved her lips. "You should. I am only trying to help you see what is best for you. And for your sister."

My hands were in fists, my teeth clenched. "Rest assured, I *am* doing what is best."

"Have you *accepted* Mr. Pendleton? That is all I want to know."

I walked to the door, opening it fully for her to leave. "I have not. *Yet.* I am still considering his offer. Go and tell your gossiping throngs the news with my best regards."

Georgiana stood and sauntered to the door. Had she slowed her pace any more, the door would have surely hit her on her way out. As it was, I stomped directly to my bed, throwing my face into my pillow to stifle the scream that arose in my throat.

I felt like a coward as I entered the drawing room before dinner.

Before I had the chance to find Peter, Lady Demsworth pulled me into an embrace.

"My darling, I heard the news. How exciting! David seemed absolutely delighted by you. If only he could have stayed for the ball tomorrow. I just know you two shall be the happiest of companions."

"I have not yet accepted him," I said loudly, in case anyone overheard our conversation.

"Yes, but you are just being modest, and that is quite amiable, dear."

Beatrice caught my eye from across the room and nodded toward Peter, who sat at his usual chair at the hearth with his nose in a book. She smiled as though to encourage me.

I had nothing to lose. If Peter no longer wished to be my friend, I would still be in the same predicament. But was he changed now that David stood between us? It was utter foolishness to pine after Peter Wood's friendship with an engagement on my horizon, but I missed my friend. And I was not ready to let him go just yet.

When I reached him, I sat on a stool across from him. "What are you reading?"

"A book," he replied, flipping a page listlessly.

"How intriguing." I leaned forward, willing him to see me. "You seem motivated to continue reading."

The crease in his cheek deepened. "I need a distraction. To get lost in a book."

My heart sank. His voice was not angry, nor was it unaffected. In fact, it sounded rather melancholy. I could not bear it. I leaned in closer, lowering my voice. "Shall I write you a story? So we can be sure you are getting lost in all the right places?"

He looked up at me. His brilliant green eyes searching mine. Sighing, he tilted his head at me. "Once upon a time there was a man—"

"A curiously wealthy man—" I smiled, not missing a beat.

"Who traveled the world in search of home."

My heart ached, flipping over in my chest, and speech suddenly failed me.

Peter continued, "He was always looking for something, someone, who would fill the empty spaces within him. Only, every time he thought he held her close enough, she slipped through his fingers, like water or air, unable to be held. And he was left alone, sitting in a chair reading a book about trees and agriculture."

"How boring," I breathed. I'd only sought to jest, but

Peter's story was too real. To know he felt this deeply was agonizing. My heart pounded in my throat. It felt as if Peter and I were alone, our heads leaning together, and the crackling of the fire behind me.

"Let us go in," Lady Demsworth declared from the front of the room, interrupting the mood between us.

Peter stood, but did not offer his arm to me. Instead, he looked around the room.

Could we not still be friends? At least for what time remained?

"Won't you take me in?" I hoped he did not hear the pleading in my voice.

"Amelia, you are nearly engaged." His seriousness was back, an honorable side to him he'd sworn he did not possess.

One day. That was all we had left. I could not let my last memories with Peter be of this forlorn man. Could we not part as friends? I had to try.

"Women get proposed to all the time." I shrugged, attempting an easy smile.

"This is different," Peter said on an exhale, not meeting my gaze.

Looking about the room, I saw we were the last to pair off. There was no longer a choice in the matter. Peter stretched his shoulders and looked to his boots. Hesitating, waiting. Finally, when the others had reached the door, he gently threaded my arm through his.

I could not keep a grin from my face. "And now you must engage me in conversation," I teased, lifting my chin.

"Any conversation I please?" Peter peeked sideways at me.

"Anything," I replied. *Anything at all.*

"Do you know Mr. Pendleton well?" Peter asked, walking slowly to the front of the room.

Anything but that.

"I only met him yesterday."

A light grew in Peter's eyes. "So you do not love him?"

I huffed. "I do not fall in love, Peter. I've told you this."

"You have," he agreed. "But I do not believe you."

"Believe me now. If I accept Mr. Pendleton, it will be entirely for his money, and he knows as much." I blushed as the truth burst from me like jam in an overfilled pie.

He hesitated as we stepped out into the foyer. "It is true, then. Your stepfather is dying?"

I froze. He knew. But who had told him? Who had discovered our secret? "Any day now. Any moment, really."

Peter tugged me backward, motioning to the butler to wait a moment for us before closing the door. He dropped my arm and faced me. "He leaves you nothing? No money or living? Is that why you would agree to marry Mr. Pendleton?"

Though I owed him no explanation, my heart begged me to explain. "Lord Gray leaves us nothing. A few days ago, I received a letter from our butler and another from Lord Gray. My stepfather's illness is severe, and he has given our things to his barrister for delivery . . . wherever we go next. We are never to return to Brighton." My voice broke on the words, but I held back my tears. "Do not pity me, Peter. This is exactly what I've always expected. But I am horribly embarrassed to have it all unfold now. To be abandoned here."

Peter raked a hand through his hair, his eyes severe and heavy. "I will go to Gray House immediately and speak to your stepfather. This is not right, Amelia."

"No," I pleaded, clutching at his arm. "Please, do nothing of the sort. It is done. I am fortunate to have found security elsewhere. Many women are not so lucky."

"If you feel so *lucky*, then why do you hesitate to accept him?" Peter tugged at my hands, pulling me closer to him, and the fire of his touch consumed me.

The butler cleared his throat, and I blushed.

"We should go in," I said, breaking away from Peter's hold.

As I composed myself at the table, I couldn't keep my eyes from wandering over to Peter. He hadn't looked at me differently when I'd confirmed my poverty. He knew I had no dowry, and still his eyes had grown warm when they found mine.

But Georgiana had said Peter was looking to marry a wealthy woman. Why would she say such an untrue thing? Did she really hate Clara and me so much she would lie to pull our families apart? Did she feel no guilt in attempting to twist Clara's confidence against making a match with Sir Ronald?

Regardless, I thought of only one thing throughout dinner, and again as we played charades in the drawing room: Nothing about me was too much for Peter. The more I admitted, the closer he moved. That, at least, was the truth.

But was he truly so unaffected by my poverty? Was love enough? I had one more day to find out, and I could not waste a single moment.

Chapter Twenty-Six

Dressed in white with an emerald spencer buttoned tightly around my bodice, I set out early the next day to find Peter. Most of the company had already eaten breakfast and sat on the lawn watching Sir Ronald and Mr. Bratten play battledore. They played with such force, I worried the shuttlecocks might run straight through them.

"He is in the stables," Beatrice called, pointing east. I did not need to question her further, nor acknowledge that my efforts were that embarrassingly obvious.

Sure enough, I found Peter standing at Summer's side, brushing her mane with a thick brush. As I pushed the door to the stall open, it squeaked.

"Where were you at breakfast?" he asked, not looking up.

I racked my brain for an excuse. "Making sure my hair was just so."

"Liar." He tsked. "Tomorrow you must wake up with the sun for once."

"Tomorrow I intend to still be up when the sun rises," I joked.

"You plan to dance all night, do you?" He gave me a crooked smile.

"Only twice, actually."

"Is Mr. Pendleton coming, then?"

I inhaled deeply, groaning on the exhale. "I meant with *you*, Peter."

He faked a grimace. "But I have not asked you."

I took three long steps toward him, pushing him back with both hands and slapping his shoulders. "You irritating man!"

His eyes were wide with humor as I pelted him, which only served to anger me further. "I'm sorry?"

My shoulders slumped, and I felt as defeated as I had when Mama had thrown my music in the fire. "I want to spend my last evening here dancing with my dearest friend. Is that so much to ask? Why does anything have to change between us now?"

Peter stilled, his smile dropping instantly. "Forgive me, Amelia. I only thought—"

"Stop thinking." I crossed my arms, frowning at him. "I like you much better when you don't."

Peter nodded once, looking both terrified and pleased. "Would you like to brush Summer?"

"I would," I said forcefully, loudly, and much too swiftly. I took the brush from his outstretched hand and moved around him.

Peter coughed. Or was it a laugh?

I could hear him rustling behind me, like he scuffed his boot back and forth in place upon the dirty floor.

"*Dearest* friend?" he asked suddenly.

My neck flushed, but I only had one day left. And I wanted it to be perfect, one way or the other. "Yes."

Peter grabbed my free hand, spinning me around to face him. His eyes were beaming. "Amelia?"

I swallowed, finding it hard to meet his gaze.

"Would you give me the pleasure of your first dance tonight?"

I raised my chin, suppressing my smile. "Yes, thank you. And I shall take your last as well."

Peter squeezed my hand before releasing me. "It is yours."

We spent the entire afternoon together, returning to our usual easy conversation. I loved the way Peter simply understood me. Even when I lacked for words, he knew what I meant. And when I moved awkwardly or fell out of step, Peter always adjusted to make up the difference between us.

Evening fell before I had time to catch my breath, and Mary laid out my ball gown. It was cherry red with a simple V-shaped neckline, hugging my figure and flowing out behind me. Mary pinned a spray of white flowers at the back of my hair and painted my lips with a dab of Rose Lip Salve. I pulled on the ivory evening gloves Peter had given me and followed Clara down the stairs.

My pulse quickened when we reached the top of the final floor. We were the first of the ladies to descend, and thus the first to be admired by the men. Sir Ronald escorted Clara to the back of the room, whispering something in her ear that made her blush.

Peter waited at the base of the stairs, hands tucked behind his back, moving forward as I approached. "Miss Moore," he said, "there are not words to describe your beauty tonight."

I would have thought him teasing, if not for the red upon his cheeks and the parting of his lips as he received me. Was it true? Did my appearance affect Peter as his did me? For the handsome wisp of his hair, the fine cut of his suit along his broad shoulders, and a heightened smell of pine and soap were entirely affecting me tonight. Only, tonight I would not avoid his charm.

Tonight, I would let myself fully admire Peter Wood.

Peter led me to the carriage parked on the drive, and I caught him stealing glances as we walked. He chuckled when I pinched his arm.

"I am sorry," he said on a laugh. "I am desperately trying to stay honorable."

"Perhaps I should find a different dance partner?" I teased.

"You are not leaving my side tonight, Miss Moore. Not for a moment."

Beatrice and Mr. Bratten joined us soon after we settled in, and our carriage departed.

Listening to Mr. Bratten prattle on about some business of his, I felt Peter's stare once more. His eyes, when I met them, were firm and serious, and I lifted my chin under his scrutiny. He did not look away for a long moment, but held my gaze with admiration and—could it be?—affection. I bit my lip and moved my gaze to the window beside me. The stars were just beginning to shine.

When we arrived at the Levins' house, Peter helped me down from the carriage, pulling me close. I hadn't expected such a crowd in such a small town. The house was large and filled with fancy dresses and flowers, and the hustle and bustle reminded me of London. I clung to Peter for balance.

Our first country dance was every bit like our secret waltz. Neither of us could contain our smiles, and we danced with as much enthusiasm as we could muster. My cheeks ached from laughter, and when Peter pulled me close, my nerves tingled and flurried. Everything felt right again. My heart alternately settled then leaped to be with Peter.

I caught his eye through every subsequent dance, so that it felt as though we never truly left one another's company, despite changing partners. Clara and the rest of our company danced and conversed amidst the crush, and not a frown existed among us.

"You look no less exercised than when we first arrived," Peter said, nearly out of breath when he found me in my chair between dances. "To think you tried to trick me into believing you could not climb a hill on our second day."

I laughed. "Is it time for our next dance already?"

"It is nearly one in the morning, so yes, it should be about time. But I am exhausted. I need a moment's rest, or I shall fail you entirely. These women do not dance with such grace as you."

My heart flipped in my chest. "Is that so?"

"Come," he said, tugging on my hand. "I need out of this place for a moment."

Peter led me through the crowd and out onto the veranda where a small group of people mingled. His breath steadied, and he leaned against the railing, fluffing out his hair.

"You look very handsome, Peter." I bit my lip, admiring

him fully. Never would I meet another man as handsome as he.

He straightened, smiling. "You are different tonight."

"Am I?" The evening breeze cooled my cheeks.

"You are happy and amiable and . . . free, I suppose."

"Are you fishing for more compliments?" I leaned beside him against the rail, and he brushed his arm against mine.

"From you? Always." He winked.

I smiled back at him and stretched my shoulders.

Peter sighed. "Why did you not tell me of your circumstances, Amelia?" I sensed a hesitation, but also a need in his voice.

I looked down at my ivory gloves. "I suppose I was afraid of losing your good opinion. And Georgiana said . . ."

Peter tensed. "What did Georgiana say?"

I met his gaze. If I wanted to learn the truth, I needed to say the words tonight. Tomorrow would be too late. "She said that a dowry was important to you. For your income. And that you needed a wealthy match, otherwise you would be forced to work in London like your father did. I would never want that for you."

Peter rubbed his face in his hands. "Why would she say that to you? Georgiana knows nothing of my finances. Gads, Amelia. I am so sorry."

"So, it . . . isn't true?" Could Peter marry for love alone without too great a sacrifice? I didn't dare let myself hope.

He looked at me in earnest. "I told you. Money is not something I have in short supply." He shook his head in frustration. "I want a family and a home. I couldn't care less how much it costs me. Can you trust that? Can you forget what Georgiana has said?"

I nodded, staring intently into Peter's pleading eyes, but then a set of music tore me away from the dream. "Oh, Peter, our dance!"

"Drat," Peter said with a wicked grin, his countenance reverting back to his easygoing nature. "We shall be forced to stay out here."

I pointed at his chest. "You missed it on purpose."

He shrugged. "I am tired, and you are so much better a dancer than I."

"You horrible man," I teased. "You owe me a dance."

Peter stood up from the railing, lifted my hands above us, and spun me. I did not stop for several rounds until I was so dizzy I tripped on my shoes.

He caught me in his arms, laughing, and leaned back against the railing again. My breath was heavy, my mind whirling and my heart pounding in my ears.

"Careful or we might truly be banished," I said, remembering our jest from the night we danced under the stars. But Peter did not release me. He looked at me with a serious expression, like he studied me as though to sketch my likeness.

"You know that story you wanted to write for me? This is how I would end it." Peter bit his lower lip, his eyes clear, sincere, hopeful. "I want a picture of you spinning and smiling at me like this forever."

My legs suddenly lost their strength. I studied his chest rising and falling in a pattern that matched my own, so much so that I hardly noticed a throng of people suddenly crowding the veranda.

Peter nodded toward a break in the railing behind us. He took my hand in his, pulling me behind him. Four steps led us down onto the soft grass, and Peter glanced over his shoulder, as though to watch for following eyes. He cast me a smile, as happy as it was mischievous, and I returned it easily.

"Where are we going?" I whispered.

"There is a garden just around the house. The Levins light it with lanterns at night. I thought you would like to see it."

As we rounded the corner, the light from the party dimmed. Was this a good idea? Running off alone with Peter with so many eyes watching?

"What if we are seen?" I tugged back his hand.

Peter slowed, glancing over his shoulder as he contemplated the thought. I watched as realization grew in his eyes. Of what could happen if we were caught alone together at a ball.

"Your mother," he said slowly, solemnly.

My mother hardly knew my father when they kissed on the balcony. Peter would not be so careless with me. If there was anyone in the world who made me feel safe, it was him.

"We can turn back." He shook his head as though he thought himself daft for recommending the garden.

"No," I heard my voice say before I could stop it. "Let's not."

Peter studied my eyes with intensity, as though searching for something unsaid. A slow smile spread across his lips, and he laced our fingers together.

My heart fluttered wildly in my chest, and I felt like a child—free, fearless, and completely happy. As though nothing in the world could harm me. As though life had shown me no sorrow.

Peter hurried his steps, and moonlight swept over his features. He became my shadowy companion, only our hands connecting us, until the first lantern appeared at the entrance to the garden. The scene before me was breathtaking in its beauty, captivating in its perfection.

The lantern lit the rolled gravel footpath beneath it, casting light upon the soft peach-colored roses blooming nearby. Peter said nothing, only watched me as I smelled the first rose I came upon, and I could not help but laugh in delight as we walked into this secret, hidden place. Another lantern hung a few paces ahead, even with the height of the flower bushes, which had grown taller upon walls of cedar wood.

"Look up," Peter said after we'd been walking hand in hand for a time, and I obliged.

A million stars shone above us, and I drew in a breath of surprise at the majesty of their endlessness. We were encompassed entirely by beauty without description, and I spun on my toes to take it all in. When I looked to Peter, he was leaning against the nearby wall of flowers under a lantern, chuckling to himself.

"Are you laughing at me?" I asked, defensively.

"At you? Not in the least."

"Then why are you looking at me like that?" I crossed my arms, but he only smiled bigger.

"Come." He stood from the wall and reached for my hand. "The best is yet to come."

I narrowed my eyes at him playfully as he grasped my hand again. The garden was endless, or perhaps our pace was so slow it felt like we journeyed for miles. Peter pointed out his favorite flowers, and even showed me a constellation named Cassiopeia.

Distant music met our ears, and I knew we had reached the edge of the garden again. Peter slowed his steps and turned to me. Under the light of a lantern, his features glowed, his eyes near desperate and full of some emotion I could not name.

"Amelia," he said suddenly, swallowing.

He clearly meant to tell me something, something serious that intimidated him, and a strange nervousness overcame me. Why was Peter looking at me as though none of the beauty around us mattered? Like I was the only thing his eyes could see? Watching him hesitate, I felt as if I could see some storm raging within him, just under the surface. I had an inkling of what he wanted to say, but I could not be sure. All I knew was that I wanted to hear the words behind the look he gave.

My voice came out soft, barely above the whisper of music floating in the breeze. "I have had the best fortnight of my life with you, Peter."

Peter lifted my hand between us, and, turning it over gently, he lifted it to his lips and pressed a kiss in the center of my palm.

"I love you," he said, as tenderly as I'd ever heard his voice.

My heart flew into my throat. "Peter—" My voice cracked.

"Please let me speak. I must or I shall regret it all my life." He took both my hands and pulled me close, kissing them again, his own hands shaking.

I could not breathe. Love, or the illusion of it, had ruined my parents. It had forced them into a choice they might not have otherwise made if they had had time to sort out their feelings sensibly.

But would I not make this choice with Peter? Again and again and again? I loved him with every bit of me. Could I choose my own future regardless of the risk?

Standing in front of the only man I'd ever loved, I wanted to. Oh, how I wanted to.

Distant noises broke through the far-off music. Peter looked over his shoulder, listening intently to the sound. A shout, it seemed. Panic.

"What is it?" I asked in a whisper, training my ears to the noise.

"Wood!" Mr. Bratten's voice called. "Peter, where are you?"

Peter looked to me, unsaid words still on his lips, until footsteps approached, crunching on gravel.

"Wood?"

"Just here." Peter held my hand as long as possible, before our hold gave way.

"It's Georgiana," Mr. Bratten called, breathless. "You must come immediately."

"What has happened?" Peter asked, worried.

"She and Demsworth. A kiss. In front of everyone."

Stepping backward, I gasped. A kiss?

Clara.

Without a second thought, I raced from the garden, barely aware that Peter called my name as I passed him.

Chapter Twenty-Seven

I clutched my skirts, heading straight for the veranda, skipping steps as I ascended to the ballroom.

Beatrice was the first person I saw. She leaned against a doorframe, her lips parted, her face pale as she stared ahead.

"Where is she?" I gasped as I approached her, breathless from exertion.

"Upstairs," Beatrice answered in a daze. "She nearly fainted. Mrs. Levin is attending her."

"Thank you," I said, stepping forward.

"Amelia," Beatrice called out, and I stopped. "Forgive me. This is all my fault."

I reached for her. "Whatever do you mean, Beatrice?"

"That night, all those days ago, when we talked of your parents. I told Georgiana how romantic their kiss was. How indeed such a scandal was worth its happiness in the end." Tears threatened to spill from her eyes. "I knew Georgiana was desperate. I could see it in her eyes tonight."

"No." I grasped her arm soothingly. "Whatever happened tonight, you are not to blame."

Beatrice nodded, wiping her eyes, and I hurried upstairs. If anyone should have seen Georgiana's desperation, it was I.

A servant led me to the library, where Mrs. Levin sat on a settee beside Clara, whose face was buried in a cloth.

"I am here," I said when I saw her, but when she looked up at me, I was not prepared for the pain in her eyes, the devastation writ across every line in her face. "Oh, Clara. What has happened?"

Mrs. Levin stood, kindness softening her features. "You must be Miss Moore. I am glad you found us. I believe Miss Clara has suffered a reaction from being privy to a scandal in the middle of my ballroom. Please allow me to apologize again, most fully. If I had expected such a circumstance, I would have never invited Mr. and Miss Wood into my home."

"Please, you must explain. I was not present." It could not be as bad as it seemed. Surely someone was mistaken.

Mrs. Levin smiled sadly. "Forgive me. The simplest explanation is that Miss Wood—"

"She kissed him." Clara's voice was rough and broken. "In front of everyone."

"In the middle of the final set." Mrs. Levin shook her head. "I can only hope he planned to marry her; they certainly will be forced to now."

Clara stifled a sob, burying her face into the wrinkled, tear-soaked cloth she held.

"Is there anything I might do to help?" Mrs. Levin asked, offering me her seat. "I wish I could offer refuge here, but unfortunately our rooms are entirely full for the event."

"Thank you, Mrs. Levin. For everything. If you could

send Lady Demsworth at her earliest convenience, that will do."

Mrs. Levin nodded. "You may stay here as long as you need. If I can do anything to help, please send for me."

I nodded my appreciation before she crossed to the door, closing it behind her. As soon as the room was silent again, I sat beside Clara, and she fell into my arms.

"I feel like such a fool," she cried. "He must have declared himself for her to be so openly affectionate."

Rubbing her shoulders, I held her to me, trying to keep my own tears from falling. "You are most certainly not a fool, Clara. You are brave and kind and incredibly smart."

"Love is folly. You said it a million times, but I never listened to you. I hate him, Amelia. And I hate her most of all."

"Don't be like that, dearest. Do not let bitterness replace what once was."

"There is nothing left inside me but bitterness. I shall never love anyone as I loved him. And he led me to believe I was not alone in affection."

"We have not yet heard the entire story. We must be patient and hear what Sir Ronald has to say."

"I want to leave," Clara said, dabbing her face with her cloth. "But wherever shall we go, Amelia? We have nothing . . . nowhere . . ."

My heart fell, my thoughts instantly turning to Peter.

He loved me.

He loved me.

But he had not asked for my hand. And even if he had, how could I accept him now?

I could never have Peter. Not like this. Not after

Georgiana simultaneously sealed Sir Ronald's fate and broke Clara's heart. The pain a match with Peter would cause Clara would be too great.

There was only one thing I was certain of, only one thing left for me to do.

"I will write to Mr. Pendleton. He is expecting us." I kissed Clara's head.

"You shall have to marry him." Clara's voice was flat and certain. "Forgive me, sister, for everything I said against you. Where would we be without your practicality?"

I winced at the word, one I'd so often used against Peter. For once in my life, I could not agree. Practicality had wounded me greatly. And I would never recover. "I am only grateful his need matches ours."

A knock sounded on the door, and Lady Demsworth quickly stepped in. "Ladies. I hardly know what to say, or where to begin. I must offer my sincerest apologies for Miss Wood's behavior tonight. We have all been quite caught off guard."

"Did she act on her own?" I asked as Clara wiped her eyes, sniffing.

"Oh, yes." Lady Demsworth knelt beside us, more casually than I'd ever expected she could. "Miss Wood's actions were a shock to us all. But I shall not trouble you with what you already know."

"We were unaware of the circumstances, actually." I cleared my throat. "Your clarification would be most welcome."

"Oh, dear." Lady Demsworth pressed her hand to her chest. "It pains me to think of the hurt this has caused you both. What can I do? Mrs. Levin has no rooms here, and I hate to think you are uncomfortable now in our home, but I insist you return so I may take care of you until you leave us. You must trust that I will not allow any discomfort to come upon you. I will keep every guest from your room so you may have the privacy I am sure you desire. I know Ronald will wish to speak with you both."

"Where is he?" I asked.

"Mr. Wood insisted they leave at once. The three of them took a carriage back with Lieutenant Rawles and Mr. Bratten. If you are willing, we shall share a carriage with the Turnballs. As soon as you are ready."

"I am so embarrassed," Clara said, wiping her nose.

"No more than I, my dear," Lady Demsworth said. "You have nothing to be embarrassed of. I know how you cared for him. You have every right to your tears."

"Shall we go, Clara?" I asked, squeezing her shoulders. "Get you to bed? This will all feel less sharp in the morning."

"All right," she said weakly. "Thank you, Lady Demsworth."

Chapter Twenty-Eight

When we entered the carriage, Beatrice and her mother were already waiting inside, both looking at us as though they'd seen a ghost. Lady Demsworth rapped on the carriage roof, and we rolled away from the ball.

Though Clara's tears were blanketed in darkness, I could hear her sniffles. I pulled her close, and she leaned her head on my shoulder. This was all my fault. I should have prevented this. Had I not left the ballroom with Peter, I could have seen Georgiana's intentions and stopped her before she followed through with the kiss.

But what were *Sir Ronald's* true intentions? Did he love Clara? Or was he content to be stuck in a forced marriage with Georgiana? As much as I wanted to know, I equally wished we'd never know the truth. How love stung.

And how it changed a person. To be loved by Peter was proving to be the most painful love of all. I shook my head free of the picture of him and rubbed my hands until the feeling of his fingers intertwined with mine faded. I pressed a hand to my middle, trying to hold it all in, but in vain. My tears fell as freely as Clara's. How could something so perfect, so enlivening, cause such pain and heartache? I would not recover from this love. Peter had a piece of me now.

I stroked Clara's hair, listening to the quiet whisperings of our company.

". . . had no cause for rushing. Who could have guessed?" Lady Demsworth said under her breath.

"You are incredibly calm. I could not keep so even a temper were I in your position," Mrs. Turnball said.

"My hands are still shaking, Julia. I do not know what Mr. Wood expects. Nor what Georgiana intends. And Ronald? If he rejects her, he is ruined."

"Indeed." Mrs. Turnball paused. "What choice do you have but to remain strong and hold yourself together?"

"I shall try, for his sake."

Their conversation faded, and I heard Beatrice shift in her seat. I wanted to ask her what she saw, how exactly the aftermath of the kiss had played out. But I could not be sure Clara slept, and I did not wish to wake her in case she did.

Before long, the carriage pulled up along the drive to Lakeshire Park, the windows alight with candles. When we reached the grand staircase, voices carried from the drawing room a few doors down. I hesitated behind Clara.

"I will not leave this room. We shall stay here all night." Peter's voice was deep and serious. More firm than I'd ever heard him speak.

"Then let us stay," Georgiana replied.

What was going on in there? I had half a mind to march in and call out Georgiana for the mess she'd created. But Clara looked back at me with such desperation, and I quickly followed before she too could hear their voices.

"Misses." Mary opened the door to our bedchamber, eyes low as she curtseyed. She must have learned what had happened when the others arrived.

She closed the door behind us, quietly assisting Clara in taking off her gown, and then helping me out of mine. Our nightclothes were laid out on top of our beds, a cup of hot tea on our nightstands.

"Thank you, Mary. We will not have any visitors this evening," I said, pulling Clara's covers tightly around her.

"Yes, miss. Shall I pack up your things this evening, or wait until morning?"

Our things. Of course. The moment was here, too early, too soon. "The morning will do."

I crossed to the desk, candle in hand, and pulled out a single sheet of paper, some ink, and a quill. This letter would seal my fate—and break my heart for good. But I had no choice. David was our only hope. "A connection with the Woods would be worse than servitude," Clara had said. How could I ask her to sacrifice so much for me? Such a bond would break her, if Sir Ronald had not yet broken her entirely already.

After three failed attempts to find the right words, I opted for a simple approach:

Dear Mr. Pendleton,

I am writing to accept your proposal of marriage. My sister and I will arrive by late afternoon. I hope you will forgive such short notice.

Trusting you are well,

Amelia Moore

Letter sealed, I addressed the outside with David's proper name. I stared at the paper. I did not know David Pendleton, not really. And he was not Peter. Still, I closed the inkwell.

I have no choice. One person could not walk two paths. And I could not—I would not—leave Clara behind.

"Mary, I want this letter sent out at first light." I said the words, but they were not at all convincing.

"Are you sure, Miss Moore?" She took the letter, staring at the address. "Once this is sent, it cannot be undone."

I paused, my shoulders falling. "I am aware."

Mary nodded. "Of course, miss. I will send it."

After Mary said good night, I rolled onto my bed, facing Clara. She lay with her back to me, her shoulders rising and falling in sleep.

Try as I might to silence it, my mind reviewed every second, every touch, every look, every word I'd shared with Peter. How I longed to hear him speak those words again. To bind the cords that pulled us together, to knot our lives as one. But to do so now, with Clara and Sir Ronald severed, would be torture for my sister. I could not ask her to live with Georgiana's brother. Nor to be subject to Georgiana's life with Sir Ronald, played out right in front of her face.

I shifted in my bed, holding my pillow. Georgiana had ruined everything with one kiss. What excuse had she given? Was she perfectly happy now, having tied herself irrevocably to Sir Ronald? And was Beatrice right? Did Georgiana mean to recreate my parents' scandal as a means to win Sir Ronald? If so, I could only blame myself. I'd painted my parents as a love story, and Clara and I as happy, lucky even, to have resulted from scandal. The truth was far from it. I had neglected to admit the pain, the heartache, the sacrifices that came with their choice.

I sat up in my bed, fiddling with my unkempt braid. What was being said downstairs in the drawing room? Georgiana was now ruined through no fault but her own. If she had indeed acted on her own, Sir Ronald might suffer if he chose to reject her now, but he could recover. He had a choice, unlike my mother and father. Did he know as much?

Clara loved him still, I was sure, and if he loved her as well . . . *they* could recover from this. I needed to speak to Sir Ronald.

I slipped out of bed, throwing on a simple day dress and an unbuttoned pelisse before donning slippers and retrieving my candle.

"Is everything all right?" Clara stirred beside me. That she asked at all told me her sleep was not as easy as I had hoped it would be for her.

"I am just blowing out my candle. All is well, Clara."

Perhaps the lie would ring true tomorrow. I covered my candle with a hand, waiting for a beat before leaving the room.

Down the stairs I raced, a new energy feeding my muscles. Georgiana would answer for what she had done, I would make sure of it. And Sir Ronald would have to make his intentions clear, once and for all.

The double doors to the drawing room remained closed, but dim lighting shone from the crack. I did not hesitate.

I pushed opened both doors as I entered, taking in the scene before me.

"Miss Moore." Sir Ronald stood from his chair, surprise

registering on his face. His hair looked like he'd nearly torn it all out, eyes bloodshot and afraid.

I ignored his greeting, seeing Georgiana standing in a back corner of the room, facing Peter. Her frown deepened, eyes wide.

"What have you done?" I asked loudly, pacing toward her.

Georgiana stepped closer to Peter, grabbing his arm. "This is a private matter, Miss Moore."

"You know full well it is not." My voice was harsh, full of spite.

"Miss Moore, might I have a word?" Sir Ronald asked, now standing at my elbow.

I flicked my gaze to Peter, the only one who had yet to speak. His eyes were heavy as he rubbed his jaw, unwilling to meet my gaze. Did he regret his words earlier in the garden? Perhaps Georgiana had changed his mind.

I looked back to Sir Ronald. "I have only come to spare my sister from having to see you in the morning. I've written to Mr. Pendleton, and we shall leave at first light." I turned, intent on leaving the room. I made it back to the door before Sir Ronald stopped me.

"Miss Moore, please." He begged. "Please, wait. You must allow me to explain."

"I will not hear your apology."

"And yet I offer it. I plead with you to forgive me. This night—what Georgiana has forced upon me, was not my intention." Sir Ronald looked behind him, where Georgiana and Peter stood in intense conversation.

My lungs finally took a deep breath. "Then why would Georgiana feel a kiss would be permissible tonight?"

"I have yet to receive an answer. She suggests I—" He shook his head. His eyes were as broken and weary as his voice. "She suggests I moved first. But I did not. You must believe me."

Judging from the reactions of the others, I had no reason not to believe him. But why did he work so hard to convince me of his truth? What was he not saying?

"Do you love my sister, Sir Ronald?"

"Miss Moore," he breathed as though mere air was not enough to satiate him. "I love Clara with everything I am."

I willed myself to remain calm, to not break down and weep for what should have been my sister's fate. My Clara, who would not take a pence more than she was owed, had been robbed of her heart's greatest desire.

"Then what is to stop you from her now?" I asked.

Sir Ronald dropped his head. "I can hardly hope she would accept me as a ruined man. To abandon Georgiana is dishonorable, and I could not ask Clara to stand beside me and endure the gossip and ridicule that is sure to follow me."

Was that all? "She has endured far worse, I assure you."

Sir Ronald looked up at me, a new hope in his eyes.

"But can you abandon Georgiana?" I asked. "I know you care for her, too."

He shook his head. "I have never loved Georgiana as I love Clara."

I raised my chin. "She comes with nothing. We have neither inheritance nor dowry."

"I know. And I don't care. I will turn things around soon,

and money will never worry my family again." His eyes were sincere, willing me to believe his words. And I did.

"Then what will you do? For either way you are ruined, but only one path will unbreak my sister's heart."

Sir Ronald took my hands in his. "Do I have your blessing? Might I offer for her?"

"Only if you do so this night." I squeezed his hands, my lips finally finding a smile that he claimed for his own.

He turned from me to Peter. I followed him a few paces before stopping, waiting.

"Wood," he said commandingly. "I am unable to sit idly by while you attempt to persuade Georgiana. I must offer my regrets in the form of a thousand pounds and declare that I am unwilling to accept the arrangement I am sure you expect of me. I hope we can remain friends. If you'll excuse me."

"Ronald," Georgiana gasped as Sir Ronald offered a deep bow.

"Keep your money. I wish you well, Demsworth," Peter said solemnly.

Sir Ronald turned from the room in a run, out the doors and out of sight.

Peter held Georgiana in his arms as she sobbed freely, and I turned to go.

I paused outside the door, listening to the sounds of Peter comforting his sister. In a way, we'd all lost. Only the innocent were redeemed.

Slowly, I climbed the stairs. I'd hoped to give Sir Ronald and Clara time, but with every step, greater unrest tensed my nerves. I needed to escape this place, if only for a moment.

When I reached the top of the stairs, Mary paced outside the study a few doors down from our room.

"Miss Moore, I could not stop him."

"It is all right, Mary. His intentions are just." I heard Clara's soft laugh from behind the door, and I could not keep from smiling.

"It is after four in the morning. I fear none of us shall sleep before we must leave. I'll have to rush to pack your things if we are to depart at first light," Mary said, wringing her hands together.

"I think I am the only one who will need packing up. And I will not be rushed."

Mary looked to the door, realization dawning. "Then I am glad to hear it."

The sun would rise soon enough. After all my jesting, it appeared I would be awake for dawn after all. "I'm going out for a walk. I shall return in an hour or so. Do not worry after me. I am sure Clara will need you soon to help her dress more appropriately for the day."

"Yes, miss. Of course."

Chapter Twenty-Nine

Out in the brisk morning air, dew glistened as far as the eye could see, and the chirping crickets and baby birds awakening to their morning meals stole me away from reality. To hide from the ache in my heart, I focused on the sounds of nature and the sweet-smelling grass as I walked. I allowed my feet to propel me forward off into the distant field, farther and farther, until I was as lost and alone as I felt.

Love was indeed pain. And to love so deeply meant to be susceptible to an equally deep agony. It took my breath away. Just as it had when I'd lost Father. When I'd lost Mama. And now, Peter. To have one more day with Father, I would not hesitate to give away every possession, every ounce of pride. My love for Peter ran even deeper, if it were possible.

So why did I hesitate to risk everything for him? Why did I not believe him when he said he loved me? I did not know Peter's intention, whether he wished to marry me or not, but I knew my own feelings. I wanted Peter for a lifetime. I ached for him in every moment.

Sunlight peeked over the horizon. The moon still hung

in the east, surrounded by only its brightest stars. It was the most beautiful sight. Two worlds colliding at once.

I stood in the middle of misty green pasture, watching the sunrise and torn between a practical arrangement and risking my heart. If I chose my heart, Clara would be furious with me. Hurt, even. But was my happiness not as warranted as hers?

Yellow turned to pink and orange in the blue of the sky, lighting the greens and browns of the earth below. The new day's first light. I thought of the letter I'd written to David. Mary would surely be sending it at any moment. I was out of time. If I wanted Peter, this was my final chance.

Could I be brave?

My heart beat loudly in my chest and my ears, and I rubbed my eyes to clear them of traitorous tears. I took a deep breath to calm myself.

Was Peter, his love, worth fighting for?

I did not wait for my mind to catch up with my heart. In an instant, I turned and raced back toward the house. To Mary. I needed to stop her from sending that letter, but could I catch her in time? Could I reach Peter, and offer my heart, before it was too late?

A stitch pierced my side, heart beating like a drum. I was so focused on my feet, I did not realize I was not alone until I finally looked up.

A horse drew near with galloping speed. Shadows veiled the man's face. Whatever news he bore, it was urgent judging by the swiftness of his speed.

Was I imagining things? Could it be—?

Stopping a few paces away, Peter dismounted and

dropped his reins. His jacket was undone, and he looked like he hadn't slept in days.

"What are you doing all the way out here?" he asked in a worried, hesitant voice.

How had he found me here? How did he *always* find me? I froze, catching my breath and collecting my thoughts. "Did I not say I would watch the sunrise this morning?"

He took a few steps nearer, then stopped as though he'd reached the end of a chain. "My man is loading our carriage."

Already? Time had truly run out. It was now or never.

Peter frowned. "I needed to see you. To apologize for everything. For the pain I have caused you, and all that Georgiana has done."

"You have nothing to apologize for, Peter," I said with a sigh. None of this was his fault.

He dropped his head, lifting his hand to the back of his neck.

"Stop doing that." I reached around him, tugging his hand away. "You will rub your neck into oblivion."

A corner of Peter's mouth lifted slightly, but sadness remained in his eyes. Clearly, he was trying to say goodbye.

What should I say? What if he rejected me? I turned away, facing the start of a new day. I'd hardly noticed the sweet-smelling flowers nestled in the grass surrounding us, their beauty only magnified by the sky transforming overhead. I could not bear it.

Peter's warmth brushed my back, his hands finding mine. His words were barely above a whisper. "What you said in the garden about our time together . . . did you mean it? I do not want to wonder for the rest of my life if you care for me as I care for you."

Breath stilled in my lungs. My heart stopped before regaining a steady beat. What had Peter just said? I felt him inch closer to me, his chest against my back, like he wanted to be nearer to me but was afraid I might break. My heart, though, had never felt so alive, so free in all my life. I could not stay silent any longer. I did not want to.

"I love you, Peter." I leaned back into him, feeling his nose against my cheek as he nuzzled into my hair. But just as I turned to face him, he stepped back, the chill morning air filling the empty space between us as he walked back to his steed.

I frowned, speechless, and my heart beat feverishly in my chest. I wanted Peter's warmth back. I wanted him holding me again. But I was too late. Peter was leaving, and I would never see him again.

But instead, he unbuttoned a satchel dangling from the side of the horse's saddle and dug inside. He turned around, clutching something in his hand. Eyes set on mine, he lifted a paper, offering it to me.

I noticed the scrawl right away. It was my own handwriting.

"Where did you get this?" My hands shook with surprise at holding David's letter again.

"I went looking for you, and your maid gave it to me. Or I took it, rather, when she told me of your plan." Peter's voice was deep and husky. He took a hesitant step toward me. "I am trying to be honorable, Amelia. I want to do what is best for you. To give you what you want and what you deserve." He swallowed hard, scraping a hand through his hair.

I was about to protest, to admit that even I did not know what was best for me anymore, when he said, "But I don't want to be honorable. I don't want to do what is best for you. I want what is worth fighting for, what makes me the luckiest man alive. And that is loving you." Peter let out a breath as though he'd released a great weight he'd carried, his arms hanging loosely at his sides.

We looked at each other for a beat, breathing in tandem.

My lips parted. Rushing heat overwhelmed me as his words registered in my mind and then my heart, paralyzing me. Peter was fighting for me. Why wasn't *I* fighting for him? For us? I took a deep breath, feeling it in my stomach and in my toes. My fingers itched to touch his chest, his shoulders, his neck. But I had one thing left to do.

"Do you know what I want?" Hands shaking, I ripped the letter in half. "I want apple orchards, and the best apple pie." I tore the pieces into fourths, and the corners of Peter's lips twitched. "I want to go to Paris, to learn French, to see the Seine." With each statement, I tore the letter again and again, until the pieces were small enough to float on the wind. "I want a life full of laughter and scheming and dancing underneath the stars."

Peter's eyes held mine as the air carried away my words, and he took a step forward. The rising sun hit him perfectly, illuminating his face as confidence grew in his eyes. We were inches apart, and the desire between us was tangible.

Lifting my hands to his coat, I brushed over the buttons that lined his chest, then grasped his lapels, leaning as closely as I could without touching my lips to his.

"I want *you*," I whispered, and his stoic form broke free.

Before I could think, before reason found its place, Peter wrapped his arms around my waist, clutching a handful of my skirts, and pulled me close to him. His lips found mine as easily as though he'd kissed me like this a million times, so fervently and so deeply and so very uncontrolled.

My hands reached his shoulders, curving around his neck and into his hair. He slid his hands up my back, laughing into the kiss as though he too couldn't believe he was kissing me in the middle of a field under a masterpiece of a sunrise. He kissed my jaw and the crease of my mouth, lifting me and turning me toward the sun, before pulling me close and starting all over again on my lips.

When my knees were weak and I was thoroughly kissed, I pulled back, breathing heavily against him. How had I spent my entire life not knowing how this felt? How had I lived before now?

"Amelia," he said softly, burying his nose into a soft spot on my cheek. He kissed my cheek, my forehead, my lips. "Marry me."

I leaned my forehead against his. "Georgiana will hate me. Clara will be mortified by the connection."

"Yes," Peter breathed, nodding in full agreement. "We will not outrun our share of trouble."

Leaning back, I looked into his clear green eyes.

Despite the growing urge I felt to laugh with joy, I was struck by the sun touching the earth behind us. Behind Peter. The gloriousness of a light unparalleled in beauty.

I let my smile lift my lips fully and unabashedly as I said, "I don't mind the trouble. As long as I'm with you."

Chapter Thirty

By the time we entered the clearing, full sunshine lined every blade of grass.

My ears were full of sweet declarations and even sweeter promises, my happiness overflowing like high tide in the afternoon. Peter stole ahead of me for the hundredth time, catching me in his arms and covering me in kisses.

Love was bliss. And I never wanted it to end.

Hand in hand, we approached his carriage.

"I wish I could stay," Peter said somberly, pressing his lips to my forehead.

I wrapped my arms around his neck. If begging made any rational sense, I would plead for him to stay. But Georgiana needed him right now. Her broken heart needed mending.

The rest of Peter's days would be mine soon enough.

I pressed my nose against his. "Will you send for me? As soon as you can?"

"The moment you allow it. I imagine you will want to be with your sister until she is wed."

I smiled into his kiss. "I shall have to convince them to wed quickly."

A forced cough sounded from behind me. Peter pulled back, grasping my hand as I turned.

Clara raised a gloved hand to her gaping mouth, while Sir Ronald chuckled at her side.

"Amelia?" Her shocked voice was a squeak.

I froze in equal shock. What could I say to her? What she knew of Peter rang false on every account, and much of that had been my own doing. How could I convince her to open her heart?

"I assume congratulations are in order, Wood." Sir Ronald stepped forward, forcing down his humor. "Otherwise, I shall have to banish you from my house a second time."

Peter and I exchanged an amused glance.

Clara was not as amused. Her frown wrinkled her face. "What is the meaning of this?"

I reached out to her, about to release Peter's hand, when my feet grew heavy. As much as I ached to comfort Clara, to make her understand, letting go of Peter was just as painful. Clara's future was secure, her heart held by a man who would, if necessary, conquer the world for her. Did I not also deserve that same happiness?

Stepping back, I drew even with Peter. "Forgive me, Clara. I know I have kept many things from you this past fortnight, and I give you my word, I never shall again. But if there is one thing I should have told you, one thing I hid even from myself, it is how much I love this man." I let out a sigh, full of all the affection and admiration I'd carefully bound since we'd met. "I cannot live without you, dear sister, but I also cannot live without him. I hope in time you might come to know Peter as I do and love him for the good man that he is, regardless of what his sister has done."

Peter squeezed my hand, and Clara looked between us, confused and sad.

After a few moments, she turned to Peter, chin raised. "You cannot have her."

Immediately, I opened my mouth to protest, but she continued, "I will not prepare for my wedding without her. Nor will she prepare for hers without me."

Stunned silence filled the air. Then Peter let out a loud laugh.

Clara added, "We shall return her to you the day before you wed, and not a day sooner."

Peter pulled me to his side, gratitude evident in his easy smile. "Thank you, Miss Clara."

"Then it is settled," Sir Ronald said amiably as though nothing amiss had occurred only hours previous. "Shall we leave them to offer their goodbyes, my darling? Cook has set out breakfast."

"Indeed," Clara said, a smile on her lips.

Sir Ronald kissed her hand before lacing it through his arm and leading her back into the house.

"I think she and I are becoming friends already," Peter said.

I nearly pinched him. Despite it all, his confidence was unyielding.

"You shall have to write me letters." I tried to sound brave, but my heart threatened to crack. Love was indeed cruel, taking away my Peter so soon. Cruel, but worthwhile.

"Every day. Indeed, I shall hire a man for that very task. We've only four hours between us. He can wait for your response and return to me in the same evening."

"Are you in earnest?" I feared I sounded like a lovestruck schoolgirl, but I didn't mind.

"Tomorrow morning, your first will be on its way." Peter leaned in for a kiss.

"Stop that, immediately." Georgiana banged through the front door, her hair a wild mess, holding a handbag and a small blanket in her arms. Red splotches painted her face, but she did not look up as she crossed the gravel. "Into the carriage, Peter."

"In a moment, Georgiana. You might offer us congratulations, you know."

I shook my head pointedly at him, not wishing for any further tension. Georgiana would come around. But now was not the time.

Georgiana's face contorted. "Perfect timing for you, is it not, Miss Moore? My brother's house is very large. I daresay you will be more than comfortable."

Peter tensed.

"Thank you, Georgiana." I smiled sweetly before he could reprimand her. She entered the carriage as though unaware of my response. I spoke louder, "I look forward to years of time together."

Forever, actually.

"No one else would tolerate her." Peter shook his head. "It is one of the many reasons I love you."

My heart soared. "I should like a list of the rest of your reasons in my first letter."

"Then you shall have it. You shall have your heart's desire for the rest of your days, my darling."

"Speaking of which, you still owe me that favor, as I recall," I teased, and he kissed me, enveloping me in his arms.

"Lord, help me. Do not include Georgiana this time. Not for another six months at least."

Laughing, I said, "First, we shall see how good of a husband you are. Perhaps she and I are better schemers as sisters."

Peter's gaze grew serious, sincere. "How did this happen? How, in the most random of places, on the most random of errands, did life bring me to you?"

I walked Peter to the carriage, straightening his cravat and feeling the width of his shoulders one last time. We savored another kiss, knowing we must make it last.

He moaned, and held me tighter in his arms. "Are you certain you cannot come? I can situate you at a nearby inn, or a house of one of my neighbors. We'll send for Clara as soon as she's had her fill of Demsworth."

Confined in his embrace, I'd never felt so free. "Soon," I said. "And then you shall never be rid of me."

With his thumb, he stroked my cheek, my brow, my lips, his glinting green eyes washing over me as though memorizing every inch. "Take care, my love. My Amelia."

"I love you, Peter." Slowly I released him, huffing a pitiful breath as he closed the door behind him.

I stepped back, watching as the carriage drove away, holding my middle.

I felt safe. Unimaginably happy.

Free.

Chapter Thirty-One

Dearest Amelia,

Was it all a dream? I fear it was, and that this letter will have you quite confused when you receive it.

I slept nearly the entire drive back. Georgiana had a much harder time relaxing. I cannot decide what to say to her, or how to ease her pain. I am not sure I can.

I am miserable without you. Has the party there dispersed? I must ask you to keep away from Lieutenant Rawles. He's had eyes for you since our very first day, and I do not wish to duel a soldier.

My estate is just as I left it, but for piles of work upon my desk. At least I have plenty to keep me occupied. I hope you like it here. There is much improvement to be made, but I shall leave that to your taste.

You are in my thoughts in every moment. Your smile, your laugh, the way you purse your lips when you are unamused with my teasing. You are the bravest, smartest, and most thoughtful person I have ever met. You care little for the opinions of others, and yet you deserve their very best. To detail your talent, your kindness, your loyalty—to say nothing of your beauty—would take pages. How have I convinced such a woman to love me? I shall spend a lifetime wondering.

Yours, etc.

Peter

My darling Peter,

I must have watched the window for hours. Your poor messenger is on a walk to stretch his legs from such a journey. I do hope he recovers after traveling to and fro.

Clara and Sir Ronald have set a date for a week from now. Sir Ronald procured a common license as they do not wish to draw more attention than necessary after the scandal. Perhaps we should do the same?

Our things from Gray House will be arriving in a few days. Prepare yourself for my many trunks. Did I tell you I love to collect seashells?

Only joking, dearest. I can hardly wait to see your estate and imagine you as a child there. It is lonely without you, now that all the company has gone. Sir Ronald is a busy man, but I am pleased with how hard he works to recover his estate. I can see why the two of you are such good friends.

Give Georgiana time. Loving her will do for now.

How I miss you. How I long to be in your arms again.

Ever yours,

Amelia

Dearest Amelia,

Our license is settled. The bishop was more than eager to offer it as he believes Georgiana is in need of a proper lady's influence. I have all but given up. I am only her brother, and I cannot say I am certain of what our father would say to her if he were here.

Is that Pendleton man still available? Perhaps we should pen him, with an emphasis on her dowry?

I took a walk along my favorite path today and thought of you. I am certain you will love the view overlooking my estate. It is green as far as the eye can see.

I see it all with new eyes. I wonder what the trees will look like, the grass, the orchard, the sky, when you are here with me.

I find you wherever there is beauty.

Yours, etc.,

Peter

Dearest Peter,

Georgiana's letter was well-received. Clara's heart is too big to stay angry for too long, and Sir Ronald couldn't care less after having won his prize. If your sister is sincere in her apology, I believe our wedding shall be a happy enough occasion after all.

Speaking of weddings. Two days until Clara is wed!

I am full of butterflies. Clara chides me as I write, for I am late to dress for a full day of duty to her. We shall confirm arrangements for the wedding from the shoes she will wear to the individual flowers that will be pinned in her hair. I confess I care little for the details, but I am steadfast in my duty. I hardly have time to miss you, but my heart aches all the same.

My things from Gray House arrived yesterday, not long after your messenger departed. With them was news of Lord Gray's passing. I fear there is something wrong with me, for I feel little sorrow. In truth, I almost feel relief. I wish him no ill, but I hope he now sees how wrongly he treated us. And I hope my mother is giving him a stern lecture.

I love you, Peter. So very much. Five days more.

Your Amelia

Dearest Amelia,

Georgiana says I have become "snippy" without

you here. I, of course, reprimanded her for the insult, only furthering her resolve. I suppose I have been more frustrated than usual with the distance between us.

Only four days more, and I shall have you in my arms again.

There is absolutely nothing amiss with how you feel. I know you won't care to hear it, but I am sorry to hear of Lord Gray's passing. Though I share your disfavor of him, I am grateful that he kept his promise to your mother, that he kept you safe all this time. If there is anything I might do to ease your worries, send word straightaway. My man is paid handsomely for his ceaseless rides between us.

In other news, Georgiana has finally left her room for some time out of doors. She seems to be improving, though she still will not take calls. The estate is well and waiting for you.

I love you, my Amelia. I hope Clara's wedding is as beautiful and joyous as possible.

Yours, etc.,

Peter

Dearest Peter,

The wedding was everything I'd hoped. Clara was radiant. Mary tucked flowers in her hair just so, and she was covered in lace. I fear I shall not come close to rivaling her beauty. The ceremony was short, the company small, but it was perfectly lovely. Sir

Ronald stole her away for the afternoon, and I helped Mary organize my things. I am so glad to have her join us. Thank you for keeping Mary on.

Three days, my darling. I can hardly wait.

All my love,

Amelia

Dearest Amelia,

Georgiana's first call was a disaster. Society has wasted no time in divulging the details of her scandal to the world. She handled the questions with grace, but I fear she will not leave her room for another few days now.

I am glad the wedding was as happy as predicted. I am sure I think of little else but our own.

And I cannot wait to steal you away for the afternoon.

Yours, etc.,

Peter

Dearest Peter,

My things are in trunks upon my bedroom floor. I do not expect to sleep at all, for tomorrow is finally approaching, but I shall try.

You will not believe what came yesterday from Gray House. A box of my mother's things. She kept a journal, and I am halfway through reading it, and her feelings are entirely heartbreaking. She loved my father, Peter. Ardently. I do not think their love was immediate, but in reading her words, I see she grew to love him. Perhaps his stories came true after all.

Thank you for letting Clara and Sir Ronald stay with us. I hope Georgiana truly does not mind. I know it will be difficult for her to see them together so soon, but Clara is so happy, I am sure all is already forgiven.

I shall see you when you wake.

Yours,

Amelia

"Are we nearly there?" I asked Sir Ronald, who sat opposite me in the carriage beside Clara.

My hands were shaking. I'd already asked Sir Ronald to check his watch above two dozen times, but Peter had said four hours, and I would hold him to it.

"I know this bend. You shall see the estate any moment," he answered with a grin.

Clara laid her head on his shoulder, and I sighed.

Soon.

Staring out the window, I relished the sight of green trees upon green hills lush with green grass, just as Peter had described. I tried to picture Peter as we rolled by, the bend in the distance drawing closer. Did he ride these hills on horseback? Take walks and get lost in the open fields?

"Ah, yes. I remember visiting here as a child. Any moment

now." Sir Ronald leaned toward the window, looking out at the landscape.

My heart beat in my chest. Would Peter be waiting for me? Did he know I'd be arriving at any moment?

"There!" Clara pointed. A rectangular brown house towered in the distance. It was beautiful, serene, regal. "Look at those pillars. Darling, why do we not have pillars lining our entry?"

Sir Ronald muttered something about structural integrity, but I did not hear him as I was focused entirely on Peter.

He stood, arms behind his back, dressed as though he awaited a queen, with the grandest grin upon his face. His hair fluttered handsomely in the wind.

I nearly opened the door myself.

Sir Ronald dropped out, helping Clara from her seat, and Peter stepped forward.

I let him help me down, but wasted no time closing the space between us. Kissing his lips was as easy as breathing. His arms held me, lifting me in the air, and he spun me around as we laughed in each other's embrace.

When my feet touched gravel again, I took in the vast height of the house, the perfectly trimmed landscape that seemed to stretch for miles on end, and the sweet breeze that rustled the yellowing leaves amongst the trees. "This is heaven," I whispered.

Peter took my hand in his, lifting it to press a kiss in my palm, and said, "This, my love, is home."

Acknowledgments

I am foremost grateful to my Father in Heaven, who blessed me with creativity and inspiration when I needed it most.

Amelia's story would never have made it to completion without the vision and help of so many lovely people to whom I owe a heap of gratitude:

Thanks to my dear friend Marla Buttars, who opened the doors of the writing community to me and encouraged me to learn my craft. And to countless others who've supported me in this journey, including friends, beta readers, and the wonderful team at Shadow Mountain.

To my sister Chelsea Ashdown, who willingly and lovingly read my first draft with encouraging eyes and support. You pushed me forward, sis, and I love you.

My momma, my sisters Jenn and Erin, my dad, my amazing in-laws, and all my extended family for their excitement and love throughout my lifetime.

With all the love in my heart, I owe profuse gratitude to my beautiful critique partners (too much, guys? I just love you!) for all their thoughts, time, talent, and efforts shared on my behalf. Arlem "Time Traveler" Hawks, Joanna "The Greatest" Barker, Heidi "Shock Factor" Kimball, and Sally "Indie Fabulous" Britton—you girls are my best friends. Thanks for enduring my bad jokes, modernisms, and terrible comma placements.

And most of all—Thank you, Ted, for everything. For our children, our home, and all the love and support you've given me throughout this process. I would not have even tried without you in my ear telling me I could do it. I love you.

And of course, to my perfectly silly kiddos who let me write in exchange for TV time—Sophie, Owen, Henry, and our angel Simon.

I hope you read this one day and love it.

Discussion Questions

1. Amelia worries about making certain her and Clara's futures are safe and secure. How does trying to maintain control help her? How does it harm her?
2. Peter listens to Amelia's plea to check Winter's airway after the other men disregard her as being overly emotional. This is a significant moment for Amelia because she feels heard and seen. Why would women in the Regency era feel unheard? Do women in our day experience these same feelings? When and why?
3. Amelia struggles with Peter's little sister, Georgiana, throughout the book. Why do you think Georgiana acts the way she does? What about her and Peter's family background might cause Georgiana to behave the way she does? Do we judge people without knowing their story?
4. Lady Demsworth requests a casual feel to the house party at Lakeshire Park. How does this casual environment encourage Amelia to be herself?
5. Peter's watch is engraved with the message "Time is not guaranteed." It is meaningful to him because of his father,

but how else is this phrase meaningful in the story? How is it meaningful in your life, and what changes could you make to apply this ideal?

6. Amelia wrestles with telling Peter how she feels because she believes that love is a potentially painful risk. In what ways is she right? Why do you think she chose love in the end? What meaningful relationships in your life are worth the risk?
7. At the start of *Lakeshire Park*, Amelia is very protective of her sister and would choose Clara's happiness above all else. By the end, Amelia steps back and chooses Peter despite the discomfort it will cause Clara. Why was this significant? Why is it sometimes important to create boundaries with those we love?
8. What do we learn about Amelia's mother from this story? Do you have sympathy for her? What about Lord Gray? Why or why not?
9. Amelia carries the burden of Lord Gray's impending death, and then his letter, almost completely alone. How might things have gone differently had she confided in Clara?

About the Author

Photo by Trisha Shelley Photography

MEGAN WALKER was raised on a berry farm in Poplar Bluff, Missouri, where her imagination took her to times past and worlds away. While earning her degree in Early Childhood Education at Brigham Young University, she married her one true love and started a family. But her imaginings wouldn't leave her alone, so she picked up a pen, and the rest is history. She lives in St. Louis with her husband and three children.